D0491898

SELDOM SEEN

SARAH RIDGARD

SELDOM SEEN

HUTCHINSON
LONDON

Published by Hutchinson 2012

2 4 6 8 10 9 7 5 3 1

Copyright © Sarah Ridgard 2012

First published in Great Britain in 2012 by
Hutchinson
Random House, 20 Vauxhall Bridge Road,
London SW1V 2SA

www.randomhouse.co.uk

Addresses for companies within The Random House Group Limited can be found at:
www.randomhouse.co.uk/offices.htm

The Random House Group Limited Reg. No. 954009

A CIP catalogue record for this book
is available from the British Library

ISBN 9780091944124

The Random House Group Limited supports The Forest Stewardship Council (FSC®), the leading
international forest certification organisation. Our books carrying the FSC label are printed on FSC®
certified paper. FSC is the only forest certification scheme endorsed by the leading environmental
organisations, including Greenpeace. Our paper procurement policy can be found at
www.randomhouse.co.uk/environment

Typeset in Fournier MT by Palimpsest Book Production Limited,
Falkirk, Stirlingshire

Printed and bound in Great Britain by
CPI Group (UK) Ltd, Croydon, CR0 4YY

For Mum and Dad

I

BACK OF BEYOND

I should never have started crawling around in ditches, kicking up people's secrets. I used to be afraid that if I tripped and fell, I'd crack my head open and they'd spill out everywhere. The stuff I knew, the secrets. That they'd lie on the road in shock for a moment, trying to get their bearings, until some got caught up in a gust of wind while others went crawling off under hedges, into ditches to wash up in people's back gardens, or in the gutter outside the village shop for all to see.

'Dolly, you'll never guess what I've just heard,' Sadie Borrett would say over the fence, looking over her shoulder towards the back garden where a secret has just landed on her buddleia like a Peacock butterfly. 'That Pam White has been carrying on with Bernie from the garage. Been at it for years, apparently. They were seen in the back of a van which was brought in for repairs from out Bedfield way.'

Or further up the road by the council houses a gang of kids would be skipping and chanting, 'We know who went with the Peaman.'

I got too good at being able to disappear, that was the problem. It took years of practice, this trick of the breath. I breathe in deep, hold it, then let it out, slow, flat and even. I breathe out through my skin, all over. That's the way animals do it. Rabbits, hares, rats. They breathe out and flatten into the sides of verges, become part of the field. It's like the edges of me begin to fade away and the colour behind leaks through. I can take on the pattern of cowslips in a ditch, or a shelf of tins in the shop, all the time feeling safe down there, tucked away behind my ribs.

That's how I found out about Pam and Bernie long before anyone else. I'd seen them a couple of miles out of Worlingworth parked

3

up in a layby one evening. You couldn't see them from the road. The Ford van was on the concrete next to the ditch, hidden behind a ten-foot-high pile of sugar beet, its lights turned off except for a small one inside above the windscreen. I was on my way home, walking the ditches between two fields with the faraway names Malaga Slade and the Back of Beyond, remembering where to avoid the drainage pipes and the small fridge that somebody had tipped down there months ago, now invisible in the dark. I was on a level with the van's tyres, the suspension. The near right looked a bit soft as the van rocked around, its chassis creaking, the springs pinging up and down. I wanted that clamp to give way and a ton of sugar beet to come crashing down on to the pair of them. He didn't do that to me. Bernie Capon didn't make the car rock and roll for me. He'd never even given me a lift home after pushing into me against the rubbish bins out the back of the village hall.

There's a stack of them in my head, other people's secrets, solid up to the roof like hundreds of straw bales wedged in tight. Take one or two out from the bottom and they'll all come tumbling down, bales exploding all over the place. Like when you cut the baler twine if they've been baled too tight and the straw busts out the middle, becomes twice, three times the size, dust flying up everywhere.

TANNINGTON STRAIGHT

Our house stood out in the middle of nowhere, surrounded by fields that stretched for miles. A Suffolk prairie, some people called it. There were no trees or hedges left. They were grubbed up when the smaller fields disappeared, so that even the spindliest elder stood out like an oak tree.

Every time I slid down a bank, it felt like I was slipping into a crack in the earth, a place where I could hear and see things properly. Where everything above ground grew to three, four times the normal size. Boxing hares could look like two grown men having a stand-up fist fight in the middle of a field, and the underbellies of vans could look as big as juggernauts seen from a ditch. It was the only place where thoughts slowly trickled back into me, where I could hear real sounds – like that noise the clay makes after it's been raining, a soft sucking noise, a bubbling from underneath as if the field is smacking its lips.

The best ditches were the ones over at World's End on the edge of Worlingworth. Three brothers and a sister worked the farm: Walter, Edgar, Hubert and their sister Ivy. They'd always kept cows and pigs, a few red hens. The water ran clear into their ditches and was thick with pondweed and frogspawn by the start of spring. Ducks came over from the drinking pond to feed there sometimes, wading down banks full of primroses and oxlips.

But then there were ditches like the ones either side of Tannington Straight, deep lifeless ditches full of rubbish. I never went in them if I could help it, tried to avoid going down the road altogether.

I'd found some bad things in those ditches. Porno mags with their pages all stuck together. Used johnnies. Stained mattresses that were tipped straight in, some left to stand there on end. With hundreds of acres of flat field either side, people knew they wouldn't be caught out, surprised by cars swooping round a bend or people out for a stroll, because nobody ever walked down the Straight, not even with the dog for a stretch of the legs. People only walked down it for a purpose, like me or Walker. Car drivers had a clear view in every direction and if they couldn't see anybody, then nobody could see them. An open road, a clear throw, so they wound the windows down, or stopped to open the boot, just long enough to lob something into the ditch. Like a baby.

Everybody was talking about it. I could hear them wherever I went.

'Have you heard? There's been a baby found. Up by Tannington Straight.' On the streets, in the village shop, over garden fences. It reached as far as Fram where people whispered about it in Carley & Webbs.

'A newborn baby, dumped right out there in the middle of nowhere. Who would ever do such a thing?'

'Nobody's been carrying round here, not that we know of. It must have been someone from outside. Poor little mite.'

On and on they went. What was its mother thinking of? How a poor little defenceless creature didn't deserve an end like that. I knew what they were on about. It was me who found the baby down there in the ditch that day.

'It was lucky you happened to be passing on foot,' people said. 'That baby could have been down there for days. Deep ditch out the way like that.' Then with a shudder, 'Oh, it doesn't bear thinking about, does it? Such a terrible thing. Was it a boy or a girl, I wonder?' All eyes turned on me.

It was a still morning in early-March when I found the baby, the first day of the year that the sunshine felt strong enough to start taking the chill out of the ground. The wind had been in the east for the past week, sheeting across the fields and in through the gaps round the window frames. But overnight it had disappeared, and the morning was so quiet, you could hear voices from miles away: the noise of children playing outside the farm cottages in Brundish, the ducks on Fram Mere. It felt like everyone was coming out of their houses into the sun for the first time that year. Blue sky, no wind, a perfect spring morning. It wasn't long before the crop sprayers arrived.

By mid-morning the spray was hanging heavy in the air. It soaked into the fields, sank into the ditches to settle on the water.

'First fine day,' my dad sighed. The spray booms swung close up to the edge of our garden, a fine wash of pesticide landing on our fence, the edge of the goat shed.

'I do wish they wouldn't come so close,' Mum said, as she made sure all the windows were closed. But still those fumes found their way in. A thick smell like burning plastic crept through every hole and crack till the pesticides seemed to fill the whole house and caught against the back of our throats.

I had to get out of the house, find fresh air somewhere away from all the spraying. In the end I decided to take a bag of feed to the two chickens who were living wild by the side of a field towards Horham. They'd fallen off a lorry some time ago when the driver skidded on ice on a back lane, and ended up in the ditch. Me and Dad came across the crash minutes after it happened, saw broken crates and a mess of chickens spilled all over the road. A few days afterwards, when the road had been cleaned up, we saw the two birds that had got away, sheltering under a nearby hedge.

'Winter nights will finish them off,' Dad said. 'They'll be dead by Christmas.' But they did survive. They'd got through the winter, and had plumped up with thick feathers from living in that strip of hedge.

It took me over an hour and a half to walk the few miles. I took the longer route so I could get off the roads and go down the bridle-ways and footpaths across the fields. The chicken boys were scratching around on the verge when I got there, but scuttled off into the field when they saw me. They were still wary after all this time, but as soon as I threw the feed and moved off a little way, they came over to peck at the corn. They were like an old married couple, sticking close together when they weren't sure what to do, whether to run and which way, or whether to come and feed. It was the smaller bird who usually took the lead, the other following close on his stumpy tail feathers.

It was late afternoon by the time I started heading home, not thinking clearly about the route I was taking. Before I knew it, I'd rounded the bend and the endless grey stretch of Tannington Straight lay ahead of me.

They were growing rape in the fields either side that year. It was already knee-high, like dull grass. The sky had clouded over and the feel of spring was long gone. I put my head down and started walking as fast as I could.

I was halfway along when I saw Bella Creasey, the last person I wanted to meet out there on my own in the middle of nowhere. She was wheeling her bike in the distance, just approaching the top junction. I slid into the ditch without a second thought and landed by a huge pile of bottles. There were always a few empty cans and bottles in there, Tolly Cobbold, Watneys Pale Ale, but this must have been a pile of at least twenty London Gin bottles. The smell of gin was so strong it could have been running off the field that day, getting mixed in with the ditchwater and the pesticides. It wasn't long before I started to feel queasy. I took a quick look over the bank and saw Bella Creasey hadn't turned down the Straight after all and had disappeared from sight.

That's when I saw it just in front of me. Half in, half out of the water. It was a package, wrapped in pages from a *News of the World*, lying underneath the land drain pipe. It looked like a bag of fish and chips but for some blood showing through. I was wondering if it might be kittens as I prised the paper open with a stick. A photograph of Prince Charles and Lady Di in her blue engagement suit had been covering the body. The face was blackened in places, blotchy, and some newsprint had rubbed off on to the belly, a faint tattoo of Lady Di's face on the chest. But the baby had a lovely sticky-out mouth with perfect lips as if she was about to reach up and kiss someone, and a tuft of dark hair with a slight curl at the end. She had no arms.

'Nobody's been expecting round here.' People were going on and on about it. Suddenly they were noticing me, that quiet White girl, stopping me for a chat, asking me how I was. But underneath all their questions about me, my mother, how Dad was getting on in his new job, I could tell what they really wanted to ask me. What did it look like? What colour was it? Was it black, white, yellow? What about its hair, its eyes? Did it look like anyone round here?

I was a walking lump of clay for weeks afterwards, people pressing questions into me, trying to push their fingers into my head and have a good delve around inside to see what they could find. But I never answered people's questions.

'Baby was dead, that's all,' I mumbled. I didn't tell them that some of her was missing. I wanted to bury her deep, keep her down there safe and quiet, where nobody needed to know anything, safe as long as she was down there behind my ribs.

If it hadn't been for the ditch baby, I often wonder how different life would be now. That maybe none of those terrible things would have happened that summer, or everything that's happened since. From the day I found her, it's as if that baby climbed aboard a runaway train and sat astride the engine as it hurtled off in all crazy directions, mowing down people and houses in its path, and leaving tracks scorched into the ground behind it. I might not be fourteen any more, but it worries me, the way that train is still going strong after all these years with no way of knowing where it's headed next.

THE BEET CLAMP

She came over and lay next to me in the church today. I stopped off on the way home from work, and as soon as I sat beneath the picture window, I felt her come over to me. She's like a lone peewit, always landing close by when there's bad weather on the way – yet more of it heading in my direction. I've got used to her over the years. How she chirrups next to me on the pew, just beyond my line of vision. How she has good days and bad. Sometimes I think I can catch her shadow, the faint outline of her tufted hair sticking up like a black feathered crest. Though as soon as I turn to look, she shifts out of the way, just enough that I can never pin her down to see her properly But she's there all right. I can smell the ditchwater on her tiny body.

At this time of day in early-spring, the sun just about reaches the window, strong enough for the colours from the stained glass to catch on the wall opposite. It's not like any other church window. There are no crucifixions or people praying in long robes. Instead it's a picture of two men out working in the fields. It's autumn in one half of the window, and a man is sowing seed by hand, the old-fashioned way, with blackbirds hopping round his feet, a cock pheasant and a chicken nearby. Next to him it's summer and the farmworker is cutting the wheat with a scythe, surrounded by poppies and cornflowers, and working in a cloud of blue butterflies. In the very top corner of the window, a pair of Suffolk Punches are pulling a plough. If I look hard enough, I can usually spot some tiny detail I haven't noticed before, like the black seeds in the centre of poppy heads, or the pattern engraved on the horse brasses.

'I'd give anything to be there right now, wouldn't you?' I said.

Peewit was squirming on the floor near my feet, the colours from the stained glass beginning to climb the wall behind us as the sun went down.

'I'd sit on top of the hill and watch everything going on down below, the pigs and the sheep, and those men out working the field. You could lie next to me in the shade from the wheatsheaves.'

We made an odd pair, sitting there together, but I liked talking to her. Nothing ever disturbed us in the church. It wasn't used much these days, just a service every fourth Sunday, and I liked to tell her about my day. She didn't get impatient and tap her fingers, didn't butt in with questions and corrections. I spoke to her the way some people talk to their dogs, like Fred Bugg does with Vegas.

'Zelma's been on at me again today,' I said. Peewit was so close now I could feel her warm baby breath on my shoulder. 'She reckons the shop won't last the year. "For goodness' sakes, Desiree, sort yourself out. Find yourself another job while you've still got this one. You don't want to suddenly be without a wage, do you? Life's difficult enough as it is without that to worry about as well."'

I turned round in the pew.

'I suppose that's why you're here now, is it?' But Peewit was off and away, playing in the colours on the wall somewhere behind me.

Zelma couldn't work it out.

'The shop should be busier than ever with all these new houses going up and people moving in from outside,' she said. 'You'd think the village would feel full of life, not be shutting down.' The village pubs will be the next to go, she says.

But maybe the village is like one of those shrubs you get in full bloom, when it looks more healthy and alive than it's ever been, while underneath its roots are rotting and it flowers in a last desperate effort to seed itself before it dies off.

Beatrice the goat woman didn't make things much better today either. I only went round after work to see if she needed any help. She was burning the horns off a pair of four-day-old Saanen kids when I turned up. She was in the goat shed, turning two long-handled irons over a Butane burner.

'How's the sciatica?' I said.

'Murder,' she said, without looking up, and pressed the red-hot irons straight on top of the kid's head. She could have been stamping a library book except for the smoke curling around her face from burning hair and bone. It took just a few seconds and then the kid shook herself and ran off to her sister with two black craters on her head.

Beatrice looked up as I put some ash branches into the main pen and the goats ran over to start stripping the leaves. She had her white coat on ready for milking, and her hair bundled up on her head like a hay net, grey strands forced into smooth shiny squares through the mesh she laid tight over the top.

Beatrice has a pedigree herd, mainly Nubians and Toggenburgs. Her prize goat, Holkham Hebe, won Best in Show at the East of England when she was a goatling, and the other two, Juno and Artemis, have all won prizes as milkers. Nancy has always looked a bit shabby next to them with her bent hocks and raggedy coat. She's a Golden Guernsey, a rare-breed pedigree. Just not a very well put together one, as Dad used to say.

'I'll milk them while I'm here,' I said, and drew up a stool to the milking bench. Nancy was the last to go up, with her lumpy udder and teats like beer-pulls. I liked to take my time with her, talk to her the way Dad used to.

Beatrice was tying a new salt lick to the pen gate behind me. She startled me when she spoke.

'A word, Desiree? If you're not in a hurry? It's about Hilary,' she said without waiting for me to answer. 'My brother . . . the one who farms out in Norfolk. Rare breeds. Goats, pigs, cattle. The lot. Looking for help. Interested?' She always talks like someone out of a black-and-white war film, in rapid-fire bursts of Morse code. 'He's happy to see you. Take a drive over. See what you think.' Rattle rattle, she went, hammering me with good pay, decent boss, lovely spot. Beatrice paused a moment. 'It's at the tip of north Norfolk,' she said, more slowly. 'Too far to travel every day but it comes with live-in accommodation. Nothing fancy, but he'd look after you. He and his wife, they're both good people.'

I pressed my forehead against Nancy's side after Beatrice left the shed, feeling so tired I could have lain down in the pen there and then. I listened to the belch and gurgle of Nancy's stomach as she brought up more cud. We stayed like that a while together.

The sun had gone down, and it was time to go home. The pigs in the sheds half a mile from the church were squealing, their shut-up stench blowing over the graveyard and into the porch where it was pooling in the corners. The pigman had turned the machine feeder on, and they were screaming for food. Mum would be waiting for me.

'See you soon, then,' I said. Peewit chirruped from somewhere near the font as I closed the door to head home. She wasn't going anywhere. Peewit never leaves church, and she'll probably never leave me either. She's got nobody else. They never did find out who her mother and father were.

For years I used to wish that somebody else had found her so that she could have latched on to them like a motherless chick instead of me, because I know how angry she is. I can feel it in the church some days: how the air spits like just before a storm; how on the bad days she'll shove a pile of hymn books to the floor or beat at the window panes, furious at being born into this world to be dumped in a dirty old ditch. If only I'd never gone down the Straight that day, I wouldn't have got caught up in her fury and brought it upon everyone around me.

Mum was reading in the front room when I got home. I parked the car and watched her through the window a while, working out what I was going to say.

Nobody else knows how bad Mum is, how much worse she's got

recently. For ages she wouldn't go anywhere without me; now she won't go anywhere, with or without me. And to think, there was a time when she couldn't bear to be indoors at home.

'Somebody give me a ride. Tony, take me out before I tear this house down with my bare hands. I am going absolutely crazy! Tony, teach me to drive. Please?' But Dad always said he couldn't afford her wearing out the clutch on the Morris Marina.

Our house looked so small from the road, like a tiny brown dolls' house with only the pylons for company. They march across the back field from Sizewell, thirteen miles of them, heading in from the coast to pass the end of our back garden, so close you can see the black-and-yellow 'Danger of Death' signs screwed to their struts, a row of stickmen being electrocuted over and over till the pylons disappear out on the horizon.

They're growing rape around us right now, which will stink to high heaven when the flowers die off in early-summer but it's worth it for the few weeks the fields bloom bright yellow, when the house feels like it's sunk in the middle of a seabed.

Mum dipped her head to look at something more closely in the book, and I saw the line of her scalp neatly dividing her hair in two like the white lines down the middle of a road. I hadn't noticed it before. Or that she seemed shorter, as if she were shrinking. She wasn't going to want to hear about my day, about the shop dying on its feet or Beatrice's offer of a job.

'Moving to Norfolk?' she'd say. 'But this is your home, Desiree. You live here.' And there would be tears. 'I can't cope on my own. Not here. You know I can't get about without a car.'

'So come with me then, Mum.' But then she'll be wide-eyed with terror, gripping on to the back of a chair or braced against a wall.

Or she could go the other way, her mouth pressed to stop her from saying anything, but it's building up behind teeth clamped shut till suddenly they shatter under pressure and out it comes at last.

'You can't leave me! I've got nobody else. Your dad's gone.' And after these years of silence, I wait for her to say it, to talk about that day which was buried straight after it happened. 'It's your fault,' she'll say. 'Remember?'

Mum got up to draw the curtains. I didn't want to go indoors. Instead I wanted to curl up there by the side of the road, burrow my way into a beet clamp and never go home. It would have to be one of those clamps that's as big as a mountain, hundreds of tons of sugar beet covered over with earth and straw to keep the frost out, so huge that they whittle away at it from one side till it becomes a three-sided drive-in clamp. Like the one Bernie and Pam parked in on bingo nights. That's the sort I want to be in, safe and cosy inside with only rats running over the top of me for company. No noise, no people except for Walker passing by twice a day on one of his looping thirty-five-mile walks, or Fred Bugg who comes along mumbling to himself and Vegas. He'll be having a go at her for rolling in something. 'You can't leave well alone, can you? I'll have to get you in the bath when you get home, you mucky little bugger.' A warm bath about to fix everything.

Then maybe when it's my time to come out, things will have moved on without me, life will have changed without me having to be there, ready for me to pick up like a bag of washing from the launderette, and everything will be all right again.

I walked into the warm fug of a house where the doors and windows have been closed all day.

'How was your day, Desiree?'

'Quiet,' I said. 'Nothing new.' Mum waited a while as I took off my boots, her hand pulling at the skin on her throat over and over till she couldn't wait any longer.

'So who was in today? Anyone new?'

'No,' I said. But I told her about the people who had bought the barn at the back of the pub, that Zelma had found out they were a pair of retired civil servants from London, and that Pam came in for a box of Black Magic, with a new perm and a pink lacy bra on show through her V-neck top. 'She's having another one of her Tupperware parties,' I said.

Then there was Milly Doy who came in for bleach. 'She was still in her housecoat,' I said. 'The blue one.' Though she looked more yellow than blue, more sour around the mouth than ever. She was turning into a lemon before our very eyes. She never looked at me when I served her, never even looked up when Walker passed by on the road outside. Her own son. But then again, nobody did. Nobody sees Walker, not any more. He's like the telegraph poles and the flattened shadow of dead things on the road. They stopped seeing him a long time ago.

'Is that it?' Mum said. 'Nobody else? It can't have been that quiet surely.' But I wasn't going to tell Mum about her sister Shirley who came in looking so huge in her maternity dress, the black one with gold buttons, that she might have been carrying twins this time. Or about Bella Creasey in a white tee-shirt with blue-and-silver flowers on the front, a tight skirt all bellied out, and bare legs that looked like a pair of cod fillets. I had to get away, get into the stockroom at the far end of the shop when I saw her come in, but not before I'd smelled the sour beer on her and she'd managed to shout, 'How's your mother, Desiree?' holding a bag of Birds Eye frozen peas out with one hand. I wanted to shut her mouth with the bag rammed in tight, shut her up for good.

'These cracks round the frames, they're getting worse. The windows are going to fall out soon if they get any bigger.'

'I'll see what I can do,' I said. 'I'll ring the farm.'

Before bed I went out to put a blanket over the car windscreen. I feel like Dad more and more these days, that I'm turning into him, as I sit at the wheel of the same Morris Marina and drive to work; carry the bags of shopping in afterwards, sometimes a sack of potatoes slung over one shoulder just like he used to do. And every night when I lock the back door.

We were in for a frost now that the fog and cloud had rolled away.

It would have been a good night to sit out and watch shooting stars when it was clear like this and the sky reached right down to the edge of the fields. That's how I found out about the wires, the electricity, found out something that nobody else has ever mentioned. Out here I can see weather coming across the fields from miles away; hear where it stops and starts, how the wind can suddenly blow itself out. I've been here when the wind has got caught up in the wires and they've been singing away like a woman. Then all of a sudden the wind has stopped. Everything's still. And yet the wires are still singing away. Until it's as if they hear the silence all around them, and then they stop. But not before I've heard it. How the wind and rain have caught them out, how electricity doesn't need the wind and the rain to let rip with its roaring and singing. It's got a life all of its own.

IPSWICH HOSPITAL

'Have I ever told you the story', Mum would say, 'about the time I got to stay a whole week in Ipswich Hospital?'

'A thousand times,' we'd say, always wanting to hear it again, one more time. 'But don't forget the bit about Shirley's arms,' after she'd tried to miss it out one time.

'The summer of 1964. Wednesday the first of July. I'd just given birth that morning and had been wheeled on to the ward with all the other new mums. "You should get some rest, Mrs White," the nurses said, but I lay there for hours, wide awake. It was so warm up on the top floor, they had all the windows open, and even the traffic noise was being drowned out by crying babies, nurses marching up and down, and trolleys banging through the swing doors. There was no hope of me getting any sleep. Instead I lay in bed, listening to the visitors and what they had to talk about. It was one of the happiest times of my life. All the nurses were so kind and caring.

'"How are you, Mrs White, can we get you anything? Do you need any help with feeding the baby? He's such a pet, have you thought of a name yet? He can't be Baby White for ever." I've never had so much fuss and attention. I cried when your father arrived to take me home. "Baby blues," the nurse said to Dad, "she'll be fine in a few days."'

But Mum would have given up an arm or a leg to stay there, we all knew that. She always said she could see herself living in Ipswich so clearly, her and Dad moving into a little terraced house just down the road from the hospital, leaping on to a bus or train whenever the fancy took her, for a trip over town or somewhere beyond. 'Just think, an hour and forty minutes on the train and you're in the middle of London,' she'd say.

Then there'd be the shops and cinemas up the road, and we'd have neighbours, lots of neighbours close by, who'd pop in and mind us children for an hour or so while she and Dad went out together. She had it all worked out to the smallest detail, this other life.

'But instead we came back here.' And she'd sweep an arm wide into the space around us, at the grey line of horizon that wrapped itself round our house like a rabbit snare. 'And your father had been tidying up for the big homecoming. He'd swept and dusted, even washed the bedroom curtains. But just as I walked through the back porch with the baby in my arms, all wrapped up in a yellow cot blanket, I tripped over the sack of spuds that he'd left right there in the middle of the floor, and went flying. If it hadn't been for your Aunt Shirley standing in the kitchen doorway with her arms outstretched, I'd have gone headlong through the plate glass in the door and probably killed the both of us. And as your father was cursing the sack of King Edwards, kicking them out of the way, and I was sitting in shock at the kitchen table, I said, "Edward, now that's a nice name."'

Mum dropped the 'King' under protest from Dad and Shirley, but there he was, Edward White, 'our little baby potato'. And the funny thing was, she said, he did kind of grow into one after that. 'He'd wave his little arms and legs around in the bath and look for all the world as if he'd chitted little tubers.' Then when I came along a couple of years later, there was a sack of Desirees in the porch, and eleven months after that a sack of Maris Pipers. That was Pipe, my little brother.

So there we all were, the potato family, and it seemed like nobody took much notice of us, living where we did, or ever wondered what we got up to, until that day I picked the baby up and wrapped her in my jumper to take her to the nearest phonebox.

The attention wouldn't let up on me in those first few weeks, especially after I took a Saturday job in Worlingworth shop. I usually managed to dodge out of the way whenever I could sense talk of the baby was about to start up again, but I was never fast enough for Sadie Borrett who lived three doors down from the shop, and came in all the time.

'You must be made of very strong stuff,' she said, looking right into my face one day. 'A very brave girl indeed. It must have been awful, finding a baby like that. I'd have been laid up in hospital for a month if that had been me.' But for all her talk of nerves, I could see she was dying to ask me in a whisper on the side, 'So go on then, what did it really look like?' And then I heard her complain to Zelma, 'She's a right clam, that girl. I can't get a thing out of her.'

'You know what she's like,' Zelma would say, 'best left alone.' Though she'd had a good go herself, trying to find out things like what the baby was wrapped in, whether it was the *East Anglian Daily Times*, the *Mirror* or the *Telegraph*, because her sister was married to the paperman and knew exactly who took what. I always said I couldn't remember.

It wasn't horrifying though, not like people thought it would be. It was like finding a featherless bird fallen out of its nest. The baby was tiny, especially without its arms. And it wasn't as if I'd never seen anything dead before. Dad always killed the male kids as soon as they were born, knocked them on the head before they'd drawn a first full breath.

'They're no use to us, just cost time and money feeding them, housing them properly. Kinder this way,' he'd say.

There were so many dead things around that you stopped seeing them after a while. Myxi rabbits mowed down on the road; rooks on sticks out in the fields. Ed slung rabbits on the porch floor when he came back from shooting out in the stubble fields at night, and come winter there was usually a brace of pheasants hanging underneath the shelf. They were only fur and feathers, meat laid over a few bones.

The baby didn't live for long, the police said, a minute at most; that she was born so early she would probably never have survived even in hospital. At least the baby hadn't been swung by its ankles against the corner of a house or placed in a sack and drowned in a pond. I wanted people to let her be. It wouldn't have changed anything for the baby, knowing who dumped her there that day. It wouldn't have stopped her feeling hard and cold as a frozen chicken when I folded my jumper around her. By the time I got to the phonebox, my shirt was wet as she soaked through the wool. I was freezing cold. But as I held her upright against my shoulder so I could use the phone, her body seemed to give slightly, her head coming to rest near my neck as if I'd managed to warm her through just a little.

I thought it was never going to stop, all the fuss, the questions. It seemed to go on for ever and that whichever way I turned there was always somebody waiting round the corner to catch me out. It was like being wheeled about in a cage, '*Roll up, roll up! Here she is, come look at the Potato Girl. See how pink she is. Ladies and gentlemen, just ten pence a go to see if you can get her to talk . . . but no poking with sticks through the bars, please.*'

Yet in all those weeks and months, nobody ever thought to ask Walker. Not a single person mentioned his name or thought for a moment it might be worth trying to stop him for a chat. The police didn't question him when they should have done. He might have liked to talk about one of his walks. He might have liked it if someone had shown an interest and asked him what sort of things he saw on those thirty-five-mile-long tramps of his, thinking that perhaps they'd been useful after all. He might have had something to say, because he was there that day.

Walker didn't want to hang about on the Straight either that afternoon. I'd been following him after I left the chicken boys, trying to see if I could catch him up for once, and didn't think about where I was headed until it was too late. By the time I turned on to the Straight that day, Walker was long gone.

I never saw him coming back. I never heard him either, not even the tread of his boots on the road as he drew close. I was down in the ditch, pressed tight into the bank next to the gin bottles, willing Bella not to have turned down the Straight and be heading straight towards me. I was about to poke my head out and check when, before I knew it, Walker had gone past, and as he did, I swear I could feel a light breeze that lifted the hairs on the back of my neck.

NEW ENGLAND

Ed and Pipe couldn't get enough of all the new attention.

'So it was your sister that found the baby? What did it look like? Did it have its guts hanging out?' The boys swapped stories with everyone at school till the baby was unrecognisable, with club feet and half a brain.

It was thanks to Peewit that Ed got his first girlfriend, Pam Hawes, who lived with her dad in Southolt and wore a leather jacket with a tassel fringe. She never took it off even in a ninety-degree heat, and she bleached her hair white till it crackled like barley straw. Pam and Ed had known each other for years, gone to the same schools, been in the same class, yet barely spoken a word to each other in all that time. But suddenly Pam started taking an interest in him overnight as if he'd turned into somebody worth talking to.

And then there was Bernie, Bernie Capon, who'd never so much as looked in my direction or spoken a whole sentence to me from the day he turned thirteen.

Bernie lived out by the double bends, in a row of cottages halfway between us and Worlingworth. His family were our nearest neighbours, living in the first house you came to just over a mile from our place. When we were very young, they still grew beans around us which covered the fields in black-and-white flowers by early-June. On summer evenings when the damp was just beginning to rise, the perfume from the bean fields was so strong and sweet, it drew everyone out of doors. We'd step out as a family for a walk up the road; take the goats with us sometimes so they could graze the verges. We often bumped into the Capons halfway, sometimes the Buggs and the Rumseys as well who lived in the same row. The grown-ups would stand around talking for a while in the middle of the road, laughing and smoking rollies, while we played with Bernie and his sister Cheryl. When it was time to say goodnight and head off in opposite directions, our mum and dad would hold hands while we ran backwards and forwards like dogs fresh off the lead.

Bernie had just turned seventeen and, when he wasn't sleeping or eating, he was usually round at our house. He and Ed were best friends and spent every weekend talking about cars and horsepower, their heads jammed together under the bonnet of the Cortina that sat on breeze blocks in the front garden. Ed wanted to get it going by the time he was due to take his test in July. They'd both been driving since they were twelve, taking old bangers over the stubble fields at the end of summer. 'I'll only need a couple of lessons,' he said.

'Ed around?' Bernie never said anything else to me when he came to the back door. To Bernie Capon I really was invisible, though I never minded. I could stand just ten yards away and watch them fiddle around with the engine. Bernie was much thinner than Ed, straight up and down. When he bent over the car with his shirt off, his back reminded me of a skinned rabbit, the ridge of his spine pushing hard at the skin.

In just a few weeks they'd managed to discuss every girl and woman they knew this side of Stradbroke, trying to work out who could have had a baby.

'Remember that girl who worked in the pub in Dennington?' Bernie was talking to Ed who was lying underneath the car. 'She was fat enough, and then she lost all that weight really quickly, do you remember? Said she'd been on a crash diet . . . but she could have been up the duff. It could have been her.' I was leaning against the goat shed when Bernie stopped what he was doing and turned round. 'All right, Desiree? Got back from somewhere?' I was so surprised, I just stood there.

'Nowhere in particular,' I said, a moment later, and went straight indoors, their laughter at my back.

After that, I couldn't come and go as I pleased. Bernie had suddenly started to see me. He made me feel hot and uncomfortable whenever he looked up from under the bonnet with an expression on his face which I couldn't work out. And he'd say things, like where he'd seen me the day before, or ask where was I headed when I was about to set off for a walk, and how that must have given me a fright, finding a dead baby when I was all by myself.

I started to keep out of Bernie's way, only watching what he was up to when I was upstairs at the window. But it got so I started to see how his jeans turned black and greasy where he wiped his hands on his legs, got to thinking how that oily shine on his thigh would feel – hot and smooth to the touch. I began to like the way his hair flopped over his face as he bent over the engine or crouched down on the grass to fiddle with a tool box. He never hooked it behind his ear like a girl. He'd open his hand, palm wide, and scoop it off his forehead, in a broad sweep to the back of his head. I watched as his hair slid forward again seconds later, falling dead straight like a plumb line. He never seemed to notice.

In May the ditches began to dry out with the warmer weather, and I started going up to the double bends in the evenings just to try and catch a glimpse of him. It felt better that way, me seeing him from down in the ditch without him seeing me, and he did look a lot bigger from down there.

The ditch ran along the bottom of long gardens that belonged to the row of cottages. It was good to sit in, deep and dry in the summer, and well hidden by vegetables and compost heaps as everyone had lawns up near their houses. I could easily spend hours down there, picking up so much goosegrass and vetches on my clothes, I looked like I'd sprouted roots.

The Capons lived in the end house, immediately next-door to Fred Bugg, Dawn Capon's dad, who grew flowers instead of vegetables: roses, Sweet Williams, Night Scented Stock, all the old-fashioned flowers that smell at night; all the ones his wife Bessie used to like.

It was a Friday night, and Bernie was taking Ed to Speedway in Ipswich. Bernie was flipping through a car magazine on his bed, sitting beneath his life-size poster of Barry Sheene who was astride a motorbike dressed in red leathers. The breeze coming in through the window lifted a corner of the poster and made Barry ripple slightly. Cheryl was in her bedroom next door. She was frantically backcombing her hair, scrubbing at the fringe with a comb. She had a boyfriend with a car, Stan Larter from Charsfield. Every Friday night he turned up at seven on the dot, honked his horn and stayed in the car, watching her come to the window and give a little wave from upstairs. After a while he'd open the car door as if he was about to get out, but instead he'd stick one of his lanky legs up on the dashboard where it would jiggle away and make Cheryl scrub at her hair even faster.

It was nearly dusk and Fred Bugg was calling in Vegas who'd been let out for a run round the garden. He bent down to scoop up her mess with a trowel and stood by the back door. He was wiping his feet as if about to go indoors when he flicked the dog mess over the fence. High up in the air it flew, landing next to Donny's freshly dug-over potato bed. They'd obviously had another of their fallings-out. It had been going on for years, this game of volleyball, whenever things got bad between them.

Fred would fling dog mess over to Donny's side who'd then curse and mutter under his breath, whenever he found it, and throw it straight back. Then, after Donny had gone indoors, Fred would scrape it up and chuck it back over the fence. And so on, until one of them gave in or it disappeared altogether. But in all that time, I never heard Donny shout at Fred about it, even when he knew his father-in-law was nearby, usually standing just inside his back door with his bony pigeon chest all puffed out, watching the shit fly.

If it was cat shit from the Rumseys' cat, that was a different game. For some reason it never buried the stuff like normal cats. That used to pass down the row of houses, like Pass the Parcel.

'Hundreds of pissing acres of field out there and it has to come and crap in my garden!' yelled Donny as he chucked it over the fence to Fred who flung it on to Jimmy Stannard next door to him. If the cat did its business in Fred's garden, Fred chucked it on to Jimmy who flung it over to the Rudds who hurled it clear over to the Rumseys, the last house at the other end of the row, and it was their cat anyway.

In a slam of doors and a reek of hairspray, Cheryl was gone for the night, off with Stan for a drink at The Volunteer in Saxtead. Bernie was lifting dumb-bells in front of his mirror. He ran a hand over his muscles, ducked his head under each armpit and changed his shirt before heading off up the road to pick up Ed. Dawn drew the curtains downstairs. A quiet night in for her and Donny.

'They've gone out,' she'd be saying to him, 'got the place to ourselves now,' with a nod to the bedroom upstairs.

Mum and Dad were on the sofa together when I got back. The *East Anglian* was open on Dad's lap, a page of it resting on Mum's knee as I sat down on the floor by her feet. She brushed the grass and soil off my clothes, untangled the burrs from my hair.

'You look as if you've just been dug up from the garden,' Mum said quietly. Dad had nodded off but every now and then she ran a hand behind his neck, tracing the lines there which criss-crossed to make diamonds. They started from underneath his hairline and ran to the base of his neck.

'You're a marked man, Tony White,' Mum used to joke, and she'd kiss the back of his neck where X marked the spot.

When the last burr was out of my hair, and a pile of goosegrass balls lay on the arm of the sofa, she gave me a pat like a spaniel. 'There, you're done, you'll do,' she said.

The next day Mum came home from Fram, all of a clatter with bags of shopping, eyes shining, and two bright pink circles in her cheeks.

'You'll never guess who talked to me today.' Nobody spoke. 'Only the Americans.'

Mum had been wanting to talk to them for months, ever since they'd moved into Shirley and Guppy's old farmhouse on the road out of Brundish, renting it for the year. She was desperate to find out where they were from.

'How can they have been living here since last year and none of us talked to them yet?' Though she must have been thinking that if she hadn't fallen out with her sister three years ago, then she'd already have known everything about them. She'd have had the perfect excuse to go round as Guppy's sister-in-law, to check they were settling in, offer to help with any teething problems.

'Their life is on the base,' Dad said. 'They get all their food from there. The girl goes to an American school. That's how it is with the Americans round here, you know that. They keep themselves to themselves, and never get to know anyone local.'

'Well, she knew who I was. She asked if I was the mother of the girl who found the baby. She came over 'specially to say hello. She sought me out. I couldn't believe it.'

'They're not royalty, Pearl. They're just normal people like you and me.' Dad always got snappy when the subject of the Americans cropped up. It was their fighter jets, the A10s. They came screaming low overhead, frightening the goats half to death.

Mum put the shopping down and marched straight over to the globe in the front room.

'If only I could have found out which part of America they were from.' She pushed the globe in irritation which made it wobble on its axis, then stopped it with the flat of her hand to check the distance between America and Britain as she did most evenings.

The globe lived with us like one of the family. Dad bought it for her one year from a sale at Wickham Market, and that started something all right. It had a special stand, and was so huge it took up a whole corner of the front room, and never had a moment to gather a single speck of dust. Mum spun it slowly in the evenings, backwards and forwards, reading out the distances marked on the dotted lines. New

York to Southampton, 3,118 miles; or Trinidad to London, 4,010 miles. She said the lines looked like footpaths over the sea, ready for when the water dried up, and then maybe we'd be able to walk to Holland one day.

Mum liked to think the world was getting smaller, drying out and shrivelling like a walnut, and recently she'd discovered tectonic plates. She showed us on the globe how Africa was sliding north-west and slowly drifting into the east coast of America, heading back to where it first came from; that Europe and Asia were heading south while Turkey in between was travelling westwards. The way she talked about it, Turkey was being squeezed so tight, it was about to shoot out from the middle like a piece of soap across the bathroom floor. 'Those plates,' she said, 'they're moving about all the time, slipping and sliding under one another and taking those countries that sit on top with them, all those cities going for a ride.' We could tell what she really wanted, though. For America to shift closer and closer to us, shrinking the Atlantic till its eastern coast washed ashore, landing right on top of Ireland like a fat old bull seal, flippering still nearer till New York was just outside Stowmarket.

'Winona, that's her name,' Mum said, 'Lance and Winona Makepeace. And I was just about to ask them where they were from and did they know New England at all, but I couldn't get a word in edgeways. She was on about the blessed ditch baby . . . how she never imagined that sort of thing would happen in England, right here in our beautiful countryside, that it was more the sort of thing she expected to happen in their cities back home, babies getting dumped in the trash cans or caught up in storm drains. And did people round here have any idea how it got to be in the ditch in the first place?'

I never told Mum but I'd talked to the American girl once. It was in Tannington church just a few months after they'd moved in. I knew who she was because I'd seen her riding about on a horse often enough, going places she shouldn't have been. She didn't seem to notice that she was trespassing as she galloped over fields, never seemed to care that she was trampling over crops, but it seemed to keep her busy, exploring all the hideaway places, the pillboxes and the broken-down cartsheds.

I was sitting on the pew at the front when she walked up behind me. I hadn't heard the door open and wondered how long she'd been inside the church.

'What do you see in that window?' she said. 'I've been watching you for ages, from back there.' She was pointing at the curtain which closed off the bell tower. 'I thought you were some crazy, maybe in a trance or something weird.' She didn't seem to realise that maybe people sat in churches to think quietly to themselves about Jesus, or that they might have somebody buried out in the churchyard and want some time alone to think about them.

She sat down heavily on the pew behind me, her thighs spread wide in riding jodhpurs, so meaty they looked like tubes of liver sausage.

'I'm Melissa,' she said, and put her muddy boots on one of the embroidered kneelers. 'What's your name?'

'Desiree,' I said. 'I've seen you around. On your horse.'

'Oh,' she said, surprised. 'I don't recognise you.' She looked up at the window, at the sun shining through the cornfields and the poppies. 'Shame it doesn't look like that round here. It's a godforsaken hellhole, this place, don't you think? How can you bear it, living here all the time?'

'What do you mean?' I said, not wanting to hear her talk this way, to have her run the place down when she'd only been here five minutes. But at the same time, I was wondering how she managed to drawl like that, speak sentences with such long drawn-out words they could have been made of elastic, stretched so tight you could see right through them and out the other side. 'I've always lived here,' I said. 'I was born here.'

'But it's so desolate. What have you done with all the trees? And the mud . . . My God, the mud. It's everywhere.'

'It's only bad this time of year with the sugar-beet harvest,' I said. The lorries had just started carting the sugar beet off the fields, and in the last week the roads had disappeared under mud and lumps of clay. I told her it would wash away soon enough.

'And the fields . . . they're so churned up. It looks like a battlefield out there.'

'So where are you from then?' I only asked because I was thinking of Mum, how excited she'd be when I told her I'd found out.

'San Diego,' the girl said. I hadn't heard Mum talk about that place. She'd been willing them to be from New England or San Francisco. She'd have put up with Los Angeles or Tucson, but San Diego? That was bound to be a disappointment. 'Though my folks are in the army so we move around a lot. They're up at Bentwaters right now.'

'I know,' I said. 'You live in the pink farmhouse on the edge of Brundish.'

'Oh my God, you people know everything about us. How does anyone get any privacy round here?' She didn't look too worried about it though as she sat there with her arms along the back of the pew, her chest pushed out till the buttons on her jacket looked about ready to fly off.

'Thank God I'm away at school most of the time. I'm only home a few days for Thanksgiving but I can't wait to go back. I miss Billy the Kid though. I left him outside in the churchyard. He'll be all right out there, won't he? Nobody will mind?'

I told her he'd be fine so long as he couldn't get at the box hedge or the yew. She did know they were deadly poisonous to animals, didn't she?

That did the trick. That got rid of her soon enough. She was so loud and full of herself, so puffed up with air like a turkey, the church felt more empty afterwards than it usually did.

She hadn't seen me though, not properly. She hadn't seen me staring at the poppies in the window, staring so hard at the seeds in the middle and the sunlight on the scythe that my eyes were starting to burn. And then it happened. The poppies moved. My eyes watered and the flower heads wavered in a breeze, the scythe sliced through the wheat, and the rooks flapped up and down before settling on the ground. I sat in bright sunshine and watched the horses move slowly up the field while butterflies danced around my feet.

WORLD'S END

The pea fields were in flower by June, tendrils and shoots hooking on to one another as the pods began to appear.

'A few more weeks, then we'll be in for some restless nights soon enough,' Dad said. 'There'll be no getting away from the pea harvest this year.'

He'd been working in the chicken factory for six months. Dad was a stockman, had always worked with cows ever since he left school, but he'd lost his job at the farm just before Christmas.

'There's no call for stockmen any more, not round here,' he said. 'Everyone's getting rid of their cows. I'll just have to take what I can get.' But it turned out the only job going was at Sunshine Chickens near Eye.

Mum took one look at Dad after his first day in the new job, and laid a hand on his arm.

'It's a stopgap, Tony, till we get back on our feet.'

But after the first week, he never talked about the factory, and we stopped asking. He always washed his hands when he came in but the water would roll off invisible chicken fat. I could see it there on him still, turning white like lard.

He was tired in the evenings, short-tempered. Dad was fretful, Mum said, because he was worried about money. But she was less understanding when he started to have a second or a third beer in the evening.

'Do you have to drink every night, Tony?'

'It helps me to unwind,' he said. But the more he relaxed, the more wound up she became as if his day was pouring straight into her.

'Why don't you do something of an evening, instead of sitting there with a bottle in your hand? And anyway, we can't afford it.' Dad took a long drink. 'It all adds up,' Mum said, 'and the boys don't stop eating. I could afford driving lessons with your beer money.'

'I'd have to drink a lot more for you to afford those,' he said with a laugh. Mum's face coloured up in a rush.

'The problem with you, Tony, is that you never could hold your drink. Never. I don't know why you do it. You're no good at it.' And she stormed off up the road for over two hours.

The stained-glass window was going to brighten things up at home, if just for a short while. I thought carefully about my pattern in the art class at school, used cellophane in the same colours as I'd seen in the window in Tannington church. I knew exactly where my stained glass was going to go and how it would catch the sun.

With its plastic corrugated roof and glass walls, the porch was like a glass bubble tacked to the back of our house. It was a sun trap in the morning, catching the sun on its way up over the back field and as it passed overhead before it disappeared on the other side by the afternoon. It got so hot in there some mornings, Mum said we should cover the floor in sand and pretend to be in the Sahara Desert. 'We could be a thousand miles away, right here in our back porch.'

The only problem was the lack of privacy. Anyone could see straight into that porch from a way up the road to either side, or from the field behind, and make out what was on our shelves down to what type of spuds we were eating or whether Dad's work boots were in the usual place. From over a quarter of a mile away on the road heading for home, I could see Mum in there some days, staring out over the field and the line of pylons to the horizon, all the time twisting and fiddling with the fly curtain, winding the strips round her fingers or her feet till they were coiled halfway up her leg. Some days that fly plastic seemed to cling to her as if it were never going to let go.

It didn't seem to bother her that the porch was see-through. Or perhaps she didn't know.

'It's like being on display in a shop window, Mum,' I should have said. 'Anyone can see in.' I wish I had done. Those few words might have changed everything.

The coloured window was just the right size when I brought it home. It covered the entire pane of glass in the porch door, top to bottom.

Mum was at the kitchen door the next morning, standing on the lintel. She turned to me.

'Have you seen this, Desiree?' She stepped to one side to let me through. 'It's like a cathedral. It's wonderful.' The concrete floor of the porch was covered in patches of blue, red and green that merged into a bigger puddle of turquoise, then into blood-orange that ran all the way across to where our boots were lined up in the corner. We stood there in the light, laughing at the colours on our bare feet.

The sack of King Edwards turned from orange to red as the sun moved overhead. Mum stood in front of the window, her face pressed close to a blue square in the centre.

'Wouldn't it be the best thing in the world,' she said, 'if that was the Indian Ocean right outside the back door? If all we had to do was step outside and take a boat over to Zanzibar?'

All I could see was a field of blue peas and a pylon standing right in the middle of it. But if there really was an ocean out there, I knew we wouldn't see her for dust.

'Right, come on, we need to clear this porch out.' Mum passed the broom to me. It was worth sweeping the floor and clearing the shelves for such a spectacle, she said.

Mum spent the rest of the afternoon in the porch. She cleaned every pane of glass and even got Pipe to climb up the side to wash the roof down with a yard brush and a bucket of water.

'Your dad won't recognise the place,' she said.

'What's the special occasion?' Ed asked when he came in.

'Desiree's window,' Mum said. 'Didn't you notice it? All those colours in the porch?' But he was already lifting the lids off the saucepans to see what was for tea.

'Dad not back yet?' he said. 'I thought he was on early shifts this week.'

Mum said perhaps he'd stopped off to feed those two chickens and forgotten the time.

We waited a while, but were already halfway through tea by the time Dad got in over an hour and a half late. He hadn't even looked in at the goats, to check if they'd been fed and watered or that I'd done the milking. He seemed to take for ever to get his boots off in the porch, even longer to wash his hands, then just sat at the table, staring at the plate in front of him. Nobody said a word. Suddenly he pushed it away with such force that it skidded up the table and landed at the other end in front of Ed.

'For crying out loud, Tony, what's wrong? It's not chicken.' Dad couldn't eat chicken any more, not since he'd started work at the factory, said he simply couldn't stomach it after the stink of them, day in, day out. Pipe was none too keen on eggs since he'd burst open some rotten ones he found in a blackbird's nest, and Mum had gone off pork because of the pig units. Me and Ed were the only ones who ate everything. Ed could combine his way through anything that was put in front of him twice over, and still be hungry.

'Are you sickening, Tony? Is that why you're so late back?'

'A man lost his fingers at work today.' We all looked at Dad's hands, our own, then at each other's. I thought of Bernie's fingers, the black oil under his nails, the swell of his knuckles. Ed was staring at Dad's plate which was touching his own.

'He got his cuffs caught and the machine sliced right through them. Nobody could do anything about it. One minute they were there, on his hands, the next they were on the floor right there in front of us.'

The boys wanted to know more, I could tell. What did they look like? How much blood? Did it spray everywhere? What noise did they make as they fell to the floor? Did they lie there spread out like proper fingers, or point in all different directions like on a clock?

'Marcus Chapman. He's got a wife and three kids.' Dad sat with his head in his hands.

There were four chipolatas on his plate, lined up in a row next to mash and peas. Someone must have picked them up off the floor, four fingers on a paper plate that rolled around slightly from side to side as they were carried carefully from the factory to the office, like a plateful of special party food for the secretaries.

'If you don't want your tea, Dad . . .' Ed said quietly, then tipped the food on to his own plate when Dad shook his head.

Nobody talked much afterwards. Dad had a beer and sat in front of the television for the rest of the night. I saw the back of his neck when he sat forward like a little old man to try and get himself off the couch. The diamonds looked wider, flattened out, as if he were carrying a heavy load on his head. He looked more like Fred Bugg then, the way he had to rock forward a couple of times before he could finally get up.

Dad couldn't stop staring at his hands in that first week after the accident, turning his palms over one way, then the other. He snapped at Ed to stop cracking his knuckles which he did at every mealtime, squeezing one fist, then the other. After that was done, Ed would yank hard on each finger at the tip, making every bone snap one by one till it seemed they were about to come clean away from their joints.

'You've got to stop doing that right now, Ed, I'm telling you.'

Dad's fingers twitched whenever he sat down in the evenings, as if they were no longer a part of him. Mum held his hand on the sofa to try and still them, but that just seemed to make the free hand even worse; one finger jerking, then another, till all five fingers would go into spasm at once and make us jump.

His hands only seemed at rest when he was doing things outside with the goats, or picking greenstuff in the evenings. They were light by then, and we often went out after tea to pick food for the goats from the verges around the back lanes.

We had five goats: three milkers, Nancy, Bentley and Hawk, and two goatlings, Poppy and Ariel. They needed greenstuff on top of their hay and cereal, more than they could get from being let out in the garden or taken down the road to graze the verges for whatever they could find. So me and Dad would drive out in the evenings and pick leaves and branches, anything he thought would keep their milk up, keep them healthy.

'Ash for milk, elm for cream,' he always said. 'The goats would love some of that.' And he'd point out milk thistles and yarrow, or say that we needed some ivy because one of the goats was off colour. 'That's too strong,' he said, weeding out wild garlic. 'It'll taint the milk.'

We drove around the lanes outside Worlingworth, usually finishing up at World's End where the hedges were thick, and the Lings didn't mind us helping ourselves. They'd said it was fine for us to pick whatever we needed, that we kept their hedges good and thick with all the pruning.

The Ling brothers all looked the same: tall beaky men with noses that dripped dewdrops in the winter. They wore grey-green overcoats, tied round the waist with baler twine, which only came off around June time and were always back on by the middle of September. Walter, the eldest, got to wear the airman's jacket from the Second World War. He always looked as warm as toast out there on his old grey Massey Ferguson, even when the wind was in the east and blowing straight in from Siberia. As for Ivy, she wore summer frocks the whole year round. Her arms looked red-raw in winter as she walked around the hen huts in the front field, collecting eggs, her legs covered with a rash up one side from sitting too close to the fire. The brothers hadn't talked in years, so people said.

They had their own places around the farm, their territories marked out long ago like the barn cats who lived half wild outside. Walter, the eldest, had the end of the house and the tractor shed. Ivy had the kitchen and the hen field. She also had the patch by the back door where she kept a herb garden up against the house and the table she used for plucking cockerels, an old door laid over a pair of sawhorses. Edgar, stone deaf since he was a boy, was most often out in the fields with the cows or in the pig shed, while Hubert, the youngest, had the hay barn and his peacocks, Percy and Susan. He'd given his birds the same names as far back as anyone could remember. Not that anyone ever saw much of Hubert to talk to. He was shy of people anyway, but terrified near to death of women. He turned and fled whenever any girl turned up at the farm wanting to buy eggs, even the older village women he must have known all his life.

'They're the way a lot of old Suffolk farming families used to be round here,' Dad said, 'living and working so close the whole time, they can never get any air in. All it takes is for some argument to blow in, take root, and before you know it, nobody's said a word to one another in years.'

It was a warm Friday evening when Dad finished that bad week at work. The verges on the way over to World's End were high with cow-parsley and campion. Dad parked in the lane and said he was going up to the farm to get some eggs off Ivy. I was going to pick ash and a couple of armfuls of willowherb.

'I'll meet you back here to load up the car,' he said.

I walked along the edge of the barley field which bounded the cow field, a deep hedge and ditch between the two, and headed for the spot where the willowherb was thickest.

There was a hole in the hedge which had been patched up with bits of old brass bed to keep the cows in, everything wedged in tight with an old bed frame. From a distance, the bed end looked like a fancy gate, until you got close up and saw the mother-of-pearl. It was under a circle of glass in the centre, and was as big as the palm of my hand. I always gave it a wipe to see the shine of it amongst the mud and the undergrowth. From there I could see straight into the hay barn, into Hubert's hideaway place.

It was where he kept his feathers, the duck and chicken feathers he collected from the yard: bantams', muscovies', mallards' – hundreds of them stuck upright into a straw bale. Percy's tail feathers waved tall as ferns in the middle of them all.

The loose bantams roosted in the barn, high on the rafters or on the old pieces of furniture which were scattered around inside. They perched on the chest of drawers where Hubert kept his tools or on the carved backs of old dining chairs, a white pyramid of chicken shit below each one. Next to a heap of sand just inside the doorway stood a wooden cradle which the Lings had probably lain in as babies. It was stuffed with straw now and used by the broody bantams when they were sitting on eggs.

Dad was talking to Ivy in the front field, red chickens scratching round their feet. I had a good armful of greenstuff and was about to head back to the car when I tripped over a stump next to the bed end and fell into a patch of young nettles that stung me all the way up my neck and one side of my face. I was cursing away and pulling up docks by the root to rub at my cheek when Hubert came round the corner of the barn, shuffling in his big work boots. Percy was scratching around in the doorway. Hubert stood a moment, watching him, then put his shovel down and reached out towards the bird as if he was about to give him some corn from his hand. But Hubert picked him up under one arm instead, and after a few paces began to sway from side to side, just inside the barn doorway. Hubert Ling was dancing. In his clumpy work boots and overcoat, he was twirling around with his peacock whose tail feathers lifted with the rise and fall of their waltz to fan Hubert's face as they swung past the feather garden and the pyramids, kicking up a cloud of straw dust and sand.

If it hadn't been for those enormous feathers and Percy's big claws hanging down by Hubert's waist, I could almost have thought he had a woman in his arms that evening. It was like seeing him the way he was as a young man, long before he climbed into his grey-green coat and tied himself in for good. I wanted to sit on that brass bed end and watch Hubert Ling dance all night long.

Dad was sitting on the verge when I got back to the lane. His face had emptied of all the strain and greyness.

'What happened to you?' he said, and touched my cheek.

'Oh, that.' I'd forgotten all about tripping over. 'Just a few nettles,' I said. We sat for a while amidst the clean sharp smell of sap from the pile of branches around us.

'This is more like it,' he said.

STAR NAKED

'You won't believe this, Zelma.' Dolly Last was in the shop first thing with her husband Elmy, telling Zelma the latest about the Americans while I took my time unpacking boxes round the corner. 'They've only gone and got a pinball machine, and put it in the kitchen! Where I can trip over it, every time, without fail. A dirty great pinball machine. I ask you, whatever next?'

Dolly went cleaning up there once a week, and told Zelma everything down to the tiniest detail. The box of chocolate bars which sat on the kitchen counter and which they got through every week. Crates of Coca-Cola, lemonade, cherryade.

'It's like a Cash and Carry in their kitchen,' she said.

They both tutted over the televisions in every room at the American house, and the state of their bins. 'What they throw away would feed me and Elmy for a month,' Dolly said. 'It's the land of plenty up there. And I swear, Zelma, not a word of a lie, I could live in that fridge of theirs. Walk right in, close the door behind me and make myself at home.'

Dolly let out a long breath. She was leaning on the counter opposite Zelma, while Elmy sat on an upended bread crate, making a rollie.

'It's a shame they don't come in here,' Zelma said. 'Mr Abbott can't bear to think about it . . . reckons they could soon shift some of his stock all right. But I've told him time and again, they get all their stuff off the base. American food, not the same as what we have here. "It stops them feeling homesick," I tell him.'

'I'll tell you something for nothing,' Dolly said. 'I haven't seen the husband without a beer in his hand yet. Ten, eleven o'clock some mornings. He's even got his own beer fridge. That can't be right if what people are saying is true.' And she lowered her voice. 'About him being nuclear.'

The rumour had been going around for a while now that the Americans were keeping a nuclear bomb up at the base, all very hush-hush, and that it was against regulations for any of them to drive down the quiet back roads, for fear that if they had an accident and got concussed, they'd spill their secrets. And they couldn't get too friendly with the locals in case something nuclear slipped out over a pint of Adnams and a pickled egg. Everyone seemed to think Lance Makepeace was high up at Bentwaters, high enough to have his finger somewhere near the button.

'You wouldn't recognise the place, Zelma. I can't get my bearings some mornings. One minute I'm cleaning their fancy coffee machine and the live-in fridge as if I'm in the middle of America, the next I see Fred Bugg wandering past the end of the drive with that fat old watery dog of his and wonder what on earth he's doing out there, thousands of miles from home.'

Elmy drew on his rollie, holding it the way he always did, between his thumb and his middle finger, the end of it pointed inward to the palm of his hand.

'That field out the back of theirs is still the same though. Remember that field, Dolly? Star Naked?' He reached over to pinch her waist but she slapped his hand away and rolled her eyes at Zelma.

'We used to go up there some nights, didn't we? There was some-thing about that field, on account of it being on a rise, that some clear nights, if you lay on your back, the other fields around just seemed to drop clean away and you could swear you were in heaven and those stars were only six inches from your face. If it wasn't for that thick old clay beneath you, holding on to your boots, you'd be off up there, swimming away in the ferment. You could feel that root pull then, all right. We had some nights, didn't we, Dolly, star-watching? Saw comets . . . shooting stars . . . going off all around us like fireworks. Remember, Dolly?' His hand was on her back now. 'Remember Star Naked? Stark

43

Bollock Naked more like.' And he coughed and laughed on his fag while Dolly said she remembered no such thing. But I noticed she didn't slap his hand away this time.

Those were the best times at work, when the shop was quiet, when it was just me and Elmy and I'd fold my arms and listen to his stories of when he was a boy, the places he knew, his tales of Star Naked and Shoulder of Mutton. Elmy could name all the fields hereabouts.

'Lovelands, Featherbeds,' he said. 'That's where most courting couples would go.' Those were the hideaway meadows, where the earth was as soft and light as air. Or the faraway fields, the ones out in the middle of nowhere, like Waterloo, South Sea, and Montserrat. 'Those big old fields today, they swallowed up hundreds of those small fields to get that size,' he said.

Elmy could name every single one of them as a boy, he said. 'I was strong as anything back then, with a quick head on me.' He reckoned girls looked at him twice then, all right. 'I had curly hair the colour of conkers. That's what the wife fell for . . . getting her hands in that thick head of hair. And I could take a drink back then. I used to look forward all week to filling my boots at the weekend. Kills the worm for a few nights, you see. That worm that keeps turning in my head.' And he'd tap his forehead.

'Mind you, that worm can't complain. There's plenty of food for him inside me. Good and fertile enough to keep him going for a few years yet. And in return he aereates my brain a treat, passes a lovely tilth out his rear end.'

I noticed his hands then, the skin worn to a shine and stuck through with knuckles which had swollen up into hard knobs of bone. Then there were his veins which stood off the backs of his hands like green tunnels, as if that worm of his had been having a touch of the night wanders and taken a nice little trip round Elmy's body after kicking up all that dirt in his head.

'There was one field though,' he said. 'A dark mean old field, near

44

the back of the pub. She had a strong root pull on her, all right. Nobody went near that one if they could help it.'

I knew the one, only twelve acres or so, one of the last on the edge of the village before the prairie fields began. I'd noticed how the soil there always smelled sour after ploughing; how hares slid across its puddled clay. Dark green slime oozed into the ditches.

'It's a field that's lost its mother,' Elmy said. He reckoned it was never looked after properly, and then it was too late. 'The clay got waterlogged, bloated up with hunger and turned bad. No amount of muckspreading or draining ever seemed to put it right. That's why it was always known as Drunken Mary,' he said. 'That's a field that would take anyone down, given half a chance. Suck your boots off and spit your buttons out after.'

COSTA DEL SOL

Ed and Bernie were together that whole summer, working on the Cortina. Pam was there most weekends as well, looking bored to death as one or other of them slid under the car. She sat on an old red car seat in the garden, reading a magazine, the tassels on the sleeves of her leather jacket swinging like catkins every time she turned a page, the leather creaking with every yawn.

'You nearly done yet, Bernie? You're dropping me back home, remember, so I can get changed before we go out.' Being the only one who could drive, he was picking up Pam and Ed later on, to go and see a band at the village hall in Earl Soham.

'Do you want to come with us, Desiree?' Bernie had slid out from beneath the car, oil smeared on one side of his face. I'd hovered a moment too long by the goat shed. He was grinning at me, teasing me.

'No, thanks,' I said, turning away so he wouldn't see the colour of my face. 'I'm helping Dad.'

'Another time then,' he said.

Bernie was wearing his flame shirt when he came back with Pam after tea to pick Ed up, a short-sleeved black shirt with a pattern of red and orange flames all around the bottom.

'The boy looks like a box of firelighters in that shirt,' Dad said, watching him get into the car.

'Like his arse has caught fire, more like,' Pipe said. But Bernie always looked different in that shirt, especially those nights when he came back from the pub with Ed, the pair of them smelling of beer and smoke.

Ed was climbing into the back seat with Pam as Bernie drove off.

'I do hope he's being careful,' Dad said. Mum was kneeling on the front-room carpet, trying to fix the feet on one of her dressmaking dummies. She had several upstairs in her bedroom but there were always things wrong with them. Either the screws had worked loose and bits fallen off them, or they wouldn't stand up properly and had to lean like drunks against the wall.

'What do you mean, careful?' she said.

'Careful . . . you know. The two of them courting that way.'

'We can't stop them, Tony.'

'But Ed's so young, Pearl. He's not seventeen yet, and she's only just turned sixteen.'

'We were young once, remember? And not yet married.' Mum had put down her screwdriver and was staring straight at Dad, who was starting to look uncomfortable. I said I'd help Pipe clear up and went into the kitchen, where we both listened at the door.

'I was always careful though,' Dad said in a loud hiss. 'And you can bet Chubby Hawes will have something to say about it if Ed gets his girl in the family way.'

'But let's face it, if they want to do it, nobody's going to stop them. You, me or her dad. They'll get over it soon enough when the shine wears off. It's only sex.'

Mum then marched into the kitchen with the dummy in both arms, told me and Pipe to finish washing up and said she was going upstairs for an early night. Ed and Pam. Mum and Dad. Me and Pipe pulled faces at each other, and started flicking one another with tea towels.

Bernie said his mum and dad were at it all the time in this weather.

'It's the sun,' he told Ed. 'Makes them feel like they're on the Costa del Sol. I have to bang on the wall some nights, tell them to keep it down so I can get some sleep. That rickety bed, squeaking away. Can't believe the old man's still up for for it, but he says, "There's life in the old dog yet."'

Donny Capon, Bernie's dad, said he'd spent over half his life with his hands down other people's U-bends. Donny was a plumber, though most days he looked more like John Wayne. It was his leather tool belt.

It was meant to be round his waist, but it hung low on his hips and the spanners and wrenches clanked every time he moved. He had a wide way of walking, a swagger almost, and for laughs he'd draw a drill bit or a spanner dead quick and spin it on his finger, then ram it back tight into his belt.

Donny liked to pull up outside the house in a squeal of tyres when he got back from work. He'd sit in the van for a while, writing a few figures in a notebook, or smoking and listening to the end of a song on the radio, arm out of the window, fingers drumming on the roof, taking his time. Until Dawn came outside in one of her low-cut tops and leaned in through the window for a kiss.

At the weekends they drank Bacardi and Coke in the back garden, singing along to the radio, Donny's belly turning brown and greasy in the sun while Dawn hitched her dress up to brown off her thighs. Donny would look at his watch, give a quick nod towards the house with a smile on his face. They still had time for a quick one before five o'clock when Fred came round for tea, as he did every night, five on the nail, ever since Bessie Bugg had died of cancer a couple of years before.

The way Bernie talked about them, I thought Donny and Dawn must have had wires in their bedroom. Circus wires that hung from their ceiling, Donny on a swing, riding away, to and fro, with his bag of tools still slung around his bare hips, his feet brushing the ceiling on each upswing; Dawn laughing up at him from far below, the wind lifting her hair with each pass of the swing till suddenly he lets go and freefalls flat on to the bed, lands right on top of her and buries her laughter with his big brown belly, the waterbed slapping away, the scented candles flickering in the breeze, the swing still gently rocking above them.

We used to love the story of how Mum and Dad first met. They liked to tell it when they were rosy with drink at Christmas. One of them would set off on the tale, a gentle canter at first, then the other would join in till they were both talking over one another and hurtling towards the end where they got married.

'I couldn't wait to leave home,' Mum would say. 'Best thing was meeting your father when I did. I was desperate to get away . . . both me and Shirley were.'

Mum was Pearl Whiting back then, seventeen and living with her mother and younger sister, Shirley, in Sizewell, a few hundred yards from where the power station was about to be built. Their mother hadn't talked in years, not properly, Mum said. 'She never got over our father's death. I don't think she really noticed we were there half the time. Never asked where we were going or what we got up to.'

Then one day Mum had been on the beach, combing through rubbish, and Dad was there fishing, having cycled all the way to Sizewell from his quarry-pit house in Campsea Ashe.

'There'd been a gale blowing in from the east,' Mum said. 'There were bottles from Holland and Germany, fish crates from Hull washed high up on the beach. I was really hoping for something from as far away as Iceland.'

'And there was me all set for a day's fishing, hoping for a sea bass or a whiting, maybe a few codling, but anyway a nice bit of peace and quiet. I was looking forward to a day by myself.'

'And then I saw a nice-looking boy, sitting there with his fishing rod on a freezing cold October day. I remember his hands. They were purple with cold. He was just sat there, facing out to sea, eyes fixed on the tip of his rod.'

'I never even saw her coming. One minute I was there by myself, thinking about the fish I was going to catch, the next I'd hooked a beauty. She was wearing a dress covered in sunflowers with a big old woollen sweater over the top . . . some rubber boots. I couldn't believe my eyes.'

'And when you told me your name – well, that was it. Tony White.'

'And all I had to do was sit there and reel her in. A beautiful plump whiting.'

'And then your father picked me up in his arms and carried me over the A12 to our new home in the middle of the countryside.'

They didn't court for long. Mum couldn't wait to become Mrs Pearl White, lose that fishtail of hers, get it chopped off once and for all.

'So you just married me for my name, did you?' And Dad would pull her towards him by the waist, making her squirm and laugh, while she said it wasn't for his money, that was for sure.

He always told her she was beautiful, a real catch, and not just at Christmas with a drink inside him.

But over time the story started to change. Mum began altering the odd detail here and there. We all knew Dad grew up in an old pit, a few houses sunk in the bottom of it, nice and sheltered from any weather outside. But over time she turned it into a sandpit, a cesspit, till it became just a muddy hole in the ground. The story became shorter and sharper. How he'd not said a word on the beach, even when she was standing right there in front of him because he couldn't tear his eyes off his flaming fishing rod, till she'd nearly turned on her heel. Mum said she came that close to calling it a day, and pinched her thumb and finger together, to show us just how close.

In the end, she'd changed the story so much that by the time Dad was worn out from the chicken factory, drinking his beer in the evenings, it was more like he'd crawled out of his cave, caught sight of Mum and thought to himself 'she'll do', because she was the nearest woman and it was the closest he'd ever got to one before. To hear her tell it, you'd think he'd clubbed her over the head and dragged her by the hair all the way from Sizewell, to dump her on the wrong side of the A12 in the back of beyond.

BENTWATERS

Mum couldn't get close to the Americans that summer, though she fancied she could hear what they were up to most weekends in Guppy's old farmhouse; that she could smell their barbecues of steak and fried onions drifting over the back field.

'They'll be having burgers now,' she'd say. Or with the side of her head turned into the wind, 'That's Frank Sinatra, isn't it?' She sat in the back garden and listened out for their laughter which seemed to carry for miles, blowing over the fields in short gusts. Sometimes Dad joined her, and for a while things seemed to be back to how they were before he started his job at the chicken factory. He'd touch her knee if they were talking, put an arm round her shoulders, though she shook it off whenever he reached for a third bottle.

It was on the first Saturday in July that the Americans organised their biggest party yet. The music had already started up by the time we'd finished breakfast. There were snatches of voices and singing, a heavy bass beat, before the wind shifted just slightly and it was gone. Then it came back, another short burst of noise, clearer than before.

'Bloody Yanks,' Dad said, as an American pick-up truck went by on the road outside.

The best place for watching the Americans that day was in a ditch on the farthest side of their house where there was a view of the front and the back. And it was well away from the lane and everyone else who was hanging about. Cheryl and Stan were parked up in the farm layby at the end of the drive, and Fred Bugg was already halfway up it with a lead in his hand, calling for Vegas when I'd seen her not half an hour ago with her paws up on a windowsill, barking away because Fred had gone off without her.

It felt like the fair had come to town. There were flags strung along the front of the house, and wide American cars with rear ends like folded-up grasshopper wings, parked all the way up the drive. There were hundreds of people spilling about in sunglasses and baseball caps as if the whole of the airbase at Bentwaters had turned out for the party.

I had a ringside seat in the ditch. It was well hidden behind a patch of giant hogweed and nettles, and was just wide enough that, if I braced myself against one bank, I could plant my feet firm against the other side and avoid the wet in the bottom.

I'd never seen so much food and drink at a party before. There were seven dustbins lined up by the back door. Winona was filling them with Budweiser and Coke, 7 Up and Dr Pepper, pushing the cans down into ice. There was a hog on a spit, a barbecue covered in burgers and steaks, and plastic tubs of ketchup and mayonnaise, so big they looked like feed buckets. It was hard to believe it was Guppy's old farmhouse underneath, that it was still the same yard with a straw stack riddled with rat holes round the back, a cartshed with the roof half fallen in. It was as if someone had come along and sprayed the whole place in bright colours, piped in some city noise. They'd even covered over an old muck heap with a sheet which had stars and stripes painted on it.

Aunt Shirley and Guppy seemed to be the only locals who'd been invited. They were in the garden talking to Lance who hadn't put his beer down for a minute and was having to do the cooking one-handed. He didn't look like a man in charge of a nuclear bomb, not with a pinny round his waist, slapping people on the back with a big bellygut laugh.

'You can't go yet.' Shirley was hissing. 'We've only just got here.' She and Guppy had come into the backyard and were so close I could see the broken veins in his cheeks. I had to stop myself from getting out of the ditch and going over to them, have Shirley put her arms round me as if nothing had ever happened, hear Guppy say he had a load of new tricks to try out on me that he'd been saving up all this time. But I had a feeling Shirley would hold up a hand before I was halfway over and say, 'You shouldn't be here, Desiree. Not with us. Your mother wouldn't like it. Off you go now.' I couldn't bear the thought of that. Or, worse, of her turning away and his silence.

'Why can't Denny see to the pigs?' Shirley was still hissing at him. 'It's what you pay him for?'

'It's his wedding anniversary. Anyway, I told you I'd have to go and check on them. Those coughs could be serious.'

'I thought you meant later. On the way home. Not as soon as we got here. I don't know anyone.'

'I won't be long.' Guppy cupped Shirley's chin in one hand. 'You know Winona. You could give her a hand till I get back.'

Mum would have given anything to be at the party. It would have been a dream come true for her, all those Americans in one garden. She'd have paid to get in if she could. One of them was bound to have been to New England, maybe even knew the Ipswich there like the back of their hand or had distant relatives in Norwich, USA. If she hadn't fallen out with Shirley, she could have been there that night and had a proper chance of finding out if those places on the globe had more in common than just a name.

The wheels of Guppy's Land Rover kicked up grit and stones as he drove out of the yard, and Shirley wandered back to the edge of the party.

I could tell she wasn't used to being without her husband. She didn't know what to do with her hands. She was fidgeting with her cuffs, then folding her arms, unfolding them. In the end she reached into the dustbin for a can of beer. Shirley never drank.

'One Babycham and I get double vision,' she used to say. And less than half an hour later there she was, sticking her hand in the dustbin again.

Melissa Makepeace wasn't enjoying the party much either. She'd been skulking round the stable with Billy the Kid for a while and then just sat down in the cartshed next door. If she was a horse, I'd have called in the vet straightaway, seeing her with her head drooping like that in a dark corner.

'Melissa, I've been looking for you everywhere. What are you doing, sitting out here?' Winona stood there, holding on to a bag of frozen chicken legs.

'Nothing. Hanging out, that's all. Just leave me alone.'

'Daddy's tending the hog roast. Come on, honey, I hate to think of you out here on your own.'

But Melissa was scowling away. She looked nothing like the girl who'd sat in a pew in Tannington church with her arms outspread, as if she owned the world.

'I hate this crappy country and all the stupid people who live in it.'

Winona was still holding on to those chicken legs, staring down at her daughter on the ground. Her hands must have been freezing.

'It's the pits, this place. I hate every single thing about it, okay? And right now I hate this dumb party and all your boring friends!'

'Too bad,' Winona said, and she walked off, her face set like concrete.

Mum would have said Melissa was a right little madam who needed to be taken down a peg or two and taught some manners. 'That girl's not too old for a good slap,' she'd say.

By early-evening, the families with children started leaving. But still more people kept on coming. There were engines revving, shouts of laughter and loud American voices booming over the top of everything. There was a twelve-bore blasting away in a field nearby, so loud that if I shut my eyes, I could just imagine I was caught up in the middle of *Starsky and Hutch*.

Cars were slowing down in the lane to have a look at the party roaring away under the garden lights. No doubt Donny had already been past, wound his window down and called Fred Bugg a snouty old sod before telling him to get in the car so he could have him home in time for tea.

I was getting cold. I'd had enough of the party and wanted to go home, but I was worried about Aunty Shirley. Guppy wasn't back yet and she'd had far too much to drink. She looked so small amongst all those big Americans, as if one gust of wind would send her bowling off into the night like a dustball.

'Guppy, you out here?' Shirley had wandered into the backyard again looking for him, though his Land Rover still wasn't back yet. She had a can of beer in her hand and her words were running together. 'I'm so tired . . . I want to go home.' She'd already fallen into three potholes and bumped into an old bale elevator. It was like she couldn't see straight. She didn't even move out of the way when a car started reversing out of the yard, or when it sounded its horn. She just stood there like a myxi rabbit caught in the headlights.

I couldn't leave the party till Guppy got back. The state she was in, I was worried Shirley might fall in the pond round the back and drown in four inches of water. Either that or wander into the stable with Billy the Kid and end up getting kicked in the head.

As it was, she found it easier to be on all fours in the end and started making her way over the yard on her hands and knees. She was headed for the muck heap, and without even stopping to think about it, started making her way up the slope, crawling over the stars and stripes. She must have thought she was on a gigantic bedspread because, when she got to the top, she lay down. Minutes later, she stopped groaning. Aunty Shirley had only gone and passed out face down on top of a load of old cow muck!

I was going to have to help her back to the house now, but it looked like Melissa had the same idea. She got to her feet in the cartshed, just as I was getting out of the ditch, and reached Shirley first. Melissa kneeled down beside her. She held her head very close to Shirley's face as if to check she was still breathing. Then Melissa stood up and stared down for a moment as if unsure what to do next. If it hadn't been for the yard light, I'd have missed what happened then. But I saw her do it. Melissa toed Shirley's head with the end of her boot. Like you would an animal on the road, to check if it was dead or just stunned. She was none too gentle about it either.

'Hey, what are you doing?' I stood up in the hogweed. It didn't matter now if she saw me and asked what I was doing there when I hadn't been invited, accusing me of trespass. She couldn't do that to Aunt Shirley. Melissa looked around but she couldn't see me in the dark beyond the yard light.

Just then Guppy's Land Rover came bouncing into the yard, and Melissa vanished. She disappeared so quickly, I didn't even see where she went.

'What have you been up to, you daft girl?' Guppy was on the heap in four strides and picked Shirley up in his arms as if she weighed no more than a bag of cement. She was still out cold as he propped her up on the front seat of the Land Rover. Guppy was going to get a right earful the next day for leaving her on her own like that, pigs with or without coughs.

I walked back across Star Naked, then another few fields of wheat and barley, before the start of the peafields in the last mile up to our house.

Mum was in the front garden looking out over the road, her face held in the air like a dog, catching the faint drift of barbecue smoke. It was a cool evening and she was standing there wearing a tee-shirt and skirt.

'Just cooling off,' she said. 'Warm indoors tonight. Your dad's fallen asleep on the couch.' She rubbed her bare arms a little.

The wind shifted round slightly; the barbecue smoke had gone. There was a much stronger, sweeter smell on top of it. The viners were out in the front field against the far horizon. The pea harvest had started. None of us could have known how those peas were about to change everything.

Dad said that Shirley might as well have moved in with us after she and Guppy got married, she was round ours so much. She'd come over and give Mum a hand with the housework or the cooking, and whatever they were doing, they never stopped talking. It was like having two wives, he said.

Mum left home when she was nineteen years old. She left in such a hurry, she said, it was like she shot down the wires from Sizewell in a shower of sparks. Shirley followed a few years later after she married Guppy.

Those two first met when he pulled Shirley out of a ditch one day. 'Tony had picked me up from home and was bringing me over for Christmas, remember? And he was just saying that the roads were starting to get icy, when the next thing we knew the car slid into a ditch.' Shirley never got bored of telling the story. How there was no phonebox for miles, not a single house in sight, and to cap it all it was just getting dark and had started to snow.

'We were all set to walk. I knew how worried Pearl would be. But then along comes Raymond Savage, sat up there on his John Deere, gleaming white in his overalls. He'd been spraying winter wheat and had his face mask pushed down around his throat. He looked just like a hospital doctor up there in that tractor cab . . . so strong and hand-some, I felt my legs give way at the very sight of him. And do you know? He pulled the car out of that ditch as if he did it every single day of the week.'

Guppy had done well for himself over the years. He farmed several thousand acres, had over a thousand pigs, and always had the newest machines, the biggest tractors. He took over the farm from his parents who died years before he met Shirley. He made a few changes then. He ploughed up the smaller fields, got rid of trees and hedges, filled in the ditches and the ponds. He even got rid of an old house once because it was getting in the way; he said he got fed up of having to plough round it all the time.

It was a long old redbrick house, with a track running up to it from the road, and had its own orchard and drinking pond. The roof was half fallen in, but it still had its four walls and a full set of windows. It had a garden, and an outhouse round the back. It had been empty for thirty years and Guppy had been letting it go, like his father before him. Then one night he blew it up. He planted explosive in the cellars, and in one massive blast it was gone. People heard it from as far away as Badingham and Bruisyard. Even Dad got up that night to look out of the window, thinking a plane from Bentwaters had come down in the back field.

The explosion left a big crater and a pile of rubble in the middle of Guppy's stubble field. It took a few days to clear before he got round to ploughing up the garden, rooting up the orchard. He kept the drinking pond though. He kept it especially for Shirley. He said he'd build her a brand-new house where it wouldn't get in the way, but close enough to the pond for her to swim in it, knowing that she missed the sea so much. It even had small steps down into it, which made it look like a swimming pool.

Guppy made Dad seem as dull as a bag of turnips. It wasn't just the sticks of dynamite or the gallons of sulphuric acid he used to wilt the tops of his potato crop. It was the way he lifted us on to his shoulders and spun us around while Shirley, far below, would laugh and clap her hands, saying, 'Be careful, be careful!' Or how at the farm he let us drive his tractors and wash his yard down with the power hose. Sometimes he'd creep up behind and hurl one of us on to the top of a straw stack, just for the hell of it. But the thing we liked best about Guppy was his hair. Long and wiry, it grew to his shoulders in a thicket of curls that from behind looked like the fantail on a goldfish. And his back was so hairy, as if covered in fur, his favourite game was to lift his shirt up over his head and chase after us with arms outstretched like a big old grizzly bear, till we were half laughing, half crying.

Pipe and Ed couldn't get enough of Guppy telling them that pests and weeds were the enemy; how they had to be annihilated or they'd ruin him as a farmer, kill off all farmers, and then there wouldn't be enough food to go round.

There was a fungus, Guppy said, that buried itself deep in the ground and, if it ever got into the rape, could ruin a whole crop in days if he didn't get to it first.

'It's like guerilla warfare,' he said. 'They go underground and they get stronger so you've got to find different ways of killing them off.' He had a shed full of chemicals to do it with, a huge stack of insecticides, herbicides, fungicides, all in drums marked 'Poison', row upon row of black skulls and crossbones.

Dad didn't often get het up about things, but he did about that shed.

'Guppy had better keep that place locked up. I don't ever want to find out that you've set foot in there, do you hear me? Just one breath of those fumes could kill you. Do you understand? You keep well away.'

Guppy built Shirley a brand-new farmhouse in the end, big enough for all the children they were going to have. It was a square house with five bedrooms, surrounded by steel barns, a concrete yard, and two acres of lawn which he mowed with his tractor.

But in all that time I never forgot about the old house that he got rid of. There was a stain still visible out in the field. It got lighter some years, but just when I thought it was going for good it came back again, darker than ever, till you could almost see the shape of the footings, the shadows of the apple trees. Some people reckoned Guppy should never have been allowed to blow up a four-hundred-year-old house, but then again he never asked. He just did it. It was on his land and getting in the way, he said, holding him back.

For years afterwards I kept finding things in the ditches nearby. A rusted tin bath, a broken sink, an iron boot-scraper. I put it down to fly tippers at first. But some days I used to look at that field of Guppy's and wonder if maybe it wasn't fly tippers dumping their rubbish after all, but that big old field coughing things up and spitting them out.

THE PEA HARVEST

The temperature had shot up after the Americans' party. There were halternecks and bare backs everywhere by the following weekend, radios on in people's back gardens, the click-clack of flipflops around Fram. Everything began to slow down as people passed one another in cars in the lanes, wound down their windows and stopped for a chat, elbow to elbow.

At the row of cottages, everyone sat out in their gardens. Dawn and Cheryl lay on blankets, reading magazines, while Fred Bugg sat in his shirt sleeves in the shade with Vegas underneath the chair, her tongue hanging out like a piece of wet ham.

The days were thick and soupy with talk of the Royal Wedding. You could hardly breathe in the shop some mornings for people going on about the bride, the dress, the romance of it all. How Charles could do with being just a few inches taller.

Zelma knew every single detail about the plans for the big day. She knew the route the carriage would take, the bridesmaids, the guests, the layout of the seating in the cathedral . . . till I wondered if someone should remind Zelma it wouldn't actually be her walking up the aisle in just two weeks' time.

'Oh, and Lady Diana is so beautiful,' she would say. 'So young, so fresh-looking. And she's got so much to look forward to.'

'She's definitely a virgin,' Pipe said. 'Her uncle said so, didn't he? Announced on the news to the whole world that his niece was still intact down there.' That was the only bit of the wedding Ed and Pipe were interested in. 'They'll have done virginity tests on her ages ago.' Pipe picked up his fork from the table and, with one eye screwed shut, held it close to his face like a telescopic torch. 'I bet it was a really detailed examination,' he said

'That's enough,' Mum said. 'Not while we're eating.'

'Charles is all right though,' Pipe carried on. 'He could have been having it off with hundreds of women. But then, you can't prove it with men, can you? Not like you can with women.' And the boys would snigger away till Mum threw a wet cloth at the pair of them.

The viners worked night and day on the front field, lorries coming and going down the road past our house as they carted the peas up the A12 to the Birds Eye factory in Lowestoft. That first night I stayed awake to watch the headlights sweep across the ceiling, listening to the engine noise of the viners as they rolled in over the field and back out again, the lorries revving hard as they turned into the road with their loads of peas. It felt as if the whole house had been picked up by the eaves, hooked on to the powerlines and sent swinging off over the fields in a shower of sparks, and we were up there in a cable car, being rocked in our beds as we flew over towns, the bright lights running off the ceiling and down the bedroom walls.

Ed and Bernie nearly had the Cortina ready for its MOT by the start of the summer holidays. They'd stripped down to shorts and bare backs most afternoons. From the goat shed I watched Bernie tie up his hair in the sun, his back turning red then dark brown overnight; Ed turning pink and staying pink. I had a special pile under my bed by then. The elastic bands Bernie used for his hair. A scribbled list of things they'd needed from the garage, with Bernie's greasy thumb prints all over it. A Marathon wrapper. A piece of oily rag.

I couldn't stop thinking about Bernie those nights as the pea lorries went backwards and forwards, me turning this way and that, till the whole house must have heard what I was thinking. My head was so full of him during the day, I tried to bury him under other thoughts, but he just wouldn't stay down. The more I pushed, the more he kept coming back up till I gave up trying. If I'd had a tail those nights, like one of the goats, it would have been flapping away like crazy, knocking against the bedroom wall, and everyone would have known for sure what was on my mind then.

I lay there thinking about the places I could go with Bernie, somewhere quiet where the two of us could lie together. In a good dry ditch or in the middle of a field – except there was no Featherbeds or Lovelands any more, or any field around us that wasn't under peas or sugar beet.

There was one meadow though, beyond Watery Lane, just on the edge of Athelington. It was full of ox-eye daisies and buttercups, grasses that grew waist-high, and was bounded on all four sides by hedges thick with hazel and oak trees. That meadow was the one place I wanted to go with Bernie, where he'd lay his jacket down over meadowsweet and we'd lie there facing each other a while, our faces aglow from the buttercups all about us.

Walker went in there sometimes for a rest. I knew it was him out there in the middle of the meadow, lying flat on his back and looking up at the sky, flattening a space beneath the surrounding grasses. I could tell by the smoke rising from among the silver grass heads, the perfect smoke rings that spun out in a chain, that it was him somewhere down below, having a quick breather, then another ten miles or so to go before home.

He'd been doing those walks all his life, Elmy said.

The hot weather and the peas were making us all restless. Mum was in and out of bed, moving around downstairs, running a tap, flushing the toilet.

'This heat,' she'd say, 'I can't get used to it.' And she'd throw the windows back as wide as they'd go, sometimes leaving the porch and kitchen doors ajar as well for a through draught at night. Some mornings, I came down for breakfast to find the back door wide open. It felt like people had been coming and going in the night, having a poke around the cupboards, helping themselves to whatever took their fancy.

The houses held the heat in their bricks long after the sun had gone down. Everyone at the double bends was staying up late, sitting by their back door. The Rumsey children were allowed to stay up and play knock-around tennis on the road outside until it was nearly dark. Television noise drifted out of windows and doors that were wedged open, and everyone could smell Fred Bugg's flowers at night.

It was eleven o'clock but the blue light of a television was still flickering through most of the curtains along the row when I crept up out of the ditch through Donny's rows of broad beans, breathing in the scent of their flowers. I wanted to get close to the back path, just for a moment, where Bernie had been standing with his dad earlier, looking at the row of potatoes they'd just dug over.

Donny and Dawn were on the sofa, Dawn's feet in her husband's lap. They sat next to a sideboard covered with photos of Cheryl and Bernie on fur rugs as babies, both chubby and naked. Donny was rubbing Dawn's foot, gently pinching the toes, running a hand over her ankle. They both looked up at the ceiling for a moment. Cheryl and Bernie weren't back yet.

Next door Fred Bugg was sitting on his sofa, a bottle of barley wine and a plate of Jaffa Cakes on the low table in front of him. Vegas was sitting fair and square on his lap, getting half of all the biscuits. She was a big dog, and he was having to crane his neck to one side to see the screen, patting her head the whole time. Bessie used to sit jammed on the sofa next to him, half on, half off his lap, tucking into a bowl of biscuits, Fred disappearing under the squash of her.

He fed Vegas probably the way he fed Bessie when she was ill, coaxing her with choice morsels, all the juicy titbits from his own plate. He was like a cockerel, chuck, chuck, chuck, till Dawn would yell at him, 'Will you stop feeding that dog off your plate, Dad? You'll fade away.'

But if it wasn't for Vegas, Fred would float to the ceiling like a helium balloon, him with his high-boned pigeon chest. Maybe it felt as if Bessie was still with him as he sat there with the deadweight of a dog on his lap, her biscuit breath in his face, and the scent of Sweet Williams drifting in through the window.

Donny and Dawn weren't interested in the telly any more. His hand had moved beyond her ankle, up over her thigh, her foot rubbing against him, catching a toe of her Friday-night fishnets in the zip of his flies. It gets caught up, snags and tears.

'Bugger it,' she says, 'these were new on just now.'

'You'll have to take them off then,' he says. 'And the rest.'

Through the nets at their bedroom window upstairs, I could almost make out the shine of the circus wires hanging from the ceiling.

The house was dark when I got back, Mum and Dad already in bed. I remembered the empty packet of Players which I'd put in my pocket. Bernie had tucked something into it before he chucked it on to the compost heap. From a distance it looked like a clump of black hair, but when I opened the packet, it was several little strips of leather, frayed at one end as if they'd come away from the fringe on a jacket.

The pea viners had finished in the front field by the end of the week, and had moved over the road to start on the five hundred acres behind us. The lorries stood by at the edge of the field, drivers leaning against their cabs, one foot on a bumper, while they smoked and watched out for the next load.

Mum was on the sun lounger out in the front garden, her dress hitched up to her thighs as the garden filled with exhaust fumes and the smell of peas.

'The sun suits you, Pearl,' said Dad. Other people had noticed as well and said she had a real glow about her. Mum's hair had turned dark gold and when she wore her sun dress, the one with the daisies, it showed off more of her skin, made the fine hairs on her arms catch the light. She looked as if she'd been polished with beeswax.

'I can't tell the difference between you and Nancy now,' Dad said, teasing her.

'Do stop likening me to that goat,' she said.

'But she's in such good nick, it's a compliment. Just look at the shine on her coat.' Next to Mum, he looked dusty and worn out.

She'd moved her lounger round to the back garden, taken to sitting out there for a few minutes in the morning to brown off her legs. Before the sun got too hot, she said. Or when it was windy, she'd have a cup of tea in the porch and watch her arms and legs change colour from blue to green, as my stained-glass windowed door shifted in the breeze.

The viners moved across the horizon for the first day, getting closer by the hour until they reached our house in the middle of the night. They came right up to our back fence, swinging around and setting out again on the track to the horizon, steering their way round the pylons, always gone for some hours before they were back again.

Dad wasn't sleeping well. It wasn't so much the engine noise, he said, but the lorry drivers standing around and talking at night.

'One of them might as well have been in the room with us last night,' he said. The bloke's voice had carried through the open window so clearly that Dad woke up thinking a peaman was standing right at the foot of the bed, talking away, telling him how it had been the best day of his life, Ipswich winning the UEFA Cup back in May, better even than the day his son was born. That he'd sell his own mother to be in the same room as Bobby Robson and breathe the same air.

'For a moment, I thought he was going to climb into bed with me and your mother, right there and then. Gave me quite a start,' Dad said.

Mum was looking feverish over breakfast. Her eyes had a flat shine.

'You're not overdoing it with the sun, are you, Mum?' I said. She was beginning to make me feel edgy, shooting looks out of the kitchen window as she opened the curtains in the morning or when she drew them last thing at night, as if there was something out there in the fields, something we should be afraid of.

THE BACK PORCH

'It's probably to do with the heat,' Zelma said. 'Maybe you got a touch of sun poison at the weekend.' I'd turned up at the shop and started feeling sick as soon as I walked in through the door. Zelma wasn't having any of it. 'You go and get yourself in bed. My Michael can give you a lift home.'

But I said I needed the walk back, the fresh air, that I'd only be sick in a car.

It was the hottest day of the year so far and the road was shaking in the heat, falling away under a layer of black water that seemed to float above the tarmac, staying the same few feet ahead of me. The telegraph poles were melting, black tar leaking out of the wood. There was no shade on the way home so I put my shop coat over my head, could feel the sweat running down my back. Nobody was going out in this heat. The road was quiet. There was a car parked by Tannington church where somebody had stopped underneath the shade of the only trees for miles around and gone to sleep at the wheel. There was nothing but silence as I headed home beneath an upended bowl of white-hot sky.

I was just a few hundred yards from home when I saw her. In the porch, her daisy dress squashed flat against the glass.

The sun had caught the colours in my window just right that morning. They were so clear, so bright. My patterns of red next to blue shone on her throat, his hands. His fingers seemed to disappear into her as they moved over her body, her bare skin, turning blue as he touched underneath her neck, then turquoise on her belly, his face blood-orange on her chest. They looked like stained glass buckling in the heat.

I couldn't stop following the colours, not wanting to see the way the man was pushing against her, standing up. His hands were gripping the shelf, his boot on top of our sack of potatoes. He was bearing down so hard, he made the paper sack bulge tight till it split open and potatoes rolled everywhere. I could see his face, eyes shut, mouth open wide, my mother's back pressed against the glass in between the shelf and the kitchen door. Him moving against her, again and again, as he lifted her leg up round his waist, and the colours played on her thigh.

He left the porch quickly after, looking left and right before stepping out past the end of the house, back over the ditch to the pea field where the viner was just appearing on the horizon. He walked hard, only breaking his step to tighten and buckle his belt, a quick jerk from side to side, while she watched him from the porch, her hands fluttering over herself, smoothing her dress back down. She never noticed the split sack or the few potatoes that had rolled over the concrete floor, never spotted the one potato that had rolled into the far corner out of sight and saw everything.

I ran. I didn't stop running, though I was sick to my stomach. Her with him. Him and her. I couldn't understand why she hadn't seen me standing there by the side of the road. I felt like I'd grown into a twenty-foot giant, and as she turned her head to one side, her mouth open in a silent moan, she was going to see me at any minute, wouldn't be able to miss me. I was blocking out the sun, casting a shadow over three hundred yards long that reached right to the back door. Any minute now, as the sun slipped behind me, my head was about to land at her feet.

It was like seeing my mother turn into someone else as she'd moved up and down like that against the glass. This wasn't the same woman who slammed our plates on the dinner table when she was fed up, and yelled at the boys for not taking their boots off indoors and treating the place like a hotel. It certainly wasn't the same woman who picked leaves out of my hair and wrapped her arms round Dad before bed some nights.

I got halfway down Tannington Straight before my legs gave way and I threw up in the ditch not ten yards from the drain where I found the baby.

I sat in the bottom of the ditch afterwards, not bothering to duck down and hide away. Not this time. I couldn't stop shivering. How could she do that? How could she go with that man like that, and what would happen if Dad found out? Maybe she was going to leave us; had her bags all packed and ready to go the moment the peas were finished, when she could finally climb into the cab and ride away with him. An hour or more must have passed while I just sat there, staring up at the grey road at eye level, feeling as if I was half buried beneath it.

I saw him coming this time. From down in the ditch I watched Walker round the bend at the far end and start coming up the Straight. He was like a walking strip of water that afternoon, the way the edges of him were all wavy. His outline never seemed to get any sharper, even though he was getting closer by the second, until he was going right past me. But I saw his boots, I saw them as they passed right before my eyes. Brown leather boots as worn and weathered as his face, the near one laced up with baler twine. He was walking so fast, he'd only gone and taken off. His feet were skimming the air inches above the road, not touching it at all. He was flywalking. Big long silent strides through the air in heavy leather boots, and he was gone. There was no other noise except for a lovely cool breeze that washed right over me and made the tall grass ripple on both verges as he passed on through. It made me forget everything for a while, lifted the ache clean out of my stomach.

'I'm not eating them.'

'But they're really fresh. They were still growing on the vine a few hours ago.' Dad had bought a box of peas on his way home from work.

'I said, I'm not eating them.'

Mum was quiet, watching me from over by the sink, Dad sitting between us.

'I thought they were your favourite though.' He looked confused. 'Oh, come on, just try a few.'

'Leave her, Tony.' Mum said it too sharply. Then, more quietly this time, 'Look at the colour of her, you can see she's not feeling well.' But Mum stayed by the sink. She didn't come over to feel my forehead or hold my face in both hands so she could look at me properly. She wasn't rubbing Dad's shoulders like she sometimes did when he came in from work, squashing them down and then pressing them tight towards one another, as if to make sure he was still holding together in one piece. 'Though I'm surprised Zelma didn't send her home earlier.' Her eyes flickered towards me. It was almost a question but she lost her nerve.

'So why didn't Zelma send you home?' Dad said. Mum was rubbing the back of her neck, over and over. Restless, fidgety. 'You look as white as a ghost. Zelma should have realised you were sickening.' He cupped my chin. 'Are you upset about something? It's not me, is it? Something I've done? Your daft old dad?' He was doing his best to get me to smile. But all I could think of was those daisies riding up and down against the glass . . . 'You should have come home to bed,' Dad was saying. And of how, when that man reached under her dress with one hand, her feet seemed to lift off the ground . . . 'Next time be sure to tell Zelma if you're unwell, won't you?'

'It's probably some twenty-four-hour bug,' Mum said quickly. 'Just taken her appetite away for a while.'

I made sure I ate everything then, quickly forking down carrots and sweetcorn, even the thick fat on the chop, every single last thing, except for the peas.

I stayed up till dawn to watch the last pea lorry turn out of the back field and leave for Lowestoft. I counted them in and counted them out, wanting to make sure that every single lorry had gone and that nobody had stayed behind, no lone driver parked up on the edge of the field with his lights off, waiting.

The next morning the field was empty. There was nothing left: no machinery, no peas, no gleanings. Everything had been crushed by the viners and the pea lorries, flattened deep into the ruts.

THE PIG PITS

It took a while to get used to the quiet after they finished, especially the silence and the dark at nights. The fields were brown with stalks, the stink of rotting peas blowing in at us from all directions.

I was glad of the shop then, glad of a reason to be out of the house every day. I no longer minded Zelma's non-stop talking about how her Michael was crazing her over such and such a thing, or how so and so in the village was in a quarrel with so and so about something or other.

'You'll never guess what those new people are up to now – the Fairweathers,' she'd say. 'That man's already complaining about Elmy's cockerel on the allotments. That if it isn't bad enough to hear it every morning, he hears it in the middle of the night sometimes as well, and he gets little enough sleep as it is before having to catch the train to London every morning. Wound up like a spring he is, over every tiny thing. He's already fallen out with one set of neighbours because of their dog barking away. Yet I can't hear myself think when he's been in the shop, all those watches ticking up his arm.' His wife had told us a while ago they were for his job, and kept the time in New York and Tokyo; that he couldn't keep up with British Summer Time and our clocks going backwards and forwards. 'It's like standing next to a time bomb,' Zelma said, 'waiting for it to go off at any minute.'

I was glad of the noise filling my head for a while. I didn't even mind it when Zelma went on about the wedding and how she was going to get a Lady Di haircut next time she was at the hairdresser's. Some days there could be up to half a dozen women in the shop swapping every single detail they knew about Diana, and what she must be feeling like with the pre-wedding nerves.

'Ooh, and then there'll be babies soon enough and royal christenings.

She'll make such a wonderful mother.' They got all clucky and teary-eyed just thinking about it. 'And then all those years they'll have together as man and wife.' Before their thoughts turned to their own forty-year-long marriages and their faces would sag at the thought of them, the disappointment, and one of the women would say, 'Oh, well, good luck to them.'

I took to coming back home late even though I finished work in the shop by dinnertime. I offered to do errands for people like Dolly, only too pleased when she asked if I could drop some extra shopping off on my way home so she didn't have to carry it back herself or if I'd go up to World's End to fetch a chicken for their Sunday dinner.

'I'm so grateful,' she'd say. 'I'm run off my feet, but Elmy won't go up there, not for love nor money.' It was Hubert's peacocks, she said. He was scared half to death of them. 'He won't go within five hundred yards of that place. Hasn't been anywhere near World's End for years. I ask you, a grown man fearful of a few birds. He's always been all right with chickens though.'

I took to walking anywhere, nowhere in particular, so long as it passed the time. Walker must have realised something was up as our paths crossed several times a week, miles away from home. I took to walking the same looping walks around Bedingfield, Wilby, Worlingworth, only stopping when Eunice Breeze asked me if I'd seen her husband anywhere on my travels.

Charlie Breeze had gone simple in the head. Senile dementia, they called it, and it had shrunk his brain to the size of a ping-pong ball, which now rolled around inside his empty head. He was harmless enough, but he didn't know whether he was coming or going half the time, so Eunice tried to keep him indoors. Except as soon as her back was turned, Charlie would be off. Whenever I saw him he was usually heading towards the allotments at a half-gallop, as if he were late for work.

I'd only ever seen him come to a stop when he reached the back garden to the house where Miles Fairweather lay in bed of a night with his fingers stuffed in his ears. Charlie would lean his arms on the fence a while as if standing with one foot on a five-bar gate, then with a sudden swing of his leg, he'd be in their garden, where Eunice would catch him and lead him away.

For a while I spent my afternoons at Tannington church. I sat on the pew below the window, willing the poppies to move again in the breeze so that I could walk straight through the stained glass and out the other side, lie down in that wheat field and forget all about home. But Melissa seemed to have taken a liking to the place that summer and was there more often than not, some days asleep in a corner of the graveyard by the yew, others just sitting in the pew beneath the window. I might have said hello, but I hadn't forgotten how she toed Shirley's head at the party when she was out cold on the muck heap.

This time it was Melissa who didn't hear me come up the aisle when she was lying on a pew, curled up on her side. She was looking up at the stained glass with her thumb in her mouth. It was so quiet, I could hear the suck of her tongue as it latched on to her thumb, and for a moment I wanted to walk up to her and smack her hand away, tell her to grow up and find somewhere else to go.

At least there were places she didn't know about, like the flower meadow by Watery Lane or the hole in the hedge at World's End. I waited there for hours at a time, willing Hubert to come round the corner of the barn and gather up his peacock for one more dance. More often than not though, I ended up watching Edgar in his silent world seeing to the cows or Walter working in the fields. As soon as the weather turned cool, he'd slip on his flying jacket and be chugging up and down as if he'd fallen out of the sky and crash landed straight into the seat of that old grey tractor.

Things got so bad, I even spent some time up at the pig pits just because I could sit behind the wall there and be hidden from the road.

The pits were in the middle of Guppy's fields. The only way to reach them was up a long concrete track which ran through the fields up to a length of wall and concrete hardstand, and ended at a large square brick pool. From a distance it looked like it could be a pond or a swimming pool, but it was a slurry pit where Guppy also dumped his dead pigs. On hot days they swelled up like purple balloons and rose to the surface. We used to go over there all the time when we were younger, me, Ed and Pipe, picking up loads of flints in the field on the way so that we could chuck them at the pigs and see if we could make them explode.

One time we were there, mucking about as usual, the boys trying to hit a sow which was lying on top of the slurry, when a car turned off the road on to the track and started coming up it. Nobody ever came up to the pits except Guppy and his pigman on tractors. Nobody local anyway. It was a boiling hot day in August, and this silver car came along with its roof down. The three of us hid behind the wall.

'It's a Merc,' Ed said. 'What a beauty. Real leather seats and everything.'

There were two people sitting in the front. The man was wearing sunglasses pushed high up on his head, and a white shirt which billowed out in the wind as he drove along with one arm around the woman. They looked like a couple who'd made plans for a lovely summer's drive in the countryside, all set to have an adventure together, driving out into the open desert, roof down, her long hair blowing in the hot wind. Any minute now they were going to stumble across some secret oasis with palm trees. They looked like the sort of people who would have a picnic all ready on the back seat: a hamper full of chicken sand-wiches, and a bottle of champagne in a bucket. They had a feeling this was going to be their special place, they just knew it.

It was only after they'd turned the engine off and got out of the car that the wind shifted direction and they clocked the stench. But by then it was too late. They'd rounded the corner of the wall and spotted the large white sow lying on top of the slurry, which by then had been cooking in the sun for hours. It was the wrong moment to be standing there as the gas began to escape from both ends of that pig, making a sound like a long sigh. It was a gas leak from her back end that made the sow lurch forward. It was only an inch or so but it was enough to make the woman scream, thinking the pig had come back to life or, worse, had never been dead in the first place. She screamed even louder when a runty piglet happened to rise to the surface, followed swiftly by another then another. The slurry was only bubbling because it was getting stirred up, but the woman was terrified and turned to run back to the car, except she tripped and fell instead. Her white dress was covered in mud and slurry. We could still hear her screaming a mile away up the road. The boys were laughing so hard, Pipe was bent double and threw up halfway home.

For the rest of that summer, I walked places and waited for Ed and Pipe to get home, just so it wouldn't be me and Mum alone together, or me and Dad. I was afraid that they'd see it on my face.

'You're quiet,' Dad would say, looking at me for a moment. 'Anything wrong?' as I push a pile of peas to the side of my plate and refuse to eat them. Then, for the first time, he'd take a proper look at me and sit back with his arms folded to watch the whole scene unroll over my face, from start to finish, in full, glorious Technicolor.

'Rats. Can't you smell them?' Dad leaned in closer to the straw. 'Bloody rat piss, all over this barley straw.' We were in the goat shed, trimming the goats' hooves. I could only smell peas. Rotting, fermenting pods which had been lying under the sun for the last two weeks, a sweet sickly smell that got everywhere. 'I think we'll have a good old fire while the others are out. What do you say, Desiree? Get rid of them old rats.'

Ed had passed his test earlier in the week, less than a month after his seventeenth birthday. 'Where would you like to go, Mum? I can take you anywhere,' he said.

'Bentwaters,' she said without thinking. 'I'd love to go to Bentwaters.'

Ed looked different from Dad behind the wheel. He drove with arms held out straight, rigid, as if they'd lost any bend at the elbow and their full force was pushing him back into his seat. Dad always took it steady in the Marina, sat up straight as if there was no back to the seat, and lurched at the windscreen whenever he came to a junction. He'd check both ways and turn the wheel with one big sweep of his arm, as if he were driving a tractor.

Pipe said he'd go along with them up to the base. He'd heard there were nightjars in the forest round there.

'I'm staying home to help Dad with the fire,' I said.

Mum was in the passenger seat, fingers drumming on the dashboard before Ed had even got into the car. She was leaning so far forward, her nose was almost touching the windscreen. She didn't turn her head once as they left. I was half expecting not to see her again.

Dad heaved a sack of old *East Anglians* on to the fire.

'Might as well have a good clear out while we're at it,' he said. I raked on more straw from out of the goat shed, and let Nancy and Bentley have a run about in the garden while Dad forked on empty feed sacks and cardboard boxes.

The goats had only been outside for a few minutes when an American jet came out of nowhere, screaming low over the garden. Both of them bolted back to the shed while Dad started cursing. But there was never just one plane. Soon there was another, and another, then yet more planes but bigger and slower this time, probably packed to the roof with supplies for the base. Packets of Oreo cookies and jumbo doughnuts pressed flat against the windows . . . everything jam-packed in so tight that when they opened the plane doors, the entire freezer-food section would explode out of the hold, beef burgers as big as dinner plates spinning high into the air before landing on the runway.

We noticed the quiet once the planes had gone over, after Dad had stopped swearing. He leaned on his rake a while, both hands cupped over the top of the handle, his chin resting on top. He was staring into the fire. 'Can't beat a good old burn up,' he said.

He hadn't seen me tear down the stained-glass window earlier and throw it into the flames.

ICELAND

Iceland came out of nowhere. It suddenly appeared in the house one day as if dropped in through the roof. The globe stopped turning at just the right place so that the front-room light landed directly on it like a spotlight. The atlas fell open to that page as well. It was so long since Mum had looked at anywhere besides America and New England that even Ed and Pipe noticed.

'What's so interesting about Iceland all of a sudden?' Pipe was sitting next to Ed one evening, trying to get off the couch and reach the television to change channels, but Ed had an arm and a leg out, pinning him down. They were having one of their silent scraps, trying to appear as if nothing was going on and snorting with the effort.

Dad would have told them to pack it in, the pair of them behaving like a couple of overgrown bullocks, but he was still at work and Mum didn't seem to notice.

'Are there some Icelanders moving in?' Ed said. He was trying to control his breathing as he half lay on top of Pipe.

'I'm interested, that's all,' she said. 'They've got geysers, and volcanoes. The plates must be moving around all the time up there.'

It was also a long way away from our home: 1,100 miles from Suffolk to be precise. That's what she was really thinking. I could see it in her face.

Mum closed the atlas when Dad got back from work. She never talked about Iceland or looked at it when he was there. She went back to America then, to New England, trying to decide if it was better to live in Norwich, which was south of Berlin, or in Ipswich, which was north of Damascus.

'I could ask Winona, next time I see her,' she said, 'find out a bit more.' The problem was, Mum couldn't get close to the Americans these days. She saw them in the distance in Fram and would start to make her way over, and then they'd be gone. Vanished into thin air. 'It's almost like she's trying to avoid me.'

'Maybe they're not as friendly as you think,' Dad said.

But there was something up with the Americans. Something not right. Winona, who usually ambled around in her car happily enough, now sat behind the wheel with four fingers pressed to her mouth as if thinking of a thousand different things, and not one of them anything to do with driving. She was jerky at junctions, stalling more often than not, or went round corners in fourth gear. Melissa sat in the front with her at weekends, while Billy the Kid could have been seizing up in the stables for all I saw of him being ridden out.

Dolly said she could hear the arguments all the way up the road some mornings.

'The pair of them hoarse from shouting, as if they'd been arguing all night. They stop and say hello when I come in, all very polite, wait for me to get the Hoover out and go upstairs, and then they pick up exactly where they left off. Like a couple of terriers, nipping away at each other. I'm hard put not to chuck a bucket of cold water over the pair of them some mornings and bash their silly heads together.'

'Maybe the pressure's getting to him,' Dad said. 'Must be hard for him to relax, being in charge of that bomb.' Lance, who never seemed to walk anywhere, had taken to wandering along the edge of Star Naked in the evenings, tripping and stumbling over the ruts. Dad said he'd seen him often enough recently on the way home from work, hardly recognising him at first out of that great car of theirs. 'Looked like a fish out of water,' he said, 'walking in that field.'

But Mum wasn't listening.

'Norwich, that's the place to be,' she was saying. 'They've got South Lebanon on the doorstep, Sydney, Damascus . . . Fancy living there and saying, "I can't get what I need in Norwich, I'm off to Lebanon, they've got more choice there." Or, "I might just pop in to see my daughter in Damascus for the afternoon, but I'll be back by teatime . . ." If I could just get close enough to Winona to find out if she's ever been there, or if she knows anyone who has, she could tell me what it's like.'

'They're from San Diego,' I said.

'Or, "I'm off to the dentist in Delhi, and then going that bit further up the road to Rome, to see a specialist. We always top up with bread and milk in Berlin, that's only fifteen minutes down the road."'

'They've never been to New England in their life,' I said, louder then.

'What are you talking about, Desiree?' she said finally. 'Who's from San Diego?'

'The Americans. In Brundish. They couldn't live any further away from New England if they tried.'

'Oh,' she said. It was the first time I'd spoken to her properly for days. I'd never told her about where the Americans came from. I hadn't wanted to for fear of seeing her face droop with disappointment. Not until now.

'They've never heard of places called Ipswich or Norwich.'

'Oh, right,' Mum said.

'Or "Framingham without the L". I got Dolly Last to check. They've never set foot in New England in their life so there's no point in asking them.' Dad looked up, surprised to hear me talk that way to Mum. But she didn't say anything. She just sat there staring at the carpet.

'That difficult age,' I heard Dad say as I went outside. 'She'll get over it.'

All I could think about was what else had she been up to when she thought nobody was looking? Was that the first time, with the Peaman, or had there been others? And then there was the falling out with Shirley. What was that all about? She'd said herself enough times that they'd been so close growing up, they may as well have been twins. They couldn't have been happier to end up living a few fields away from one another.

I hadn't forgotten the times that Shirley would come over, upset and tearful as if her world had ended, and Mum would be comforting her, forgetting we were there. And it was always about the same thing. Shirley wanted a baby, lots of babies, and they weren't coming.

'It'll happen, Shirley, just you see. The moment you stop worrying, it'll happen.' Then a while later, the pair of them could be laughing away as if none of that upset had ever happened.

'We've tried everything, Pearl, believe you me. Upside down, hot baths, cold baths. Out in the open air.' More laughter, and Mum shooing us out like flies.

And then one day Shirley stopped visiting. She and Guppy didn't come for lunch any more. We stopped going over to the farm.

'It's a busy time of year for them,' Mum said, and kept on saying it for weeks on end until she became sick to death of us asking when we were going to see them next and said that she didn't want to talk about it.

'Your mum and Shirley have had a falling-out,' Dad said. 'It's just something between sisters. They need some time to get over it, that's all.' But that was over three years ago, and now it almost felt as if Shirley and Guppy didn't exist any more, rather than living just a few miles away. In the back garden I sometimes caught myself looking at a pair of pylons and thinking of Mum and Shirley, standing there facing one another with hands on hips, squaring up for a fight.

We missed Guppy more than anything: missed the bear hunts and the rides on his tractors, how he never seemed to tire of spinning us around and around at arm's length, our feet lifting high off the ground, always laughing when he set us back down and we fell over. He never said no to us having one more go with the water blaster or sliding down his straw stack, and even Shirley never minded us jumping up and down on the sofa and messing up all her cushions.

I came across them once. It was at the pig pits in November, not long before Dad lost his job at the farm.

The sugar beet was over a foot high around that time, nearly ready

80

for harvest. I was walking along the edge of the field towards the pits when I caught sight of Guppy. I recognised him by his hairy back, the golden hair falling in waves as he humped up and down, his back end just skimming the top of the beet leaves. I dropped down into the ditch, landed in green stinking water that had run off from the slurry pond.

A moment later Guppy stood up with his white boiler suit round his ankles. He bent over to do the zip back up, and that was it. I was off, crawling back along the ditch, not caring about the stinking water as it splashed in my face. I wanted to get away from that sight of his bare arse, and I certainly didn't want to be caught by Shirley, who any moment now was going to get out from underneath him, and rise up out of that sugar beet to give me a right good talking to for creeping about like that, spying on other people's business. Shirley must have felt it was exactly the right time to make a baby, and with every minute counting, hurried over to find Guppy at the pits where they soon got carried away, even as the stench of slurry washed over them.

DRUNKEN MARY

The corn harvest was well under way by the first week in August. It was so dry everywhere, huge cracks had opened up along the edges of fields, as if they were about to break away and head somewhere else.

It was easy to see where the chicken boys were by the puffs of dust rising above the verge as they lay at the side of the road, flapping a wing up against the bank. Yellow dustclouds followed the combines way out in the middle of fields.

The Royal Wedding had been and gone and Zelma was in a slump.

'I feel really flat now they've gone swanning off on their honeymoon. A Mediterranean cruise in the royal yacht . . . just imagine.'

She'd imagined it all too well though, that was the problem. She'd followed after Diana every single step of the way from Clarence House to St Paul's Cathedral to Buckingham Palace, then all the way to Southampton harbour. And now they'd both gone and sailed off without her.

'I feel like I've been dumped by the side of the road,' she said. 'Just abandoned there with my suitcase. By God, I'd give anything to be where they are right now. To be her. Don't you feel the same, Desiree?'

I didn't. I hadn't even watched the wedding, not after seeing Lady Di in her carriage all tangled up in that huge long train, and in that same instant seeing her face imprinted on the baby's ribcage, as clear as if it happened only yesterday.

And still I couldn't get away from the peas. Bella Creasey was in the shop every day, or so it felt like, always after peas, her underarms swinging in time to her every step as she headed straight for the freezer. Fresh peas. Tinned peas. Now she was on to frozen peas, and even asked Zelma to get an extra big order in now that the fresh ones were over.

'We all miss it when the viners have finished, don't we?' she said, her basket full of dried marrowfats. 'I always think I can't go back, not after I've tasted fresh. You had all those peas round you this year, didn't you, Desiree? There must have been some coming and going . . . all those lorries. I bet Pearl likes her peas fresh, doesn't she? They go well with a nice bit of fish. Nice chunk of cod or a juicy bit of whiting.' She was laughing away like a fat old witch, her eyes on me the whole time. I disappeared round the back as fast as I could. '. . . always goes down well with a man that does, a nice bit of whiting . . .' I stuffed my fingers in my ears. 'Laid out on a plate, right there in front of him.'

I felt clammy just having to think back to that day, trying to remember if there had been anyone else on the road, passing by our house. Maybe Bella had been well off her usual track, had pedalled past, and I hadn't noticed. Or her husband Lenny had been riding by on the biggest tractor made yet, sitting in a cab as high as a water tower, with a bird's-eye view into our porch. Or there'd been a diversion on the roads and a local bus had come down the lane, and as it crawled past our house, everyone on the top deck rubbed at their eyes and ended up with a crick in their necks because they couldn't quite believe what they were seeing as my mother and the Peaman rutted like dogs in the hot sun.

I didn't think there'd been anyone else. But then all I could really remember afterwards was frying to death on the road like an egg in a pan, and the emptiness all around me.

One thing was for sure: if Bella Creasey knew, then the whole village knew. She'd have hurled the gossip around and set everyone off talking. I could just picture it, all those married couples waiting till dark then whispering to one another on their pillows at night. A nudge in the ribs, faces turned to one another for the first time since they can't remember when.

'That Pearl, you'll never guess what she's been up to, stuck out there by herself. And that poor man. Shameful! Her husband doesn't deserve that. Working away in that factory all day long and her carrying on right under his nose, going with any man who happens to be passing. It'll all end in tears.' Not like us, they're thinking, grateful to have my mother to hold up as a manual on how not to do it. 'Not safely locked together like us.' And falling asleep happy for the first time in years.

'You don't want to mind Bella,' Zelma said. I was loading the shop bike to drop some shopping round to Elmy's house. 'She's always been that way. Had a bad start in life. Lost her mother when she was young.' Zelma shook an invisible bottle in her hand. 'Some people go a bit wrong, Desiree, that's just how it is.'

It was a funny thing about the Creaseys, nobody ever talked about them. But it wasn't because people didn't notice them, that they were invisible like Walker. It was more like people were afraid to, in case the whole family might be catching. *As long as they keep themselves to themselves and don't bother us.* That's what it felt like.

But the Creaseys did bother me. Bella bothered me, and it wasn't just because of the peas. She was near the Straight that day, out on her bike. She could have been pedalling up it moments before I came along, and for once it might not have been the usual packet of pig's liver lying in the bottom of her bicycle basket, all fresh and bloody from the butcher's. She wouldn't have batted an eyelid about throwing a baby into the ditch. She'd be the sort of person who wouldn't even bother to stop pedalling, let alone get off her bike. I was scared to death of Bella, of the whole Creasey family come to that. I think everyone was.

It was the smell of their place more than anything else. Depending on the wind direction, their stink would drift across the field and follow after you, along with the din of yelling and wailing. If it wasn't Bella, it was Lenny Creasey, shouting his head off at Bella or the kids, the muscles in his arms standing out like rugby balls as he waved his fists in the air. His arms were black and blue, covered with tattoos of fighting dragons that curled right the way round from his wrists to his elbows.

People said he was invalided out of the Merchant Navy, though there wasn't much of the invalid about him, not with those arms.

And then there was Lenny's demented dog. He had a thick neck and ran round in a circle all day long at the end of a heavy chain. He barked non-stop and lunged at anything that passed within range – birds, bees, cloud shadows – till you'd think he'd forgotten his chain, and his neck was about to snap clean off. The story was that Lenny had had a dog before this one, an Alsatian cross that was too friendly and didn't bark enough. So Lenny broke its neck in the crook of his arm and threw its body into the ditch.

There were murmurings after I found the baby. About Tina Creasey, thirteen and well developed for her age, plastered in blue eye shadow which made her look like a cross between a four year old playing at dressing up and an old woman not right in the head. She always looked as pasty as a Sunblest roll. Tina could easily have had a baby tucked inside those big old doughy guts of hers.

It wasn't the first time I'd wondered why the baby had no arms. Some days I thought maybe she'd decided to miss them off because she knew full well how she came about. She wouldn't have wanted kindly women bending down into the pram to have a proper look at her.

'Oh, what a little darling, such a pretty baby,' they'd say as she waved her fists in the air, only to give a gasp of shock as they backed off in horror at the sight of the tattoos, the nursery rabbits and squirrels romping all the way down her arms in green and black ink. So she stopped growing them altogether.

Dolly Last had gone to visit one of their daughters in Peterborough for two days. She was worried that Elmy was sickening, and asked if Zelma could keep an eye on him and send me round with a few bits of shopping because he was sure to forget. But Elmy wasn't at the house when I got there. He was in the field at the back, heading at a fair old pace towards the bridleway that ran along its far edge.

'There's nothing wrong with me,' he said, when I caught up with him. He was in his shirt sleeves with a bucket in his hand. 'The wife's fussing over nothing. She's just feeling bad because she knows she'll have a good time without me.'

Elmy had spotted half a dozen horses riding down the bridleway that morning, and thought he'd better get there before anyone else. I offered to hold the bucket while he lifted the horse muck on his shovel.

'This is like gold dust,' he said. 'If someone had told me that as an old man I'd go haring off half a mile for a bucket of horse shit, I'd never have believed them. We were up to our knees in it when I was a lad. Couldn't walk for stepping in it.'

We went up the bridlepath a way, following where the riders had been that morning. The wheat on the other side of the hedge looked nearly ready for combining. I could make out the Creasey place beyond that and the black smoke from a fire in their back yard that the Creasey boys had most likely started with a couple of car tyres.

Drunken Mary was under wheat that summer. The crop had ripened well though the field was bald in places, as if the seed drill hadn't been working properly. There was still some stagnant water in the bottom of the ditch, green slime up the banks, though the ditches were bone dry everywhere else I knew. I hurried on after Elmy. He was still going on about horse shit.

'This place used to reek of animals and shit,' he was saying, 'farmers busy loading it up and putting it back into the soil. And everywhere you looked, there were horses working the land. Big old Suffolk Punches.'

Elmy's father was a horseman. It was some sight, he said, seeing his father walk behind those Suffolks. 'They were built like elephants – so heavy they could make the road shake when they came past, and rattle every tooth in your head. But do you know?' he said. 'A team of Suffolks could work a field that was so heavy, that same field would pull any one of those big old tractors right under today. And they didn't go picking up mud like Shires. Smooth legs,' he said. 'Lovely and greasy they were.'

Elmy's face changed when he was talking about those horses. Something seemed to quicken about him as he remembered his father braiding their tails or tying them up in winter, and how he'd do the same with their manes. 'It kept the mud off,' Elmy said, 'and showed off a good strong working neck.'

We had two buckets of horse muck by the time we headed back over the field to his house. He stopped when we got to his back fence, and picked up a handful of earth.

'Look at this,' he said. 'It should be wriggling in your hand, it should be alive with things you can't see.' Elmy blamed the big old farmer boys who didn't know how to work the land properly, saying they never put back in what they took out.

'They got greedy and used up all the richness,' he said. 'Always wanting the land to do more work on less food. Then they went and crushed the life out of it with those heavy machines.' And I knew he was talking about Guppy then, Uncle Guppy, all alone out there in the middle of his fields with his tankfuls of chemicals, dressed in his whites and his face mask as if he was fighting some war in the desert.

'This field had earth one time that crumbled like Christmas cake.' Elmy threw the soil away like a handful of old dust. 'It's out of heart,' he said. 'No life in it now.'

I offered to take the buckets up to the allotments for him and feed the chickens while I was there.

'Shouldn't you be getting back?' he said. The allotments were in the opposite direction and I still had to walk home afterwards. Wouldn't my mother start to fret if I was late?

It was fine, I said, she wouldn't worry. Thinking Mum had far too much on her mind to wonder where any of us were or what we were getting up to.

I sat by the run a while after I'd fed Elmy's chickens. The air smelled of perfume. It was coming from the washing lines on the new estate, a row of whirligigs that stood like tipped-up windmills in every back garden, bed sheets turning like sails. The smell of fresh laundry was so strong, it smothered the stink of chicken shit.

Charlie Breeze had got out again, given Eunice the slip. He shot through the allotments right past me as if I wasn't there, with Eunice shouting for him up the road.

Charlie was making a beeline for the Fairweathers' house. Whatever it was, there was something about that place that drew him there every time, like a three year old after a bag of sweets. He made it seem like the most natural thing in the world to stop and stare at someone's house a while before climbing over the fence and walking straight through their washing lines and flowerbeds. It looked like he was sleepwalking.

This time Charlie had only managed to get one leg over the fence when Eunice caught up with him. She steered him away, talking to him the whole time as if he was a child, saying that he shouldn't keep running off like that, and what would those new people say if they found him in their garden?

'They'll call the police and get you put away in St Audrey's, that's what,' she said.

His mother and father came back to him so clear some nights, Elmy said, it was like they were standing at the foot of the bed.

There were seasons to his mother's hair, he said, the way his father scooped it up come the start of spring, a spray of catkins at the back of her head that swung in time with her walk, or when she came into flower with primroses and cowslips woven into it or, later on, forget-me-nots and blue starflowers till some days she could look like a meadow in full bloom. Then his father would start on Elmy's sisters, French weave their hair with vetches and scarlet pimpernels, scrape it back so tight it was smooth and satiny. 'Like a hoss to the touch,' he'd say.

'Father had them dressed up something lovely for Church. I used to sit in that pew behind my mother and sisters of a Sunday morning.

That was a sight to behold, I can tell you, my sisters braided with ribbons and violets, Mother with wild roses and honeysuckle. It's how I always remember those Church mornings, the scent of my mother's hair.

'Mind you,' Elmy said, 'I used to get the devil in me some days, and I'd tell my sisters it was like being sat behind a row of horses . . . those grut old Suffolk arses all pointed straight at me. That always set one of them off crying to Mother.

'Father would have a job now. Bit of ragwort and sheep's parsley would be his lot, I reckon.'

When I listened to Elmy telling me stories I'd heard before, they seemed to get louder and brighter with each telling, until they were boring into my head and taking root there; as if that old worm of his was flicking his tail end out of Elmy's skull, and, when neither of us was looking, passing some of the inside of Elmy's head straight into mine.

THE SILVER BARN

The corn harvest had nearly finished by the end of August. Some of the stubble fields already had mile-long heaps of pig muck along the headlands, ready for spreading and ploughing in. The pea fields had already been ploughed up around us, which got rid of the stink of rot, but now the house was full of the smell of pigs instead.

Bernie didn't notice the stench when he came round to drop off the invitations. It would have been worse for them up at the cottages. Their gardens backed right on to a heap so ripe you could see it steaming some mornings, like a giant Christmas pudding.

Cheryl was having her eighteenth birthday party at the village hall in Earl Soham.

'You're all welcome,' Bernie said, wiping his feet by the back door. He seemed to have thickened up over the summer, was pushing out at his shirt more, and his jeans. I had it so bad some days, thinking of him in that flame shirt, that the sight of a single box of firelighters at the shop could send my head into a tailspin.

'Mum and Dad will be getting loads of food and drink in and said you'd better all be coming.'

'We'd love to come, wouldn't we, Tony? We haven't had a night out in God knows how long,' said Mum.

'We'll be there,' Dad said. 'We can celebrate having that extra bit of money coming in soon, can't we, Pearl?'

Dad was going to sell the goats. He'd found out through the Goat Society that a prince in Saudi Arabia was offering really good money for pedigree goats from Britain. It would take the strain off them for a while, he said. 'Be less work for me, especially around kiddings.'

Though I had a feeling it wasn't the extra work he minded so much as the male kids he'd have to deal with sooner or later.

As Bernie turned to leave, his shirt was still sticking to that part of his back which had been pressed tight against the car seat, and beneath the damp warmth of his body, I was sure I caught the faintest scent of white paraffin.

The whole world was ablaze the night we left for Cheryl's party. The stubble fires had just been lit and the horizon glowed orange as Ed drove too fast down narrow lanes, past farmworkers still out in the fields, raking burning rows of straw.

'Me and your dad will be along in a little while,' Mum had said, 'as soon as he's back from work.' She was all dressed up in shiny heels and a floaty dress. She looked happy for the first time since the pea harvest had finished.

Smoke hung thick over fields and farms, columns of sparks spiralling up into the dark as a pile of dusty chaff ignited or a hedge caught alight. World's End was surrounded by burning stubble, and flames were reflected on every window of the Lings' farmhouse. Smoke was drifting across the road, and on the field opposite there was a man standing next to the ditch, keeping the fire from jumping across and setting light to the verge. He was no more than a black outline against the flames, holding a pitchfork by his side. I wondered if it was one of the Ling brothers.

'I don't know,' Pipe said, turning to look out of the back window. 'I didn't see him.' We picked up Pam on the way. She looked the same as usual, in jeans and leather jacket, except that Chubby had braided her hair into a French pleat. I was wearing a dress. Mum had put her foot down and said no daughter of hers was going to a party in jeans, and that she had a dress on one of her mannequins which would suit me.

'And why don't you wear this?' Mum showed me a silver bracelet, hung with lucky charms, lots of tiny horse shoes and love hearts. 'I had it when I was a girl,' she said. 'I'd like you to have it now.' And she fastened it on to my wrist without me saying anything.

The dress was pink and orange, and went in at the waist then out at the skirt. Ed and Pipe said it made me look like a spindleberry.

'It's got no pockets,' I said. Where would I put my hands?

'There'll be a dark corner at the party where you can stand against a wall,' Pipe said. 'No one will notice you.'

Light from the village hall was streaming out of the main door when we got there, so bright it reached all the way across the car park like the beam from a lighthouse.

'There you all are.' Dawn spotted us before we'd even opened the car doors. 'My goodness, Desiree, is that you? In a frock?'

She held on to me firmly by the elbow as we went into the hall, as if fearing I might bolt out backwards. 'Donny, Cheryl, everyone . . . come and see Desiree. She looks so grown-up for fifteen, such a picture. And to think, I can remember you as a baby in a romper suit soaked through with dribble. Where does the time go?' she said, looking close to tears.

'I don't know,' I said. I had a hand up to my eyes, trying to work out how a village hall could be so bright while Donny winked at me and said my dad would be having some sleepless nights about me soon enough.

It was the silver foil. It was everywhere. Donny and Bernie had been up ladders all afternoon and lined the walls and ceilings with baking foil, so that the strip lighting bounced off every surface.

Ed and Pipe already had beer glasses in their hands, and bought me a pint of James White cider.

'That'll help,' Pipe said, and went off next door.

'You've made this hall look a treat,' people were saying to Dawn, pushing aside the coloured ribbons that fell from the doorways in coils. There was a big banner strung up over the food tables, reading *Cheryl Capon, 18 years old today*, and balloons pinned into the corners of the ceiling.

The Ablets and the Cracknells were all turning up, the Hawes and the Stannards, all the aunts, uncles and cousins, and in the middle of it all stood Cheryl, looking like a bride in a tight-fitting white cotton dress, her hair cut short and swept back at the sides

'Ooh, she looks just like Princess Diana,' people were saying. 'What a beauty. My, but she's dropped some weight though, hasn't she?'

Everyone looked special that night. Once the overhead striplights had been turned off and candles were lit on the tables, the silver light from the tin foil made people's eyes sparkle. It took away the lines from their faces and removed the heavy chins. And the older women looked so different with their party hair. I didn't recognise Stan Larter's mother whose beehive was so high it could have been blown up with a bicycle pump. It put at least three inches on her, while the men had slicked their hair down with wet combs and lacquer and looked as many inches shorter.

And then Bernie was standing there in front of me, his mouth open. He shook his head as if he had water in his ears.

'Desiree White? I didn't recognise you there for a moment. It's that dress,' he said, though he was looking at me in such a way, I might as well have not been wearing one. 'I don't think I've ever seen you out of trousers before. You should take them off more often,' he said, but he wasn't teasing me this time.

Bernie was wearing a white short-sleeved shirt and black jeans that night, and his hair was falling straight and shiny. He smelled of lemons.

'I'll be seeing you later, Desiree,' he said, all serious, and turned away to go to the bar. I looked down at myself a moment, following where he'd been looking, and realised that he'd just seen all of me in that dress, and some more besides.

'Your mum and dad are still coming, aren't they?' Dawn was laying out extra Scotch eggs on a silver tray, plus sausage rolls and ham sandwiches.

'They'll be here soon,' I said. 'Dad should be back from work by now.' Though I did wonder if somehow they'd found out at the last minute that Guppy was going to be there and changed their minds.

He was at the bar on the other side of the room when we arrived, but not with Shirley who must have decided to sit this party out after the last one. I didn't think it was enough to put Mum and Dad off coming though. They'd got used to avoiding each other over the years, found a way of not seeing one another even when they were no more than a few yards apart.

Guppy nodded hello at the three of us when we came into the hall, and for a moment he looked past us as if to check whether Mum and Dad were following behind. He'd straightened up and sucked in a lungful of air as if he was about to slip off his bar stool and come and talk to us. I wanted him to come over, to have him make some joke about tin foil and the song 'Hi-ho Silver Lining' which was playing at full volume in the room next door; for him to say it was as if all these years in between had never happened, and that next time we were passing we should drop by and have some dinner with them both. But Dawn was still showing me off to people and, by the time she'd finished, he'd thought better of it and turned back to his drink at the bar. Pipe saw my face.

'He's probably worried about Mum and Dad turning up,' he said. 'Guppy won't want to cause any problems between us, make anything worse.'

After the cake and the speeches, people started to drift next door to dance where Donny had blacked out the windows for the disco. There was soon a thick fug of bodies and smoke, and my head was spinning from a second pint of cider.

It was clear by the time the slow music came on that Mum and Dad weren't coming to the party after all. The floor emptied and fiancés, married couples and grandparents moved in to dance up close, the rest of us standing around the edge in darkness. Ed and Pam were dancing together as if there was nobody else in the room except them and Lionel

Richie, while Pipe pulled a face at me, and said he'd had enough for one night and was walking home.

It was dark and quiet outside the back door. I was standing just beneath the kitchen window, breathing in the smell of burnt stubble on the night air, when Bernie came outside to have a fag.

'Are you feeling all right, Desiree? You look pale as anything.'

'Just a sore head, I'll be fine.' But he made me sit on the step and gently pushed my head towards my knees.

'Just breathe deep,' he said, one hand staying on my back as he sat down next to me. 'You know, you should wear a dress more often,' he said, his hand moving now, round and round on the small of my back, working its way towards my waist, nipping at my flesh a little. Then somehow we started kissing. Then a hand reached inside my bra. He'd gone down via the neckline of my dress. I could hear the material straining, the stitches creaking as the dress stretched tight across my back. He had a thick wet tongue that pushed deep into my mouth, then pulled at mine. I'd never expected it to be like this. I could feel my own tongue getting bruised at its roots. His fingers were pinching my thighs.

I pulled away a moment.

'I'm not sure, Bernie,' I said. In the light from a slit in the kitchen curtains, I could see his face. It had changed, turned runny like soft egg yolk. I thought of us being in that meadow together, Bernie laying his jacket down and carefully brushing the grass seeds off it before we sank into tall buttercups. Wood pigeons calling to one another in the trees overhead.

The concrete step was hard beneath me. And Dawn was putting me off. I could hear her in the kitchen, talking to Zelma as clearly as if they were outside with me and Bernie.

'Cheryl's not ready yet. Says if she got in the family way now, it would be the worst thing ever. But Stan wants to get married and start a family right away . . .'

Zelma was so close, I could hear every tut and click of her tongue.

'Well, it's because he's that bit older,' she said. 'Stan should realise she just needs some time. She doesn't want to be tied down, not at her age. Not like we were.'

'Well,' Dawn said, 'I don't think they've been too happy these last few months. Cheryl's lost so much weight, I've had to take that dress in twice. Stan's had a face on him as long as a drainpipe all night. My Donny's already had to have a word with him about not getting in a sulk and ruining the party, after all the money we've spent on it.'

'Come on, Desiree. Why not?' Bernie's breath was hot on my face. Why not? I was thinking. Over and over. Why not? It's only sex.

'I've got a johnny,' he said, reaching into the back pocket of his jeans, and the wood pigeons and buttercups fell away.

We went round the back, out by the bins, away from the disco lights flashing through the cracks around the blackout curtains.

It was dark, up against the side of an old coal shed. The walls muffled the thumping beat of David Essex; my back pressed hard against the weatherboards as he leaned into me. The lucky charms made a tinny noise as they jangled on my wrist. His fingers were hurting. I tried not to think of those four fingers on a paper plate come back to life as he pushed them inside me, then pulled some more at my tongue. My legs were about to buckle and give way beneath me when he unbuttoned his flies. He got hold of my leg, to pull it up round his waist. It must have jutted out past the corner of the shed, because as he butted his way into me, I was staring down at the colours, at the reds, blues and greens of the disco lights dancing on my thigh.

I sat on the low wall in the car park after it was all over. The women were clearing up, grabbing dustpans and brushes, looking tired and washed out under the bright lights. They'd shrunk back to normal size, hair now deflated and stuck to their heads with sweat.

Bernie had gone back into the hall before me. He did help smooth my dress down, and kissed my shoulder as he left, but I could tell he was in a hurry not to be missed. He didn't look behind once as he walked off. Just a quick glance down to check his flies, brush something off his shirt and he was gone. He didn't see me take the charm bracelet off and drop it into the bin.

After the final slow dance of the night, Bernie left to drive Janice home. That was Janice, his fiancée. Janice Bullock who he'd been going out with since they were both fourteen; the girl everyone knew would get married to Bernie as soon as she turned eighteen.

From the car park, I watched them drive off together. It was only sex, I was thinking, as the tail lights disappeared. Like Mum said, it was only sex.

I didn't notice Melissa at first. I saw her horse, Billy the Kid, parked neatly between a Mini and a Toyota truck, and felt surprised Cheryl knew Melissa well enough to invite her.

I was sitting amongst leftover drinks and half-eaten plates of food as I waited for a lift home with Ed. There was a dank smell drifting over from a pond or a ditch nearby as if something, or someone, had stirred up the water – stronger than the smell of half-eaten Scotch eggs and spilt lager.

People were gathering in the car park, engines starting up and coughing out exhaust fumes. Yet the ditch smell was now so strong it almost had a shape to it, like a thick foggy cloud of darkness. A feeling of sadness crept up beside me on the wall.

Cheryl and Stan were arguing.

'I'm not drunk. I can drive you home, I said.'

'And I'm telling you, you've had too much to drink. Look at your face, it's all droopy.' Cheryl looked back at the hall. 'Where's my dad? I want my dad.'

'I'm not drunk, Cheryl. I'm upset,' Stan said. Then, with a catch in his throat, 'After everything we've been through. I'm driving you home, OK?' But he looked like a desperate man, trying to hold on to her when all the time he knew she was slipping through his fingers.

Guppy came over.

'I'll take Cheryl home, Stan.'

'You will not . . .'

'And I can take you as well.' Guppy was holding up one hand to cool Stan down. 'I can drop you off after.'

Melissa was in the car park. She'd been circling the argument in the darkness, slunk low to the ground like a fox. She wasn't dressed for a party though. Instead she was in jeans and tee-shirt, with the word *Yankees* on the front and back in big capital letters.

It didn't take long to recognise the sadness, now jammed up tight against me on the wall. It was that same feeling I'd had back in March when I'd picked up the baby and sat with her a while on the verge, wanting to warm her through by holding her close. I could almost feel the tufted hair on the top of her head, slightly greasy to the touch like feathers. And then the screaming started.

There was a red stain down the front of Cheryl's dress. Melissa had picked up one of the drinks off the wall and thrown it all over her, a huge spreading Ribena stain down the front of her beautiful dress, that made her look like a clumsy three year old.

Cheryl was crying.

'What did you go and do that for?' she shouted, and turned to Stan. 'What's going on? Why did she do that?'

But Melissa had gone and the ditch smell had evaporated. The baby had gone with her.

Ed drove home slowly. He took the long way round to avoid the police who sometimes hung around Tannington Straight, ready to catch people who'd got into their cars after a Saturday night in Brundish Crown. We stopped at the edge of Worlingworth to pick up Pipe who'd left the party earlier. He'd been throwing up and had to sit in the back with his head stuck out of the window like a dog.

The fires were low, damping down with dew. They were going to be smouldering all night. I breathed in the smoke, let it wash through me, down into my lungs. I didn't feel any different from before. I couldn't understand why people went on about sex, why they would risk being seen, getting caught, for that.

We knew something was wrong before we even got inside the house. The car wasn't parked outside, and Mum was still up, sitting by herself in the kitchen.

'He's in there,' she said, jabbing a finger towards the front room before any of us could say anything. 'Your father's sleeping on the couch tonight.'

Dad had found out somehow, I was sure of it. About Mum and the Peaman. Maybe they'd turned up after all and seen me with Bernie, the dancing disco lights, and watched the whole scene unravel from Mum through to me. That would be too much for Dad to bear, one terrible scene replaying on a continuous loop with a subtitle going round and round. *Like mother, like daughter, like mother, like daughter.*

'What's he gone and done to upset you now?' Ed asked. 'And where's the car?'

'He got stopped for drunk driving. Your father got dropped off in a police car an hour ago, barely able to walk.' Mum was crying. 'And God knows what's happened to the car. Probably where he left it, in a ditch somewhere.'

They didn't make it to the party, she said, because Dad hadn't come back from work when he'd said he would. There she was, all dressed up to the nines and starving to death because she was saving herself for the party.

'So I gave him what for when he did get home. For a start he was over two hours late, and his boots and trousers were filthy . . . like he'd been rolling around in soot. And he wasn't wearing any socks. "I lost them," he said. Nothing else, no explanation, except to say it wasn't a big deal. So I said he must have been drinking, that he must have stopped off on his way home, forgotten all about me and the party, and he swore he hadn't. "But I am now," he says. And he storms off out, doesn't he? Straight down the pub.'

I looked in at Dad, asleep on the couch. I could smell the beer, the warmth of it coming off him. His feet were sticking out from under the blankets. They still had black all over them, apart from the skin on the underside of his arches which was the palest white. I waited for Mum to go upstairs to bed, then used one of her best cushions to cover his feet.

They found a body the next morning. It was lying face down in the middle of a blackened stubble field. There was a loose horse wandering along the lane nearby, with his tail and mane all singed, walking lame on one side.

It was the American girl, unrecognisable but for her tee-shirt which still had *Yankees* across the back. Melissa Makepeace had been thrown from her horse, broken her neck, and died in a heap of burning stubble in Drunken Mary.

II

NEW BUILD

Nobody talks about that August night any more. There's no mention of the American girl or her parents, or how, when the ambulance came that night, it got stuck at the edge of the field with its back wheels spinning in mud and it took four men to push it out while Melissa's body got rocked around inside.

People were very sorry for the family. *'Any death of a child . . . the worst thing that can happen to any parent,'* they'd sigh. But like Sadie Borrett said, they hardly knew them. The Americans didn't even live in Worlingworth and had only been up at the pink farmhouse for less than a year, kept themselves to themselves and mixed with all the other Americans up at Bentwaters. But it was such a shame that Cheryl Capon had had her special night tainted. *'And after all that money her poor parents spent on the party, all that time and effort.'* It couldn't have helped matters for Stan and Cheryl either who split up not long after, with Cheryl going off to art college.

But when everything was said and done, it was a terrible riding accident which happened out in the middle of a stubble field, and was best forgotten along with everything else. In the end, it felt as if Melissa Makepeace's death left no mark; that the Americans had never been here in the first place.

It was a bad year all told, people said, what with that poor baby the White girl found in the spring. Nobody ever did find out how it came to end up in a ditch halfway along Tannington Straight or who the parents were. But least said, soonest mended. And as hundreds of new houses went up in the village and the newcomers moved in with their lives from outside, all the gossip and the stories got diluted down till that year just seemed to disappear. If it hadn't been for Lady Di and her wedding dress, 1981 might never have happened at all.

But that August night changed everything for us. And Peewit never did go away. I get the feeling she'll be around for ever, stuck in my side like a tick, making bad things happen all around me.

I tell her, 'Just because I took you out of the ditch, it doesn't make me your mother, you know.' But then there are the days I could almost believe she never had one, and the memory of Peewit lying there in the ditch comes swooping down out of the sky on full throttle; of her being born too soon and being dead some while before she landed beneath that drainage pipe alongside a heap of bottles, as if she'd slid out of the guts of that field itself which had long been soaked through with pesticides and gin.

THE EMPTY QUARTER

The oilseed rape is coming into full flower, streaking across hundreds of acres, turning the countryside bright yellow. Our house sinks a little further beneath it every day. From a little way up the road, the flowers seem to lap against the upstairs windows, the downstairs completely submerged, till soon only the roof and the chimney will be sticking up out of the flowers like a trawler adrift at sea, with Mum trapped inside somewhere down below.

She was at the window upstairs as I parked the car. She'd been waiting there for a while, had to rouse herself as I walked up the path. Then she started waving at me, pointing at something to her right. Her mouth was opening and closing, her finger tapping at the window. The dustbin had blown over and rubbish had tipped out everywhere. Empty tins had rolled up to the fence, and a sheet of newspaper had blown into the field, caught against the rape stems as a double-page spread. The new bin bags left by the dustmen had blown into the ditch by the road. I'd noticed them as soon as I got out of the car. I knew that's what she was pointing at, wanting me to fish them out. But instead I stood there, wondering how long it would take for her to open the window, as the knocking got louder and she looked from me to the roadside and back again, willing me to follow.

'I can't hear you. Open the window,' I said. And then she was gone. She was still upstairs by the time I'd picked up the bin bags, cleared up the rubbish and taken my shoes off in the porch. She waited until she heard the back door close, then came to the bottom of the stairs. She had that pale unlived-in look about her, and there was a sweetish smell of unwashed jumble in the house. She'd been sorting through the bin bags of clothes again, with the windows shut tight the whole day.

'I've told you before about the bin,' Mum said. 'It always gets knocked over by the wind if you leave it beyond the end of the house, you know that. And then the rubbish blows all over the garden. And the binmen never tie the bags properly on to the dustbin, and they fly off over the garden.'

'Why couldn't you open the window and tell me the bags were in the ditch?'

'I didn't want to let the seagull in. It's been bothering at me all afternoon.'

'What gull? I can't see any gull. Look out there,' I said. 'The sky's empty, Mum. Not a single bird anywhere. Not even a sparrow.'

'There's a big brute of a bird, he sits there sometimes, trying to get in. Probably trying to pinch something.' Killer pylons, and now thieving seagulls. I turned my back on her to put the few bits of shopping away in the cupboard.

'Did you remember the foil, Desiree?'

'These are the last two rolls in the shop,' I said, laying them on the table between us. There was something different about the front room. I was trying to work it out but Mum was agitating about the foil.

'You've got loads upstairs, Mum. How much more do you need?'

'Only a couple,' she said. 'I suppose this will do for now.'

Mum's been telling me for years how the pylons could be killing us, cooking us alive from the inside out. 'The foil's for our protection, to stop the electromagnetic fields giving us cancer.' I never ask questions any more. I don't want to hear what she's planning to do with hundreds of metres of the stuff, afraid I'll wake up one morning to find I can't get out the door because she's wrapped the whole house in extra-wide Bacofoil.

'Just look at them out there,' she'd say, as if the pylons were waiting to pick us off one by one the moment we turned our backs.

I don't recognise Mum any more, not with just the two of us left together in this house, rattling around like a pair of leftover peas, all dried up and shrivelled out. It's been two months now since she last set foot outside; two months since Beatrice offered me the chance of going to look at that job with her brother in Norfolk. I never mentioned it again afterwards, and neither did Beatrice. She only had to take one look at my face to realise it wasn't going to happen, that she never should have asked.

Because if there's one thing I do know it's that I can never leave my mother, not after what I did. My one angry lungful of breath changed everything. The thought of it after all these years can still make me rock in bed at night.

'*You did this*,' I tell myself, when some days, most days, I find myself thinking, God, is this it? Shuttling backwards and forwards between a dying shop and a dying house? Ferrying everything in, everything out? '*You did this so get used to it.*'

'Miles Fairweather is off to New York,' I say, coaxing Mum, trying to bring her round. 'Maybe he'll go to New England, and I can ask him what it's like . . . if he's got any pictures to show you.' I save up stories to feed her, ones I know she'll like, pick out the choice bits and set them all before her, like the time the *East Anglian* reported that twenty minutes had been taken off the journey time between London and Ipswich after the railway lines had been electrified. That perked her up.

'It fits in with everything,' she said. 'London's moving closer, don't you see?' I didn't mention that perhaps it was the other way round and we were being dragged towards London instead. More than ever I need Mum to believe that places could come to her, if that's what it takes to get her to go out again. She might just lessen her grip on me then.

I sound more like Fred Bugg every day, the way he chucks away to Vegas, offers her the tastiest morsels off his plate.

'Come on out for a walk,' I'll say. 'There are some primroses in the ditch just up the road, some white violets.' Or, 'It's warm today. Just come out for a second or two.' Chuck chuck chuck. 'Just to the back door then, for some air.'

It's as if the fears have been creeping towards us for years, crawling in from over the fields one after another in a long line. Not once did I spot them coming. First it was the pylons giving us cancer, then it was the pig units, how she couldn't bear to think of those animals shut up in the heat all day on farm tracks out in the middle of nowhere. When she heard about five hundred pigs up Stonham way all suffering from heatstroke on a hot summer's day after the cooling system broke down and nobody went in to check on them, she stopped eating pork altogether. The very thought of eating that flesh sickened her, she said, when they could so easily have suffocated to death.

Then there was the back field. That one took us all by surprise when Mum came home one day in winter, bursting in through the door as if there was something coming after her. She was so out of breath she could hardly talk and was covered in mud down one side where she'd fallen over.

She'd taken a short cut back from Fram over the fields, she said, because it was starting to get dark. When she was out in the middle of the back field, that's where she'd felt it.

'There was definitely something out there. I could feel it, a warmth on the back of my neck. Something dark behind me. A presence, call it what you like, but I was terrified. I just dropped the shopping and ran.'

Everyone teased her about it for days. Dad said one of the new monster John Deeres had probably been left out in the field and the engine was still cooling down, but she was none too keen on walking back from Fram in the dark after that.

Fears have been erupting out of her over the years. She must be riddled with them on the inside. Even if I do manage to plug one, another will go and pop out somewhere else. The house cracking down the middle. Us getting ploughed under. Last spring it was the spray booms, so large she ducked every time they swung round at our fence as if they were about to take our roof off. Either that or the pesticides were poisoning us, giving her headaches. Then it was the bird bangers that made her jump as if she was being shot at.

The guns woke her at first light, she said, every single morning. It was like being under fire from dawn to dusk. I wished she could be more like the pigeons who weren't bothered by the noise at all. They'd rise a few feet in the air with each blast then settle back down to feed on the field.

'It's only gas and air,' I said, 'the guns can't hurt you.' But we were surrounded by them till even I began to have trouble sleeping through, and lay in bed listening to them start up at first light, the guns in other fields firing back.

It's been so long since she last left the house, people have started asking after Mum as I do the shopping in Fram on my own.

'We've not seen Pearl for a while. Is she keeping well?' They have a look on their faces, hold my gaze a little too long as they try to work it out, if maybe I've locked her in the house, or buried her under the floorboards. The thing is, they can still pick up the faint scent of death clinging to me. *'Desiree . . . you know, the girl who found that baby in the ditch? That awful summer, remember? When all those terrible things happened. Well, now her mother's disappeared. Someone should go and check.'* And in a whisper, with an excited rub of the hands: *'You know, check that she's still alive.'*

'She's busy at home with things,' I tell them, as I think of Mum raking through jumble day after day, ferreting around in the house by herself. 'Though she might as well be dead,' I want to say. I'd enjoy watching first the confusion then the disappointment slide down their faces to stop at their big, eager snouts all slippery with drool.

Even the fishman asked after Mum at the weekend and he got fed up with her years ago, since the time she was always asking after the Icelandic cod wars, and where did his fish come from? Did he have any from Iceland she could buy? She was always at the fish stall back then, or in the butcher's, or chasing after the Americans. But they've all gone now. Everyone's gone, or so it feels like some days. And now it's just the two of us, playing the same conversation every day, over and over, who I've seen, what they were wearing, till even that wears thin and one day soon we'll dry out in the silence and turn to dust.

I never told her but I did go into the back field the morning after Mum had come tearing home, covered in mud. I went to look for the shopping she dropped. It didn't take too long to find the carrier bags. There were huge tractor tracks nearby. Dad must have been right. One of the farm's new tractors had probably been left out in the field that night and she got spooked by it. But of all the shopping she'd bought, all I could find was a bottle of disinfectant, some Vim and a packet of J-cloths. Everything else had gone. The meat, the bread, and the vegetables. It could have been foxes, though I didn't think they'd take a string bag of onions or tins of baked beans.

I picked up the bottle of bleach which was half sticking up out of the earth. Someone or something must have been hungry for all that food to disappear without a trace. Even I was glad to get out of the field that morning.

'Have you read this about Sizewell?' Mum was in the front room after we'd eaten, reading the *East Anglian*. She was pointing at a picture of the plans for a new nuclear reactor at Sizewell. I came through but lost all interest in the paper. I'd just noticed the emptiness in one corner of the living room. The globe had gone. The present that Dad gave her on her thirty-fifth birthday. I knew she hadn't touched it in ages. It had been stuck on Siberia for months. She must have thrown it out with the rubbish that morning. 'It's only gathering dust,' she'd have told the binman who had no doubt taken pity on her, that pale woman at the window, and kindly agreed to come in and carry it out for her. 'I've no use for it now,' she'd have told him. It was probably cancer, the men would have agreed between themselves as they drove off.

We sat there watching television in silence, neither of us mentioning the gaping hole in the corner of the living room, each of us now feeling as hopeless as the other.

Mum won't see a doctor. 'I don't need them,' she said. I think she's afraid they'll make her do something against her will, like force her to come to the clinic after the first home visit, tell her off like a silly little girl when she refuses to go, say that she should know better at her age. What on earth was there to be afraid of in going outside? Everyone goes outside, they'd say.

If nobody else will help, I'll have to do something about it instead. I could always ask Beatrice and Elmy to come over and lend a hand. We could use one of Beatrice's plastic drench bottles that she uses to worm the goats and fill it with medicine. The minute Mum sees Beatrice standing there in her white coat and realises what we're up, spots the drench bottle in Elmy's hand, she'll bolt for the stairs. But we'll get hold of Mum by her ankle, pull her down on to the carpet. Then I'll clamp her between my knees, her head held fast, trapped by her ears so she can't go backwards, shoulders wedged behind my legs so she can't go forwards, till she's gripped so tight her head starts spinning, and then I'll prise her jaw open till we can tip a whole bottle of medicine down her throat.

'I'm trying to help you, you stupid woman, get you out of here. I'm trying to put things right, can't you see that? Undo what I did.' But still she's stramming and screaming.

'Let me go!' in a long thin wail.

'So now you know what it feels like,' I'll say, as she kicks out in panic, trying to get away from me, but I'm holding her firmly, so tight she can hardly breathe. 'You need to come outside, get some sun on your face. This can't be good for you. I can show you how to drive. I'll do anything, but not if I can't get you out of the door. What are you afraid of? There's nothing out there.' And as she spits out the medicine, convinced I'm going to kill her, poison her with an overdose,

I'll grab Beatrice's pill gun and fire tranquilliser tablets down her gullet, if that's what it takes.

I'll close her mouth and stroke her throat as she gags and retches till she has no choice but to swallow them down. Because I'm not a good person like Fred Bugg, not when people live so much longer than dogs. And even if by some miracle Paris did wash up in the back field tomorrow and we wake up to find the Eiffel Tower standing out there in line with the rest of the pylons, I wonder now if it would be too late.

Sleep didn't come easy that night. The chicken boys were scratching around in my head. I hadn't been to see them for ages. It was early-May and they had enough to eat but still I shouldn't leave it so long. They're six years old now, getting on in chicken years, especially as they didn't have the best start in life and were only meant to live for forty days before being slaughtered and wrapped up in plastic. They don't stray too far these days and I always know where to find them within a hundred yards or so from the spot where the crates smashed on to the road that night. If it's sunny, they have a favourite place on the ditch bank, where they like to lie in the long grass, pecking now and then at insects and seed heads around them, content in the sunshine, the breeze lifting their feathers. They look like a normal couple of chickens except for only having half a beak. Scratch scratch scratch.

I opened the window wide, drew a deep breath of damp air, thick with the scent of rape. The chicken boys were out there somewhere in the dark, all fluffed up close to one another, deep inside their hedge together, muttering and bickering, pecking at each other to move along a bit this way, that way. Scratch scratch scratch. What if one goes before the other? What will happen to the one left behind? I dread turning up one day and finding only one of them out there in the field all alone, the other one dead in a ditch or carried off by a fox. I've been wondering, what would I do then? Till I wanted to tear out of the house, reach deep inside that hedge and knock them both on the head. Just to get it over and done with.

Mum was rustling, moving about in her bedroom. I could hear her through the wall. What could she find to do with a hundred bin bags full of jumble? I pictured her doing something pointless, folding, refolding, making them look like brand new shop clothes, before packing them away again in a messy heap, to start all over again the next night. And she was talking to herself. By the rise and fall of her voice, it sounded like she was having proper conversations, asking questions, answering others. I haven't been in her room for years, never even looked inside, for fear of what I might see. Mum doesn't sleep in there any more. She always sleeps in the boys' old room across the landing, lying on the bottom bunk surrounded by all her foil, trying to keep her fears at bay.

Dad lost his driving licence after Cheryl's party. By mid-September, he was cycling to work. The Morris Marina sat out in the drive all day while Dad went off to the chicken factory on Ed's pushbike. Mum said she couldn't bear to look at the car just sitting there, right outside the front window. Dad must have felt the same because in the end he covered it with tarpaulin so it blurred out of shape to look like something buried under bright blue snow. If there'd been enough left over, Mum would doubtless have thrown some over Dad to make him disappear as well.

She'd stopped speaking to him, turned away when he came in through the door from work. She looked at Iceland in the evenings quite openly now, didn't bother to cover up the page when Dad came in the front room or stop measuring the distance from the tip of Scotland to Reykjavik on the globe when he sat down next to her.

Ed took over the driving. He picked up anything Mum needed in his dinner break, did the shopping with her at weekends. Dad never went along.

'You don't need me to come as well,' he'd say. I was glad he stayed at home. I didn't want him to have to sit behind them, to have to stare at the back of Ed's head or at Mum sitting next to her son.

*   *   *

The first mists had just started to appear and the black stubble fields were being ploughed up when we heard about the Americans.

'They're pulling out.' Elmy and Dolly were in the shop first thing Saturday morning with the news. Winona had told Dolly the day before that they wouldn't be needing her services any more except for a last big clean before they went.

Nobody was surprised. They'd lost their only daughter. They had nothing to stay for in this country, and the rumour was their marriage was over, that it was probably on its last legs even before Melissa's death.

Dolly reckoned the arguments used to be about money as far as she could tell, and Winona going on about getting Melissa into some fancy college back home before it was too late.

'I suppose they can't argue about that any more, not now their daughter's gone and it's all gone cold between them,' she said.

Mum dragged around the house looking hopeless when she heard the news. She took to staring at the fly papers which hung at the kitchen windows.

'Someone else will move in, maybe some other foreigners,' said Ed. But we all knew that wouldn't be enough to make up for the Americans. Mum had only just started looking into San Diego in the week before Melissa's death, and had found out it was one of those cities on the move northwards past Los Angeles. She'd been planning to talk to them about it. The hope of that seemed to be making up for the disappointment of them never having set foot in New England.

The muckspreaders were busy out in the front field, and with the slurry came the flies. The paper coils buzzed with small black flies and fat bluebottles, their legs and wings soon stuck fast on the glue.

'They seem to get in even with the windows shut,' Mum said. 'They must be crawling through the cracks.' Some days it was like they were queuing up by the back door, swarming indoors the minute it was opened, bashing the plastic strips of the fly curtain to one side.

'I really thought I'd get to know them one day, have proper sit-down conversations with Winona about America, where she was from, find out everything I needed to know. But no chance of that now.'

'We'll get the money from the goats soon,' Dad said. 'We could go somewhere. Maybe a weekend in a caravan somewhere. Just the two of us. The children are old enough to look after themselves.'

'And how will we get there? On a bus? Or get our son to drop us off like old people? I don't think so,' Mum said.

At the end of October, a man from the Goat Society came to the house to collect the goats and take them to the airport. They were off to Saudi Arabia in a couple of days, all of them except for Nancy, who wasn't good enough to breed from, so Dad said. The five of us stood outside to watch them get loaded up. In a few days they could be grazing in mountains beside the Red Sea, maybe in Mecca with a view over to Egypt, or somewhere alongside the oil pipeline that was headed for the Persian Gulf. Mum had listed all the places from the atlas. They had proper deserts in Saudi, she said, deserts with sand and camel trains, mirages and watering holes.

It was strange to think of our goats living there. They'd never been more than a few miles up the road, and that was only to Stradbroke to get their horns burned out as kids, and a mile or so further on to Horham to be mated when they were goatlings.

Mum pointed at a blank space on a double page.

'That's called the Empty Quarter,' she said. 'They'll feel at home there.' It was one of the largest deserts in the world, thousands of square miles of empty sand.

'I'm sure they'll have the life of Riley,' Dad said as he signed the paperwork. The goats were led up the ramp. Mum stood silent, with her arms wrapped tight around herself.

'And it's good money,' he said, glancing over at her as he checked the trailer door was secure. She started to cry. 'They'll have a good life, Pearl. Better than here.'

'Don't I know it?' she said, and went indoors.

* * *

Nobody saw the Americans leave but they'd gone by the first week of November. They must have slipped away one night. There was no glorious flypast for them in a Phantom jet. Instead Lance and Winona were probably winched out by helicopter, dangling from the end of a rope as they sped over our house in the dark, skimming the rooftops of Fram, the castle battlements, thinking they were leaving Drunken Mary far behind, that they could shake her off for good, when I bet she followed them all the way back to America to swamp them nightly with the horrors.

They'd left the house more or less as they found it. There were yellow circles in the grass where the beer dustbins had sat all summer, and scorch marks from the barbecues. But the volleyball nets, the big table on the lawn, the line of cars and jeeps, they'd all gone. And Billy the Kid's stable was empty.

The Americans might never have been living there, if it hadn't been for the bits of silver in the grass, all over the garden. I thought it was money at first, loose change, silver dollars that had been sprayed every-where in a final battle between Lance and Winona about money and the divorce. But it was hundreds of ring pulls, on the lawn, in the flowerbeds.

I was glad they'd gone, that they'd taken their cars with them. I hated the way they were too big, took up too much of the lanes. I saw one of them clip Walker with their wing mirrors one time, speeding past in a rush of air that made the verges ripple. With those long mirrors stuck right out like that, they couldn't miss him. But they never saw him. Walker didn't even break his pace. He just kept on going as if the car hadn't even touched him, like that mirror passed right through him.

It was different with Dad. He cursed and wobbled on his pushbike, had to stop when they drove by and put one foot on the verge to steady himself. I hated the way they made him look small, like nothing worth slowing down for. I was glad when they left in tatters and took their fat cars with them.

THE A1120

There was a heaviness in the house after the Americans left. Mum only spoke when she had to, either to say that food was on the table or that she needed someone to go to the shops. Even the goat shed was quiet now that the goats had gone, all except for Nancy. She bleated during the day, a small sound that rattled round the shed.

'She's lonely,' Dad said. 'They're herd animals. I'll sort something out soon, maybe get another Golden Guernsey to keep her company. Can't have her feeling all alone out there in the shed by herself.' On hearing that, Mum upped and left the room.

One evening when Ed got back from work, Dad asked him if he'd mind picking up a bale of hay and some goat pellets from the farm outside Earl Soham.

'I haven't got time, Dad. I'm taking Pam out. It's her birthday,' Ed said.

'It won't take you long, Ed. Please.' Dad said it quietly. It wasn't easy for him to ask when it should have been him leaping into the Marina and going himself

Ed looked at his watch.

'Oh, all right then,' he said.

Ed still wasn't back by teatime. Pam rang, wanting to know where he was. He'd said that he would pick her up by six.

'He's on his way back, I'm sure he'll be home in a minute or two,' Dad said.

The phone rang again. It was the police this time. There'd been a road accident. Ed had been in a collision with a motorbike. Ed was fine, they said. He was on his way to the hospital with broken bones. But there had been a fatality.

'What are we going to do? I can't even drive us to hospital.' Dad was sitting on the edge of the couch, the palms of his hands pressed tight to his eyes. In the end it was Pipe who picked up the phone and asked Donny Capon up the road if he could drive Mum and Dad to Ipswich.

Everyone said how lucky Ed was. Luckier than the boy on the motorbike, that was for sure.

It happened on the A1120 between Earl Soham and the Ashfield crossroads. Jason Feathers had been on his way home to Stowmarket after taking his new bike out for a spin, and had decided to open up the throttle as he turned on to the road out of Earl Soham. Everyone got a move on down that stretch of Roman road. But people who weren't familiar with the road didn't know that it had a party piece. How it looked as solid and level as a plank of wood running into the distance, until cars suddenly appeared out of nowhere coming right at you on the other side, as if they'd shot out of a hole in the ground. Those dips were always catching people out.

The police said there was nothing Ed could have done. Jason Feathers thought the road was clear, overtook a car, and drove smack into Ed who was coming the other way.

When Ed came round, the Cortina was off the road and the boy was in his arms, his head resting against Ed's shoulder. The boy's chest had been stoved in by the car bonnet, his neck snapped in two as he flew in through the windscreen. The police said Ed was lucky to be alive, that he must be made out of reinforced concrete, having the lad slam into him like that. He'd have been going at the speed of a bullet, they said.

Ed was in hospital for a week, long enough to set both legs, let his cuts and bruises begin to heal though they said his broken ribs would take a while. His face was all colours by the time he came home. Mum had made a bed up for him in the front room.

'He's young, he'll heal well,' the doctors said. But we heard him shouting out in the night, crying in pain. Mum would go downstairs and sponge the sweat off his face, spend ages down there with him some nights. He was having bad dreams, he told her, like it was happening all over again, that he kept on seeing the boy flying towards him, skimming low over the bonnet while Ed sat and waited at the wheel with both hands reaching out to him, waiting to catch Jason Feathers in his arms.

I could hear her soothing him quietly.

'It was an accident, Ed. It wasn't your fault, you did nothing wrong. It wasn't your fault,' over and over, till I fell asleep.

Where his pyjamas fell open, his flesh had turned black and yellow, exactly where the boy had landed on him. I could see Dad didn't feel comfortable around him when he came in from work, seeing his son's puffy face the colour of chicken fat. For a while none of us felt easy around Ed, knowing he'd had someone die on him. Within a fortnight he had moved in to stay with Pam and Chubby for a while. It was easier in their bungalow with his legs still in plaster, he said. No stairs, and a bedroom and bathroom at the back of the house.

Now there was no one left to drive either of the cars that sat out front of the house all day long. In that time, the rest of us cycled or walked everywhere.

It didn't take long. Within a week of Ed leaving home, the row finally broke. We'd sensed it coming for a while, making the air crackle around us.

The washing powder started it.

'I've run out of soap powder, Tony, and I need to do some washing today. Work clothes for you.' Sniping remarks shot out of Mum, one after the other. 'What am I supposed to do now? Any ideas?'

'I can go to the shop after school,' I said.

'It's not just the powder,' she said, not looking at me but at Dad. And she rattled off a whole list of things. Windolene. A sack of potatoes so we didn't run out every five minutes. Meat from the butcher's, enough to fill the freezer up. 'I don't want just a pound of this or a bag of that, anything you can carry on a bike. I need enough to stock up properly.'

'Donny says he can always drop by with any shopping,' I said. 'We only have to ask. Remember?' But Mum didn't want to remember. She didn't want help to get it all sorted. Quite the opposite in fact. She wanted it to get worse. Far worse. When Dad started to say he could do a big shop tomorrow, she didn't even wait for him to finish.

'Fat chance of me doing any of my jobs today then. Like cleaning the windows.'

'I can go out on my bike and get the urgent stuff,' he said. 'It won't take me long if I go now. I'm on a later shift this morning.' But she was shouting over him now, about how in the beginning she thought we'd cope because at least Ed could drive, that thank God somebody round here could still get behind the wheel of a car, that he should have listened to her all those times she said she was desperate to learn.

'It was the money, Pearl, you know that.' But she was still talking over him.

'Only problem is, Ed's got both legs in plaster, and even when he is better, he'll be working, and busy courting. He won't move back here when he's better, not now. What if there's an emergency, a real one? What am I going to do then? Call Donny again? Get him to be our taxi service whenever there's a problem? He'll love that, won't he?' There was spit bubbling at the corners of her mouth. 'Or if he's not there, just think, I'll have to try all his neighbours down the row, asking for help, until everyone knows our private business. Was that what you wanted when you threw all that beer down your throat?'

Dad didn't say anything. He just stood there with his head down. It was when he put his hands in his pockets and turned to walk off outside, thinking Mum had finished, that she really lost it.

'Don't you dare walk away from me, Tony White!' And she started railing at him, saying only he could be so stupid as to get in a car with all that drink inside him, *and* get caught on the quietest stretch of road in Suffolk. How it could only have happened to him. That he couldn't even hold his drink properly. She let loose words in an ugly white-hot rush, words like 'weak' and 'useless', her spit spraying in his face.

'You're no bloody use to anyone now!' she was yelling. 'I wish you'd lost your fingers like that bloke at work instead of your licence. At least then you'd still be able to drive.'

The fingers. Dad stood there, holding on to the fingers of his left hand, like he was having to protect them from her.

'I'm sorry, Pearl,' he was saying, over and over. 'I'm so sorry.' He hadn't even wiped the spit off his face.

Instead he was apologising to her as if he was the only one who had done anything wrong. How could she talk to him like that, listing all his faults and calling him weak? How could she? When all the time it should have been her apologising to him, going down on her knees and asking for forgiveness, saying that it was a mistake, a moment of weakness, and she'd never do it again.

'Ed wouldn't have been on the road running your errands that day if you could still drive.' She looked at him straight in the eye. 'You as good as killed that boy yourself.'

Dad dropped on to the sofa as if she'd just swung at the backs of his knees with a crowbar.

'At least Dad didn't cheat on you.' I said it quietly. Too quietly. They'd forgotten I was there, listening to Mum bringing the end closer with every word.

'At least he didn't go with another woman.' They both turned to look at me this time. 'Because I saw you,' I said, looking straight at her. 'I saw you with him . . . that man.'

'Don't,' said Dad. And he moved to stand between us.

'I saw you with the Peaman that day.' Now I was shouting, making sure my words curved round him to smack Mum full in the face. 'You and him together. In the porch. His hands all over you. I saw every-thing.' And then I ran out into the rain, straight into the goat shed. Pipe followed me out a moment later and stood in the doorway. He just stared at me.

'What have you gone and done, Desiree?'

THE GOAT SHED

After Melissa and Jason Feathers, there were whispers in the village. 'We're not done yet,' they'd say. 'Bad news always comes in threes.'

'Just you wait,' Sadie Borrett, was saying. 'Death will be knocking on one of our doors soon enough.'

I noticed how God had started cropping up in conversations a lot more than normal, with the older people especially.

'I'll be round on Sunday, God willing.' Or, 'We're hoping to see our Yvonne over in Wisbech at Christmas. Going on the train, God willing it stays on the tracks.' Or they'd take one look at Ed who was shuffling round like an old man after the accident, and think, There but for the grace of God . . .

Dad moved in with Nancy after the row. He slept in the goat shed for a week while Mum stayed in the house. Neither of them had anywhere else to go. Dad came indoors for a wash and brush up but otherwise he chose to sleep outside, bedding down next to the goat. He had some blankets on fresh straw, told us he was fine.

'It's just for a while till things get sorted out with your mother.' Meanwhile the Morris Marina slowly seized up under the tarpaulin outside.

Out of everyone, Nancy was looking the happiest. She'd started eating again, content to stand and chew her cud for ages with her front hooves in the feed bowl. Her coat was glossy, and her belly was rounding out. Dad reckoned she was having a phantom pregnancy. He'd let her run through for the past couple of years, not wanting to get her mated any more.

'She got a bit broody so she's gone and tricked herself into believing she's in kid,' he said. 'She'll get all big and heavy, even produce some milk, but she'll just be full of water.'

It was only when Dad came down with a cold that he finally came back into the house. We heard him in the shed one night, coughing away. Mum refused to leave food for him by the door when he got back from work the next day. Instead she pleaded with him.

'Please come in, Tony. You can't sleep out here like this. Not like an animal. We can sort things out.'

Sadie Borrett was right though. We didn't have to wait long.

The relief when it came in the last week of February . . . shock followed by a sigh of relief went right the way round the village. I could hear it from over the fields like a breath of wind, a village whisper, 'There but for the grace of God . . .' It wasn't one of their own. They could drop the 'God willing' before every trip out of the house, let Him rest in peace while they gathered their families to them. They no longer had to give short shrift to the postman and the brush salesmen knocking at the door. Because it happened to us, the Whites.

There was no need to knock. The back door was always open at our house. Death walked straight in from the back field, pushed through the fly curtain and helped himself to Dad.

Me and Pipe were at school when it happened. It was Mum who had to phone Donny Capon this time, to ask him if he could take us up to the hospital. Except Dad was already dead by the time they got him to Ipswich. He was near enough dead by the time that blue light caught him full in the face as he was stretchered up the garden path, and the ambulance set off up the road with a squirt of its siren which echoed over the fields as far as Worlingworth, and everyone who heard it could stop holding their breath and sleep a little easier that night.

The silence of that first February night. I stood outside in the garden after Ed had put Mum to bed and looked out over the back field. There was no moon, no stars, no cloud. Just the blackness all around us. And silence. Even the pylons weren't buzzing that night. It felt as if something had been blown away, kicked out from underneath us, and we were hanging there in space. As if we'd been hooked on to those powerlines after all, but instead of swinging through the night over motorway lights and towns, we were hanging over nothingness as endless as the sky above.

FRANCE

The chicken boys didn't settle all night. They were scratching away till I gave up on sleep in the end and sat in the porch a while, watching steam rise from the back field as the sun came up and burned the dew off the rape.

Beatrice's place was at the church end of the village, hidden behind thick hedges, front and sides, which she'd planted when she first moved in. They were willow and hawthorn hedges, good browsing for the goats she brought with her. She had Elmy and Dolly on one side as neighbours, and new neighbours on the other, who'd just moved in a few weeks before. That was Bernie and Janice with their new baby, Mickey Capon.

I was glad of Beatrice's thick hedges then. I didn't want to have to stare into their house every time I was in the goat yard, see how they'd set out their new kitchen with fresh flowers at the sink, or how their bedroom curtains were drawn after lunch on a Sunday when the baby was downstairs having his nap.

There was no hedge at the bottom of Beatrice's land where she had her goat paddock. Instead there was a wooden fence and a ditch which ran between the paddock and the field beyond. It was green with barley right now, dotted with rape plants around the edge which had blown in from surrounding fields. There was a bridleway at the far end of that barley field, and on the other side of that lay Drunken Mary.

I was going to look after the goats with Elmy for a few days while Beatrice went off to Guernsey to visit another goat breeder. But she wanted a proper handover beforehand, she said.

Beatrice was in the yard when I turned up, trimming Nancy's hooves and talking away to her.

'You'll feel as good as new after this, like you're walking on air.'

She cut off the long points and planed the undersides, the bone clean and white underneath. 'She'll walk better now,' she said to me. 'I let them get too long.' She gave Nancy a brush-down after she was finished and let her into the paddock to join the rest of the herd who'd been turned out after milking.

Nancy looked as if she was going down on her hocks, beginning to hobble more at the back.

'Arthritis,' Beatrice said. 'Not doing badly for her age though, is she?'

Beatrice took Nancy on after Dad died. Warm solid Nancy with her lumpen beer-pull teats. By the end she looked so heavily in kid, it was hard to believe she didn't have two good-sized offspring inside. But she had her cloudburst as Dad said she would, just two days after his funeral. I went in to check on her and she was calling to a heap of wet straw in the corner of her pen, her sides all hollow now that she'd emptied out her waters. I gave her a bucket of warm mash, some fresh hay, but she wouldn't let up nosing at the corner.

'There's nothing there,' I told her, but I waited until the morning when I could let her out in the garden before forking the wet straw into a sack and putting it in the back of the car, where she wouldn't smell it.

Beatrice didn't hesitate when I asked her if she'd take Nancy in. Mum couldn't stand her noise any longer. She'd taken to stuffing her fingers in her ears to block out the sound of Nancy bleating away at night, calling for her phantom baby.

Beatrice walked me round the goat shed, pointing out the milk rations for the kids, and the different foodstuffs for the milkers and the males. She housed the male goats in a separate shed, a couple of them kept for breeding along with four others being reared for meat.

'You will keep the door shut, won't you? Don't turn your back on them for one minute. That one,' she said, pointing out a Saanen male with a long beard, yellowing around the mouth as if he'd been chewing tobacco, 'he'll be in with the females before you know it. I've seen him clear a fence over six feet high when one of them has been in season.

'And take special care with Hebe.' That was her champion goat, a big-boned Anglo-Nubian. Beatrice wanted to make sure I stripped her out properly so her milk would be up for the Royal Show. She was the best milker by far, and had already produced three champion kids. 'She's the backbone of the herd,' as Beatrice liked to remind me now and again.

'And remember, no beet for the boys,' she said as we went back outside. 'The sugar makes them sterile.'

Elmy came into the yard with a barrowload of muck for Beatrice's roses that he'd wheeled up from the allotments. He set the barrow down, and leaned against the fence as if he was in need of a sit down.

'Let me spread that,' I said. 'You look tired.'

'It's nothing to worry about,' he said. 'Just had a broken night's sleep, that's all. It was a full moon last night, did you see it? Set all the cocks crowing for miles around. I could hear that bird of mine on the allotment, clear as day.'

It never bothered him, but Elmy said he could just imagine the Fairweather bloke lying in his bed wide awake, agitating.

'And then I expect I'll be due a visit. He'll come and have another go at me about the birds.' Elmy laughed. 'He doesn't let up, I'll say that much for him. I just let him rattle on. Makes him feel better, I reckon, hearing the sound of his own voice. And he still hasn't caught on that every time he goes on about the chickens, I go and stick another one in the pen.'

Elmy had one more load of muck to fetch and then he was going to stop for a tea break with us and see what needed doing.

'It wasn't the cocks keeping me awake,' he said, as he stuck the fork back in the barrow. 'It was that bloody worm of mine. The moon set him off, churning everything up and bringing stuff to the surface I haven't remembered in over sixty years or more. Some stuff I don't want to remember neither.' Elmy rubbed his head. 'He got down as deep as the Great War last night. I was remembering how we woke up one day and the villages were empty. All the men and young boys had gone off to war, and the horses went with them. Some of Father's best Suffolks went over to fight in France, you know. That was when Father started on Mother's hair.'

Elmy said to get the kettle on and pushed off up the road, followed not long after by Janice Capon pushing a pram, the noise of her baby's steady wail dotted with the squeak of Elmy's barrow as they trailed round the corner together.

Bernie and Janice got married the day after Janice's eighteenth birthday. They moved in with her mother, Wendy Bullock, while they were waiting for a house to come up. Then just when it seemed like they'd never get a place of their own and people were beginning to wonder if they were going the same way as Shirley and Guppy because surely they should have started a family by now, they had baby Mickey in April. They called him that after Mick Mills on account of the fact that when he was born, Bernie reckoned he looked just like the Ipswich Town captain, a long lick of hair stuck to his forehead and a bright red face, as if he'd just been running up and down the pitch at Portman Road. Zelma reckoned Wendy Bullock was glad of the peace and quiet after they moved out, though Janice still went round there every morning with the baby after Bernie left for work.

We never talked to each other again, me and Bernie, after that time at Cheryl's party. Bernie stopped coming round to ours. He didn't need to, now that the Cortina was up and running. I only ever saw him out and about in his car, usually with Janice next to him large as day. There was no blocking her out then. Bernie had put stickers in the front of the car after they got engaged earlier in the summer, *Bernie and Janice*, though it was difficult to see much of Janice beneath her name. The shadow from the letters seemed to fall over her face half the time. Either that or she looked car sick from the green strip he'd put across the top of the windscreen to cut out the sun glare.

For a while I used to wonder what it would be like to be the one sitting in the passenger seat, but never seemed to be able to picture where we'd go or what we'd do once we got out of the car. He'd have had a job finding a name plate for *Desiree* anyhow. He could have gone into Bridges & Garrard in Fram and asked them for a *Deirdre* and a *Sue*, then cut them up and rearranged the letters – unless, of course, there happened to be an empty potato sack lying around in the storeroom with my name already on it.

Bernie carried on going to the pub with Ed on Friday nights. Ed and Pam, Bernie and Janice, a neat square foursome. And he'd put his thumb up if he saw me, his fist pressed flat against the car windscreen, knuckleside up, and give me a big leery grin. But more often than not he didn't see me, and things went back to how they were before I found the baby. The few minutes behind the village hall were cleanly forgotten by both of us.

Beatrice came marching into the yard just as Elmy finished spreading the last barrowload of muck.

'Look what I've just found in the paddock by the back fence.' She was holding up a plant with a long white taproot, dangling it like a rat by its tail. 'Hemlock. Look at it. Growing right where the goats have been grazing. Never had that come up before. There's none of it in the back field. I had a good walk round. Wonder where it came from.'

Elmy said it could have come from anywhere, seeing as a single plant carried thousands of seeds.

'They could have been carried by birds or on the wind like everything else. Like that rape there,' he said. We looked out at the back field, then further beyond at the flash of yellow, just visible through gaps in the bridleway hedge. Drunken Mary was hidden under oilseed rape this year. Her ditches were deep and damp enough for hemlock. She probably had all sorts growing down there, bindweeds and deadly nightshades, long fingers of water dropwort and charlock creeping up the sides of her banks and into the fields beyond, making their way towards the goat paddock.

We were so taken up with the hemlock, none of us noticed that Beatrice had left the gate open, or that the goats were drifting through it, not until half the herd was at the roses in the front garden, and four of the Nubians were out on the road. They ran in short bursts, snatching at grass on the verge, their milked-out udders flapping like empty shopping bags. But Hebe, the prize Nubian with ears like wing flaps, decided to stop in the middle of the road with her mouth wide open, bleating away. She was blaring so loud, I only heard the lorry as it was coming round the corner.

I ended up on the verge, flat on my back with the goat on top of me, my hand still caught inside her collar.

The driver jumped straight down from the cab.

'Are you all right?' he said. I couldn't speak. The goat had knocked the breath clean out of my chest. He took hold of her collar and crouched down next to me. 'That was a close one. I nearly had you back there. You haven't bust a rib, have you?'

'Just winded,' I said, and that I'd be all right in a minute.

Beatrice came running over. She'd turned as grey as her hair, most of which had come loose from her hairnet.

'Oh my God, I thought you were under the wheels! I'm so sorry,' she said, first to me, then the driver. 'All my fault. Left the wretched gate open.'

She got hold of Hebe, and helped me stand up. 'Nothing broken, is there?' But she was talking to Hebe this time, running a hand along her back and down her flanks.

'It's Desiree, isn't it?' The lorry driver was looking at me more closely as I started to brush myself down. 'Desiree White? I thought you looked familiar. I'm Stan. Do you remember me? Stan Larter?'

It was Cheryl Capon's old boyfriend, Stanley Larter, who used to pick her up every Friday and Saturday night at seven o'clock on the nail. Stan with the shiny black Escort and the juddery leg.

I remembered, yes, I said, and that he used to come from Charsfield way.

'Still do,' he said. 'But I work up at the mill now. I was just on my rounds, making a few deliveries. If I'd been going any faster, I'd have had that goat. Had both of you. Are you sure you're OK?' He was in brown overalls, the colour of malt, and had dust in his hair, but it was Stan all right, though he looked bigger than I remembered him, broader round the shoulders and his neck had thickened up.

Stan helped Elmy to get the rest of the goats off the road. Beatrice couldn't stop apologising for them.

'Anglo-Nubians. Total airheads, every single one of them. Borderline certifiable. If it wasn't for the butterfats, I'd get rid of the lot of them.'

Stan turned to me as Elmy and Beatrice took the last two goats back to the paddock, and asked if I worked round here.

I told him I worked at the shop in the village.

'I'm in the pub here most Friday lunchtimes for a sandwich. Would you let me buy you a drink tomorrow, seeing as I nearly ran you down?'

'I'm working then,' I said, and that I most likely wouldn't have the time.

'It'll only be for twenty minutes. I'll have to get back to work after that.'

'I don't think so,' I said. 'Thanks anyway.' Thinking, why would I want to sit in the pub across the table from Cheryl's old boyfriend? What on earth would we have to talk about?

Beatrice had to go and collect a load of pea straw from Hoxne. I hitched the trailer on to the back of her car while she double-checked the paddock gate and fussed with the salt licks on the side of Hebe's pen.

I told her she needn't worry, that I'd be over at least twice a day for milking and feeding. Elmy would bottlefeed the kids while I was at work, and then we'd go and pick greenstuff in the evening. She really needn't worry, I said. The goats would be fine.

'First time I've left them in years, that's all,' she said.

She stood back as I lifted the trailer on to the tow bar.

'And how's your mother, Desiree? Feeling any better?' She knew about Mum not sleeping well with the gas guns earlier in the year.

'Still a bit jumpy,' I said.

'I had a goatling who suffered from bad nerves once. Anglo-Nubian. Felbrigg Fortuna. Could never get her into a trailer, and she hated windy weather. Any tiny noise and she was leaping about, crashing around the stall.'

'What did you do?' I said.

'Oh, I gave up on her in the end. She was far too much trouble, always injuring herself and upsetting the rest of the herd. Her nerves were contagious. And then I found out she had a double hole in her teat so that was it. I had her put down.'

'She should have tried a spot of laudanum on that goat,' Elmy said, as Beatrice left. 'That would have quietened her. Do you know,' he said, sitting down, 'I was only thinking in the night how Miles Fairweather could do with a drop of that. Set me off wondering if there was an old bottle of Father's lying out in the back shed some place. A lot of horsemen used it in their drawing oils,' he said. 'Father used it on his horses, especially when they came back from the war.'

Elmy said the horses came back to the farm like broken men. Scared of every little noise, of guns going off, and they couldn't stand the sight of men in uniforms. 'Father had to use what he could just to get those horses out in the field some mornings. He couldn't bear to see those Suffolks turned to a quivery mess of nerves.'

Janice had come back with Mickey Mills. All we could see of him through the hedge were angry legs kicking out of the pram, tiny pink fists punching at the air, though we could hear him well enough. 'Nothing wrong with him, is there?' Elmy said.

Janice was trying to soothe Mickey, talking away to him as she wheeled the pram up the garden path.

'You know, women used to give a drop of laudanum to the young ones as well in them days,' Elmy said. 'They could get on and work out in the fields then, while the babies slept strapped to their backs.'

Mickey's yells grew louder as Janice parked the pram by the back door.

'She probably wouldn't say no to a drop of that stuff right now, would she?' he said.

If Elmy did happen to have an old bottle lying around, it wouldn't last five seconds with all those takers queuing up for it. Mum could definitely do with a good dose, though she'd think I was trying to poison her.

I sat in church, staring at the Suffolk Punches who had their heads down, pulling the plough in the top field, unaware they were about to be sent off to war in France. It must have been some sight for the Suffolk farm boys when they saw those horses arrive in France, saw them traipsing through all that mud and wet, pulling the heavy guns. Those horses must have made them feel right at home.

There was a loud noise in the vestry as if something had just fallen off a table. Peewit was busy as usual, making enough noise to get herself noticed. It felt like she was taking over the church more and more these days, and that sometime soon I'd have to knock on the door and ask if it was all right to come in.

A shadow fell across the hymn book at the end of the pew.

'So what would you do if she was your mother then?' I said. 'How would you get her out of the house?' I felt something behind me, like a breath on the back of my neck, a puppy breath that smelled of garlic, and out of nowhere I thought of Shirley. She was due to have her baby in a few weeks. If I could just get Shirley to talk to Mum again . . . It had been nine years. Surely it was time to mend their row and sort things out, especially with Shirley and Guppy about to start a family.

There was a tug to the back of my head then, a pull at the fine hairs on the back of my neck. I turned round, half expecting to see Peewit this time, see her properly. Then another tug, harder this time, and I smacked a hand to the back of my neck as if to swat a mosquito. 'What's got into you today?' But I was suddenly unnerved by the echo of my own voice, to hear myself talking out loud to her. I sounded like my mother.

I sat there in the pew, not saying another word. It was like she was waiting, watching me to see what I'd do next.

THE ALLOTMENTS

There were six goats waiting to be milked the next morning before work, all with tight udders but such small well-bred teats, they were hard to grip on to. By the time it was Nancy's turn at the end, my hands were aching so much, I'd lost all strength in my fingers. I had to stop every half a minute while I was milking her, and ended up leaning into her side, listening to her heartbeat.

It had come to me in the middle of the night what was wrong with Peewit. It must have been my talk of mothers and babies in the church that had upset her, made her pull at my hair. She'd never done anything like that before. But then it struck me. She needed her mother. All babies need their mothers. What if I were to find Peewit's mother for her, find out who she was after all this time? If I did that, then maybe Peewit would latch on to her instead. Peewit could lash out at her for a change, kick and scream at her own mother for leaving her all alone in the wet and the dark. 'She'll calm down, given some time,' I'd say, and walk away. Peewit would have to let go of me then.

I had it all planned out by the time I'd finished and was straining the milk through a muslin cloth into a clean bucket. It would take some poking about, but I had a feeling it might be easier now than back then. Six years was a long time, long enough for the rawness to fade and for something to have slipped out, for someone round here to have heard a story about a woman they knew having an unwanted baby one time.

I bagged up the milk for the freezer, and cleaned the equipment ready for milking that evening.

Once I'd found out who she was, I'd get the mother to go to Tannington church. I could send an anonymous note, promising her some news, and she'll tip up, expecting a fresh grave and news of a surprise windfall, but instead she opens the church door and walks straight into a blast of ditchwater and that March day will come back to her in every tiny detail. But before she can turn and run, she gets knocked backwards by the blow of something sharp to the chest like a heart pain, as Peewit hurtles into her. It'll be her turn to carry her baby around from now on, feeling a heaviness in her chest as Peewit grows fat and sleepy on her mother's guilt.

There was an excitable atmosphere in the shop by the time I walked in to start work. Dolly was telling Zelma and Sadie Borrett all about Elmy and Miles Fairweather, how they'd had a stand-up row in the allotments the night before.

'You could hear them a mile off,' Dolly was saying. 'Miles was yelling at Elmy how that cockerel had kept him awake all night and now the hens were making too much noise as well. And Elmy was telling him they made that squawking noise when they'd just gone and laid an egg.

'"Wouldn't you?" Elmy said. He was still all calm and peaceable then. "There's nothing I can do about it," he was saying. "You can't stop a hen from laying eggs, you know. You can't just stick a cork up its arse. It'll blow up."'

But Dolly said by the time she got to the allotment, Miles Fairweather was so red in the face, it was plain to see he couldn't take a joke. He'd just got back from work and was standing by the chicken run, still in his suit with his pink-stripe shirt and his shiny shoes, those watches up to his elbows.

'He's brought this all on himself,' Sadie said. She was rocking up and down on the balls of her feet, with her fists clenched as if she were bracing herself for the fight there and then. 'So go on, what happened next?'

'I can't believe it really,' Dolly said, and stopped a moment to let me step between them to carry a box of teabags to the shelves. 'Miles had just about run out of steam and looked as if he was ready to go home when Hubert Ling's peacock started up, and that set him off again, saying if it wasn't the chickens giving him no rest, it was those damn' peacocks over at World's End. He had a mind to go over and wring their bloody necks one of these days.

'Well, I was so surprised. It was like he hit a button on Elmy I never knew existed, and I've been married to the man for near enough fifty years. Elmy just turned on him.

'"Don't you go start making a fuss over there," he said. "Who do you think you are, coming over here and interfering? If you go anywhere near those peacocks, I'll get a bloody pitchfork and come right after you." And he picked up his spade like this, and . . .'

'And what, Dolly? What?' Sadie was almost beside herself, but she had her back to the window and couldn't see who was heading towards the shop, gliding up the path in a long linen skirt.

Fidelis Fairweather must have known the women were talking about her husband, the way they fell silent as soon as she opened the door, the fury on Sadie's face that she didn't even bother to hide because Dolly had been just about to get to the good bit.

I went up to the till.

'Can I help you?' I said. It wasn't her fault that Miles was that way. She'd had it hard enough living here, having so much time on her own with two small babies when Miles was in London for most of the week.

The truth is, I felt sorry for them both, and for a lot of the other new people as well, the way they moved in all shiny and hopeful at the start. I could see it in their faces, how much they wanted to fit in, start a new life of garden fêtes and barn dances, cups of sugar being passed backwards and forwards over garden fences. How their children would be out playing in the fields till dark, riding up and down the roads on their bikes. But come the evenings when everyone else is indoors, doors locked, televisions on, that's when the shine starts to disappear off the new life. Winters are the worst. When they sit in their houses at night and hear how fast some cars take the road, flattening family cats, hedgehogs. How the village shop doesn't stock what they're used to, so they have to go elsewhere in the car. How they suddenly find themselves in the car for every single tiny thing. How they could have lived here for years but they'll always be the 'new people', those 'blow-ins', the Fairweathers, the Hamiltons and the Westcott-Joneses.

Fidelis always used to breeze into the shop first thing on a Monday morning when it was quiet. She reminded me of a dock leaf on a still day, how it can wave about on the verge, when not a single other plant is moving. That was Fidelis. Her hands wheeled in the air as she talked away, neither me nor Zelma saying much with it being first thing in the morning. She only ever bought a pint of milk or some bread, and most of the time she probably didn't need those as she did her food shopping in Eye or Diss at the weekend. I think she just needed the company, an excuse to wheel the baby up the road. She was always so chatty and bright, when half an hour before she could have been howling her eyes out into a tea towel in the kitchen after Miles had left to go to London for the week. I used to see her standing at the sink when I took a shortcut across the field some mornings to get to the shop. The windows were so huge in those new houses, you could see right in and out the other side. The problem was the birds did as well. The number of times I'd seen her come running outside to cradle a baby bird in her hand which had flown smack into those plate-glass windows, blackbirds, thrushes and tits, necks snapped clean in half, brains run through with their beaks.

She always looked so pale and washed out, as if she'd never got over being uprooted from Basingstoke those few years back.

Fidelis didn't stay in the shop long. She clearly felt uncomfortable as she stood at the counter, fiddling with her hair, winding the few strands at the back of her neck round her finger like a small child.

Sadie waited until the door clicked shut after Fidelis.

'So go on then. What happened next?' But Dolly had lost her flow and said that the row had fizzled out with Miles saying Elmy wouldn't be hearing the last of this, and Dolly taking Elmy home, having a go at him that he'd pop a vein in his head if he carried on that way.

'I can't get over it though. I don't know what got into them, two grown men shouting at each other over chickens and peacocks. Elmy's never liked those peacocks himself. He's always had that funny thing about them, hasn't he?'

'So that was it? They didn't hit each other then?' Sadie's shoulders had slumped in disappointment. 'What I don't understand', she said, 'is why Miles Fairweather doesn't go and live in London if he's so sick and tired of the travel. He's always complaining he can't get enough peace round here. They should never have moved here in the first place, should they? It's not making him happy, is it? Donny and Dawn's girl, Cheryl, she moved to London, didn't she? Why can't they do the same?'

I went into the stockroom round the back for a moment. I'd forgotten all about Cheryl – how she couldn't get away from home fast enough at the end of that summer, or from Stan Larter. How Dawn must have told nearly everyone at the party that Cheryl hadn't been eating or sleeping well for months. *'She's been as bad as Lady Di, losing all that weight before her wedding day'.*

But I wondered if there'd been something else she didn't want to hang around for, the same something that took away her appetite and stopped her sleeping at night.

Stan was still in the pub by the time I got there. He looked up from his sandwich, surprised to see me standing there, out of breath from having to run up the road.

'I didn't think you were coming.' He stood up too quickly and knocked his chair over. 'So what can I get you?' he said

I sat down and managed to get a good look at him as he went up to the bar, and wondered, Could it be him? Could he have fathered Peewit?

'I think I've seen you out and about over the years,' he was saying as he sat back down. 'You're usually striding around the place, miles from home.'

'Probably looking for goat food,' I said, 'helping Beatrice out. You know, the goat lady from yesterday.'

'Oh, right,' he said, and took a big mouthful of sandwich, giving himself more time to think of something to say.

He had a tideline on his throat where he'd been sweating and dust had caught in the folds of his neck. I asked him if it was a good job up at the mill, working it out that Cheryl would have been seventeen at the time which made him eighteen or nineteen.

'It's not bad,' he said. 'Pays all right, and I get to do different jobs there. Drive a forklift, get out in the delivery lorry, hurl sacks around. It's kept me fit.' He flexed his arms. 'I was so lanky at eighteen, I never thought I'd put on any weight.' And it seemed to have got rid of his juddery leg. They were underneath the table, legs so big and muscled up at the thighs, he was having to sit with them slightly apart.

'So what changed your mind,' he said, 'about coming here?'

I wasn't going to tell him it was because I'd been picturing him and Cheryl in the Escort together, driving down Tannington Straight, his legs shaking so much he can hardly work the pedals.

'It wasn't as busy at work as I thought it would be. I had a lunch break after all, so . . .' Donny would have killed him for getting his daughter in the family way.

I'd forgotten about the low rumble of pub noise, the smell of beer and smoke. Stan was talking about his football, how he played at the weekends with the local team, and that every match ended up in the pub. As he leaned over the table to talk, I could smell warm sweat and bonemeal. The hairs on his chest were creeping out where his zip had come undone. By the looks of it, he wasn't wearing much underneath his overalls, if anything at all.

'I'd better be off,' he said, scraping his chair back as if about to get up but changing his mind halfway through. He cleared his throat. 'How about a proper drink next weekend? It would be good to see you again.'

I thought for a moment. I could ask Stan outright after he'd had a drink or two, ask him when he was starting to look a bit flushed and least expecting it. '*So did you and Cheryl ever have a baby once and happen to leave it somewhere?*'

'I'd like that,' I said.

Mum knew straightaway.

'You smell of the pub,' she said.

'I had a quick drink with Stan Larter,' I said. 'Just a half of shandy.'

'Oh,' she said. She was quiet a moment. 'Will you see him again?'

'Next Friday,' I said. And because I suddenly felt sorry for her, I offered up that he was in overalls, but that he was wearing black jeans underneath and a bright blue tee-shirt.

The shopping list for Ipswich was on the table. Amongst other things, she'd put down a nightie and new underwear. Just seeing that list made me feel hollowed out. I knew there was no point in asking her if she'd come along this time, if only to sit in the car. People only ever did this sort of shopping for family when they were going for a long stay in hospital, or about to be locked up in prison.

CHARLIE BREEZE'S RED POLLS

'I told you, didn't I? I knew he was lying there in bed that night, getting all aereated about those cockerels.' Elmy had made up the bottles for feeding the kids the next morning and was jamming the teats in so hard, he was going to have a job getting them out again by the time he'd finished.

'Time for another hen to go in the run, then?' I said. But Elmy wasn't laughing this time. He was so fired up, the veins were standing out in his neck.

'Bloody daft boy.' Elmy climbed into the pen and started feeding the first two kids. 'Who does he think he is? Moving here and stirring things up like he owns the place. He doesn't know his arse from his elbow, that one. He'd think a lapwing and a peewit were two different birds, and tell you he was right and you were wrong. But I could tell him a thing or two about his house he wouldn't want to know. You know Charlie Breeze had his cowsheds right where their house is now?' Elmy nodded in the direction of the new estate. 'I could tell him all about how Charlie had a herd of Red Polls in that meadow. That they used to calve right where Fairweather has his tea at night, munch through the afterbirth and swallow it down right where he has his fancy glass-topped table. And Charlie had a steaming muck heap right by the back door, where their toilet is.

'"You can dress up in your pinstripe suits," I'll tell him, "but when it comes down to it, there's no difference between you and a load of animals, is there? It's all blood, shit and death in the end." He wouldn't like to hear that, would he, standing there in his smart clothes, telling me what he's going to do? I could tell him stories that would disturb him more than a few hens on the lay. What happened to the young

Doy lad for a start, right underneath where he lies spark out on his leather sofa at night. That would give him something to lie awake about all right.'

Dolly had come to see how we were getting on. She stood by the pen as Elmy fed the last kid.

'Do stop, Elmy. His wife did come round, didn't she? She said sorry, explained that he's been under a lot of strain at work. That he's not sleeping well.' Dolly turned to me. 'He's become fixated on his travel time, so his wife said. He starts working it out on the train, how long he'll have at home before he has to be back in the car to go to the station in the morning. Bound to send you round the bend, isn't it, counting down your life that way?'

I stayed on after Elmy and Dolly had gone home for breakfast, weighing the milk and writing all the weights down in the milk book, giving Nancy a brush-down.

I remembered the cow field. Dad used to take us there before it disappeared under houses, took us especially to see the cows.

'Look at them,' he'd say. 'Proper Suffolk breed they are. I'd do anything to work with a herd of them rather than those Friesians.' On a sunny day, he reckoned those Red Polls had coats that shone like rosewood. But they were a rare breed, he said, not many of them left now.

'Charlie Breeze knows how to look after his cows all right,' Dad said.

Elmy said he was only a lad himself when it happened.

'The boys should never have been in that cow field in the first place,' he said. 'The pair of them were up to no good in there, messing with Charlie's cows. The vicar's son, he'd been caught crazing animals before. He was sly all right, always leading that other lad astray.'

Charlie had a score of Red Polls by then, but Elmy reckoned there was one he always went soft over, called Ida Jane. He always gave her something extra in her feed, something a bit special. 'She liked a bit of comfort, that one, sometimes a woollen blanket on winter nights, a warm sunny wall to rub against.'

The boys had a young calf cornered by the shed when Ida Jane took one of them by surprise and decided to have a lean up against him. With his back against the brick wall, he'd have had a nice bit of give in him, Elmy said. That it must have been like leaning into a warm bag of air. A gentle bounce or two and Ida Jane sauntered off.

Charlie had just reached the gate when he heard the boy's ribs go off with a crack like firewood.

'By the time Charlie got to him, that boy was just standing against the wall, stiff and straight like he was standing to attention. Until his knees gave way and he slid to the ground like a bag of rags. Charlie said his hair was soaked through as if all the water had been squeezed out of him from the bottom up. And the blood, he said, it just poured out of him.'

Elmy turned to Dolly.

'It was the Doy lad, wasn't it? Milly's boy.'

THE SWAN

It was only going to be an evening out with dusty Stan, the same old Stan who could never be bothered to get out of the car when he picked Cheryl up but sat listening to tapes instead with his foot up on the dashboard. But it was still an evening out, a night off from me and Mum being in the house together. And there was even a chance I might find something out about Peewit, if I was lucky.

Hawthorn blossom had turned the hedges cream and pink around the village, and the verges were growing tall with cow-parsley. Walker was on his final loop back home as I left the shop to go home for tea.

I thought it had always been just Walker and Milly in that house together, that he only ever had a mother. Nobody had mentioned a brother or a father, that one of them got killed and the other ran off. The husband left after the youngest son died, Elmy had said. Ran off to Dunwich with some woman. Apparently Milly never spoke his name after that, not once.

'But you could see it in her face,' he said. 'That she wished it was him who got killed instead. That he'd kept on running and never stopped until he'd hurtled off the beach straight into the sea. She wanted him drowned like that old village, with that church bell clanging away in his ears for all eternity.'

Milly had always doted on her younger boy, Elmy said. He thought for a moment. 'But the oldest, now what was his name? Samuel. That's it. Samuel Doy. He never got a look in after the brother died. She took against him. It was like he wasn't there any more.'

Stan was wearing a white short-sleeved tee-shirt and jeans when I met him in the pub.

'Shall we sit outside?' he said.

It was a warm evening and people were making the most of it by drinking in the garden round the back.

'Over here.' And he steered me to the table by the tree. The grass had only been roughly cut by the tables. There was long grass and cow-parsley up against the pub fence, and dog roses in the hedge just beyond.

He sat down next to me.

'So you still live in the same place?' he said. He'd heard about Dad, saying it must have been hard on us.

It was five years ago, I told him, and that it was just me and Mum in the house now.

'Mum can't get around by herself so she needs me to do all the running around,' I said.

'But she's still only young, isn't she? In her forties?' Stan looked confused.

'She can't drive,' I said.

'Oh, right,' he said, with a nod of his head.

Bernie and Janice came and sat down at a table a little way away. They looked over in our direction and Bernie raised a hand to Stan. It was only when Janice said something to Bernie that his eyes slid towards me. He put his thumb up as if he was back in his van, then turned to his wife, cupping his hand over hers.

'Do you ever see anything of Bernie's sister Cheryl?' Stan was looking down into his pint as he spoke, running a finger round the top of the glass.

Not in a long time, I told him, but I knew she'd done well for herself.

'The last I heard, she was in London with a graphic-design job,' I said, and that Donny and Dawn were both really proud of how well she was doing.

'She broke my heart, first love and all that. I went a bit wild after Cheryl.' He laughed. 'The funny thing is, I probably missed her mum and dad the most after me and Cheryl split up. I went over there for tea some nights after she'd gone to college. Donny and Dawn were really good to me.'

He took a long drink of his pint and turned to me as if the thought had only just come to him. 'So are you seeing anyone at the moment?'

I shook my head. I wasn't about to tell him that I was twenty years old and had never had a boyfriend. Those five minutes with Bernie behind Earl Soham village hall didn't count.

'I don't have much time to go out,' I said. 'With Mum at home,' I added, seeing he still didn't quite understand.

'What about your brothers?' Stan said. 'I know Pipe's moved away but I see Ed around sometimes. He's still here. Can't he help out with running her about?'

'Ed's busy,' I said. 'He's got a family of his own to look after now. Pam and the twins.' I thought of him slowed down by medication. Cautious, quiet, damaged.

'So they're still together then?' Stan glanced over at Bernie, then back at me to see if I'd noticed.

'Why do you say that?'

'No reason,' he said. Stan looked uncomfortable.

'What have you heard?'

'Nothing,' he said, but he knew all right. 'I just heard that Ed got ill after his accident. It must have made things difficult at home, for him and Pam.' So he did know. He knew all about Pam and Bernie Capon, about my brother being left alone to mind the babies on bingo nights. Now it seemed everyone knew Ed's private business, everyone that is except for Ed.

We didn't speak for a moment. Bernie had an arm round Janice. She was leaning into him, and in the middle of a yawn so wide she had to use both hands to cover it over. She looked as if she had a mind to lay her head on the table next to Bernie's beer and go to sleep.

I could have told Stan that Pam stopped going to bingo three years ago, that she stayed at home now with Ed and her Tupperware parties. But it had nothing to do with him.

'I'm sorry,' Stan said. 'I didn't mean to upset you.'

'I thought only women were meant to gossip,' I said.

'But you can't help hearing things, can you?' And I wondered what other business of ours had reached as far as Charsfield.

'You shouldn't pass them on,' I said. 'It only makes things worse. How would you like it if people found out your business and spread it around?' I heard the tell-tale crack in my voice.

'I wouldn't. Though I haven't got anything to hide. I don't have any secrets.'

'Everyone has secrets,' I said, and got up from the table. Every single person in this pub, I could have told him. I could point to at least half a dozen people straightaway who had something to hide. Like Robbie, sitting at the bar, who as a boy lived next door to Zelma's niece, Tracy, big-built and large-chested like all the women in her family. Robbie used to creep into her back garden and take Tracy's bras off the washing line, then stick his face in each enormous cup, breathing in long and deep as if they were oxygen masks and his whole life depended on it. Then there was Gail working behind the bar, who had the Beauty of Bath orchard round the back and had all sorts of young boys after her windfalls, who never knocked before they went in through the side door. Everyone in the pub had something to hide. 'Even you, Stan Larter,' I wanted to say.

At least it was quiet in the Ladies. I couldn't stand it that Ed's business was being talked about by people who hardly knew him. He'd had a bad enough time after his road accident. He didn't need Pam and Bernie carrying on together and making things worse.

I'd stumbled across them in the van one night, not far from our house, hidden by a sugar-beet clamp. Pam was sitting astride Bernie in the passenger seat, her head squashed up against the ceiling, half hidden by the name sticker on the windscreen that said it should have been Janice sitting on Bernie, not her. And she was laughing like I'd never heard her laugh before. The tassels on her leather jacket were shuddering with every gust of laughter. She'd pinned Bernie's arms down on to the seat with her knees, and was tickling him in the face with the tassels on her breast pocket. He couldn't move. All he could do was snap at the tassels with a crack of his teeth like a dog going after flies. She teased him till he couldn't bear it any longer and he got hold of one of the tassels between his teeth and ripped it off.

It was always on a Tuesday, Pam's bingo night. Bernie would be off and away in his truck, heading towards some hideaway place or sometimes at the wheel of other cars he was fixing. But the clamp was their favourite, the place where they regularly made the suspension rock so hard, it shook the concrete foundations and toppled a few sugar beet off the pile. There was always a single sugar beet rolling around in the road afterwards, left there like one of Bernie's calling cards.

Ed was too ill that winter to realise anything was going on. He'd not been right after the accident, but two years on he had a full-blown nervous breakdown. He was too busy trying to put one foot in front of the other to notice the tassels thinning out on Pam's jacket.

Janice was splashing her face with water at the basin when I came out of the cubicle. She looked up at me with water running down her cheeks. It was all she could do to stay awake tonight, she said.

'Baby Mickey doesn't sleep. He's like his dad. Dawn says Bernie didn't sleep for the first two years. He's making up for it now, though,' she said. 'Bernie never hears the baby in the night.' Janice dried her face. It was her mother who'd made them come out tonight.

'But all I can think about is my bed. I haven't been able to stop thinking about it all night. Bernie should have come out to the pub by himself, and I could have had an early night.' She looked me up and down. 'You don't know how lucky you are.'

Stan was sitting forward on the bench, draining his pint, as if he was about to come looking for me.

'I was starting to wonder where you'd got to,' he said. 'Thought maybe you'd gone home.'

'I thought about it,' I said.

He moved back to his end of the bench to let me sit down, nodding to Bernie and Janice as they left.

'Look, I'm sorry,' he said. 'I'm no good at keeping things quiet, but then I don't have anything to hide. Never have done. What you see is what you get with me.' But I remembered Stan in his car on winter nights, parked up in field gateways near the double bends, the tip of his cigarette burning down in the dark as he watched and waited for Cheryl.

'So why did you and Cheryl split up in the end?' The evening was turning cool. He brushed the question away.

'Things happened,' he said. 'It got messy.' He looked down at his hands but not before I wondered if I'd caught a glimpse of something in his face, something he was ashamed of. 'It ended badly,' he said. 'That's all. Never seen her since.'

TANNINGTON GRAVEYARD

'Are you off out again?' Mum knew full well I had the goats to see to that afternoon, but she was on edge, more so than usual, unable to settle to anything. 'It feels like you've not been here all week. And you were out the other night.'

'It's only while Beatrice is away,' I said, wishing she wasn't coming back so soon. I was enjoying looking after the goats with Elmy, having an excuse to go out for something other than work. And I got to spend more time with Nancy.

It was because of her that I stopped at Tannington church on the way. There was a big patch of comfrey in the churchyard, growing over by the new graves, that I knew she'd like. It was a still afternoon, quiet as always with nobody around, yet there was a noise coming from the fresh grave nearby as if the cellophane wrapping round the flowers was being rustled by the wind. It could have been a bird or a vole in amongst the wreaths, but when I checked there was nothing. It was only as I walked away that I had the feeling I was being followed, that there was something ducking and dancing between the headstones just behind me. As soon as I stopped, whatever it was stopped as well, as if we were both playing a game of Grandmother's Footsteps.

What had made her leave the church after all these years? It was Peewit's home. It was where she lived. So what was she up to now, edging outside into the graveyard? Something must have happened.

I shut the gate firmly behind me, not that it would keep her in, not if she had her mind set on where she was headed and what she was going to do next. Nothing I could do or say was going to stop her, however badly she knew it might end.

* * *

I put Nancy in a separate pen so she could have the comfrey to herself, and told Elmy I had to go and get a carload of greenstuff for the rest of the goats.

'I'll come with you,' he said. 'I could do with a change of scene.'

Beatrice had left instructions in her notes about how much greenstuff the milkers needed, and what type, so we headed out towards Horham, stopping every time we spotted something on her list. We crushed the branches to get them on to the back seat, filling the car with the smell of damp undergrowth and elderflowers.

Elmy waved a hand towards the fields. 'You know the railway used to run out here? All the way from Haughley and Mendlesham and that way towards Laxfield. Hard to believe now, all these villages had stations. Wilby, Worlingworth. The Middy we called it then,' he said. 'And look at it now. No railways left and all these new houses going up.' And we both looked over the fields to the estates appearing on the horizon, slowly creeping out of the village towards World's End, and I wondered if the Lings checked out of their bedroom windows every night before bed, knowing they'd wake up one of these mornings to find their thick hedge gone, the cow field under tarmac and Hubert's black barn turned into a holiday home, where a family has just taken up residence for the summer like a nest of house martins.

'I don't miss much about those days,' Elmy said. 'It was a hard life, and the workhouse was always just down the road. But I do miss them old railways. Them and the horses.'

I stopped in the lane by Ivy Ling's chicken field.

'There's some willowherb just up there,' I said, pointing to the hedge alongside the cow field.

'You go,' Elmy said, and he stayed in the car with the window wound up, staring straight ahead as if he were on the motorway.

'I'm sorry,' I said when I got back in afterwards. 'I forgot about the peacocks.'

'It's not the flaming peacocks,' Elmy said. He sounded cross, as if I should have known better. 'That's something I told the wife.' He only turned to look at World's End as we were driving off. 'It's something I did once,' he said. 'Something I shouldn't have.'

There was a feed lorry parked by Beatrice's gate when we got back. Stan Larter honked his horn.

'I'm glad I found you,' he said, leaning out of his window. Elmy had made a start on unloading the car and was dragging branches of ash round the back. Stan waited until he was out of sight. 'I wanted to say I enjoyed the other night,' he said, 'but I get the feeling I went on a bit too much about Cheryl. I'm sorry if I did.'

'You didn't,' I said, thinking he hadn't gone on about her enough.

'I didn't mean to. It's just you were asking about things.'

'It really doesn't matter.' I was getting a crick in my neck, having to look up at him, sitting behind the wheel still.

'Well, that's all right then.' He hung a little further out of the cab, lowering his voice as Elmy came back for a second load of leaves. 'Would you like to go out one night after work?' I could smell the fishmeal on his sleeve, see the dust that had even settled on top of his eyelashes, like thick golden mascara. For a moment, with a squint of the eye and the sun behind him, Stan Larter looked just like Shirley Bassey.

'I'm free Wednesday,' I said.

'I was thinking about a trip out to the coast. We could go anywhere you like. Aldeburgh, Southwold, Dunwich?'

'Sizewell?' I said. 'I've not been there for years.'

'Sizewell it is then,' he said, and slapped the door a couple of times with the flat of his hand like you would the rump of a horse, before swinging out into the road and driving off in a cloud of diesel fumes.

Elmy took the last of the greens out of the car.

'Good to see you getting out for a change,' he said, and winked.

'It's not what you think,' I said, and shut the boot far harder than was good for an old Morris.

* * *

154

It wasn't anything to do with the peacocks, Elmy said, a little later that evening. He didn't stop going to World's End because he was afraid of a load of old birds.

'It was the Lings. I was afraid of what I'd done to them,' he said. 'Me and my sister Rosa were always over at the farm, mucking about with the Ling boys. Out of nine sisters, she was the most like a brother to me. She was good at killing rats, and her dress was always filthy after riding the hogs.

'They had it hard, those Ling boys and Ivy. Their father was a wicked old sod. He was bed-bound by then, filling up with poison, shouting and hollering orders from upstairs. He'd already driven that wife of his into the ground, you know. He went and wore her out with hard work and sent her to an early grave.'

Elmy had given the kids their last bottle by then and we were shutting up the goats for the night. I stuck a concrete breeze block against the door to the male shed, just to be on the safe side.

It was the look on Walter's face Elmy remembered best, and the way he never seemed to stop running after Rosa.

'Walter was very sweet on my sister,' he said. 'He'd be chasing her, doing his best to catch up with her, but Rosa was always one step ahead of him, dancing out of reach. She was like a dragonfly in them days, never settling at anything for long. Some days Walter looked as if he had a mind to stick her through with a pin. I can still remember his face when he was watching her. I was only young. I thought he was ill with griping pains in his belly.

'Mind you, he must have caught up with her one day,' he said, 'because by the time Walter joined up, he and Rosa were sweethearts. She was only fourteen to his eighteen. And then Walter Ling went off to France.'

SIZEWELL

Stan came over a few minutes early on Wednesday evening. Neither of us heard him pull up outside in the car. Mum was vacuuming the landing upstairs, and I had the hairdryer on in my bedroom. When I came downstairs, he was standing in the doorway.

'Your door was open. I hope you don't mind? I did knock.'

'We wouldn't have heard you,' I said, pointing to the noise of the Hoover roaring through the ceiling.

'Shouldn't you be a bit more careful? Two women living out here by yourselves?' He gave the handle on the back door a rattle. 'You need a bolt on the inside. That catch wouldn't hold with a good kick.'

'Are you offering to do it?'

'Any time,' he said. 'Just say the word.' He smiled.

I looked up at the ceiling. It was time to go, I said, aware the Hoover had been quiet for too long.

Stan suggested we stop on the way to get fish and chips in Leiston, then go and eat them on the beach. We drove the last mile to Sizewell alongside the dual carriageway of pylons which ran straight out of the nuclear power station, the packet of fish and chips lying hot in my lap.

It was early-evening and the car park was empty.

'I've never seen the power station up this close before,' he said. The hum of it was filling the air and the lights were on as if a small town lay behind its concrete walls.

'Mum's from here,' I said. 'She grew up in a house over there.' I pointed to a patch of bare concrete where it used to stand. The house had been knocked down years ago after her mother died.

'It looks small,' Stan said, looking at the square of foundations.

'It was big enough for the three of them, Mum, Shirley and Grandma

Jean. My grandfather died when Mum was a toddler and Shirley just a baby. He fell off a fishing boat and drowned.'

We went down to the beach and sat at the top by the marram grasses.

'You look cold,' said Stan, and gave me his jumper. It was warm and soft, smelled freshly washed, with a polo neck that rolled right up to my chin.

'You know the water's warmer here than anywhere else? It's the best spot for swimming,' I said.

'Bet it makes you glow in the dark as well,' he said. 'I wouldn't go in there if you paid me. How does it get so warm, do you think?'

It was the water from the cooling tanks in the power station, I said. That the water they used to cool down the fuel rods after they'd split the atom got flushed out to sea over there.

'So how come you know all this stuff?'

It was Pipe, I said. He was interested in anything to do with electricity. 'He climbed up a pylon one time.' Stan whistled through his teeth.

'What did he go and do that for?'

'Because it was there. And he liked climbing. He'd always wanted to see the view from the top. Mum and Dad caught him just in time. They reckoned the shock of seeing him up there nearly killed them.'

We could have been sitting in exactly the same spot as Mum and Dad when something passed between them all that time ago. Pearl Whiting and Tony White, fresh-faced and seventeen. They could have been sitting there like us, looking out to sea, Dad checking his line, Mum smoothing her sunflower dress down over her knees. They didn't know it then but from that moment they met on the beach, twenty years of married life had suddenly started spooling out ahead of them.

'My parents met here,' I said. 'On this beach.' Thinking if Dad hadn't cycled all that way to come fishing that day, and Mum hadn't been beachcombing because of those easterly gales, I wouldn't be here right now. None of us would. I rubbed at my arms through Stan's jumper. 'They were only seventeen.'

Stan ate the last of his batter, and screwed the chip papers up in a ball.

'I was all ready to start a family at that age,' he said. He held it as if thinking about lobbing it on to the beach below, but ended up resting his chin on it instead. 'We had a scare once, me and Cheryl.' I held my breath. 'I was all for it, so I thought. I wanted to get married, have children, the whole package. I even knew the house I wanted, a two-up two-down in the next village along, a mile or two away from our families for some space of our own. I didn't know any different at the time, but I was all for it. She wasn't.'

It wasn't a baby in the end, he said, but it was the beginning of the end. 'I saw it on her face when she got the test. She'd let go. She'd already left me behind.' He dropped the chip papers into the bag by his feet.

'I'm sorry,' I said, though I didn't know what for. I didn't know if I was sorry for him for not having a baby and ending up married to Cheryl, or sorry that they never had Peewit after all, because everything would have been different for her if they had. Donny and Dawn would have made things right. Donny might have threatened Stan with a bag of spanners when he first heard the news, but he'd have calmed down soon enough. And after that first shock of seeing the baby with no arms, Donny and Dawn would have taken all three of them in and made everything right.

'You're quiet,' Stan said. 'I can't see what you're thinking half the time.' He touched my forehead with the tip of his finger. 'How about I get us some tea?'

'The cafe will be shut by now,' I said.

'I've got a flask in the back of the car,' he said. He looked back at the top of the beach and gave me a small wave before dipping down into the car park.

I stretched my legs out in front of me. Six years later, did he still miss the baby and the house he never had with Cheryl? Donny would have seen to it that they had everything they needed: a plumbed-in washing machine and a brand-new tumble dryer for all those baby clothes. I could picture the house so clearly and everything in it, from Stan's polo neck jumper slung over the back of a kitchen chair to the double bed upstairs, that house could have risen out of the shingle right in front of me. Except it had my coat by the front door, not Cheryl's.

Stan flopped down next to me with the flask, and lay back on the sand while I poured the tea.

'Did I tell you I've got my own place now?' he said. I noticed the gap between his teeth. He ran a hand over his belly under his sweatshirt, gave it a slap. 'Things are going well for me right now. I've got a good wage coming in.' He went through a whole list of things, as if he was setting out his best goods on a market stall right there in front of me. How he'd managed to afford a new car, a Golf GTI, that he went on a holiday with some lads from the football club last year.

He was lying there with both arms behind his head, raising himself up now and then to look out to sea as he talked. I kept losing my train of thought every time he did that, fancied I could hear the crunch of his stomach muscles, the ping of them as he lay back down.

'. . . and I'm going to help pay for my parents to go to Florida next year for their wedding anniversary.' It began to feel like I was having a night out with one of Hubert Ling's peacocks. Once Stan had put his tail feathers up, they wouldn't go down. Instead he started wafting them like an enormous fan, dazzling me with his good life, then sidling up to me in a funny little sidestep dance, all the time crowing about wages, a nice house, a steady life, and did I know that he was even on the telly that time when he got to be in the film *Akenfield* along with the rest of Charsfield?

He sat up, one arm behind me on the shingle. I wanted to pull it round me. I wanted to feel dusty Stan's arm around my waist, his hand on my hip, except he wasn't so dusty now.

'We decided on Greece in the end,' he said, 'me and a few of the boys from the football club. Had the time of our lives, island hopping. You should go if you get the chance.'

Didn't they have earthquakes there, I said, because Greece was sitting on a plate that was being pushed around by Africa?

'Have you been there?' Stan looked surprised.

'It's my mum. She's always been interested,' I added, seeing how his eyebrows had ridden up at my talk of tectonics and earthquakes.

'My mum never talks about anything like that,' he said. 'She just has a go at me about settling down and giving her grandchildren, and says I'm not eating well enough.' That was the only thing he missed about living at home, he said, his mum's cooking. He was too tired to do much when he got in from work.

'I'm losing weight, look.' And he patted his stomach through his sweatshirt. Then, thinking I couldn't see it well enough, he peeled it up to his chest. He took hold of my hand and laid it on his bare stomach. 'Feel that? I'm wasting away. I need a good woman to feed me up.' And I could hardly listen to another word he said as the thrill of touching him had completely smothered every single thought in my head. 'I think I'm about ready to settle down now,' he said.

It was nearly dark, and the lights from the power station were lighting up the night sky behind us. I got up and brushed the sand off me. 'We'd better be getting back,' I said. And as Stan stood up he put a finger under my chin to lift my face, and kissed me on the lips. It was a comfortable kiss, better than the last time when it felt as if Bernie had grown a tongue as big as an ox.

'How about a drink on Saturday?' said Stan as we got into the car. His hand was firm on my thigh.

'I'd like that,' I said, and as he took his hand away to change gear and checked his rear mirror, he couldn't see the house following behind us on a tow rope, the moon shining straight through it.

'Thank God you're back.' Mum was shaking. 'Has Stan gone? Has he driven off already?'

'Yes, he just dropped me off. Why? What's wrong?'

'There was someone out there earlier on, someone out there in the field. I wanted him to take a look.' She was standing next to the kitchen window, flat against the wall as if to look outside would be to risk getting shot at. Her hand shook as she pointed. 'I was closing the curtains when I saw him. He was going along beneath the pylons, then he must have turned around at the far end because he came back past again. I swear he was checking the place out.'

'Nobody's interested in walking round here at this time of night. There's nothing to see. Now go to bed. It's late.'

Of course she'd overheard Stan. It was too much of a coincidence, his throwaway remark about flimsy door catches and her brand-new fear. She'd turned the Hoover off and heard every word, and now she had a notion in her head that there was something else to be afraid of, that there was someone out to get her. What was it about Mum and that field? If it wasn't sprays and poisons, or some dark presence that made her drop the shopping in fright and run for home, now it was a man hiding out there in half a thousand acres of oilseed rape. She was like a bath sponge, sucking up any fear that was going and swelling it to three or four times the normal size. But surely there were only so many fears a person could carry in their head before their legs buckled under the sheer weight of them.

I stayed in the kitchen, listening to Mum as she moved around upstairs for a while then the squeak of springs as she got into bed. I had to find some way of talking to Shirley, before it was too late. Talk to her before the baby was born. If anyone could talk some sense into Mum, then it was Shirley.

I sat in the dark with the radio on low. It was a late-night programme, playing love songs and messages for wives back home from long-distance lorry drivers working through the night, gas-rig workers out in the North Sea, saying how they were missing them every minute of every day but they'd be home soon. There was the usual crackling interference from the pylons, bursts of foreign voices from Dutch and German radio, though it seemed louder than normal, more urgent. And then I heard it. A burst of French and a noise like a baby's cry. A single cry coming through the radio, except it sounded so near, so real, I got up and checked outside the window. The pylons were quiet in the back field, not spitting or sparking, but humming away like on any other night. The moon had disappeared. Then I heard it again, a cry as if there was a baby out there alone in the dark.

Pipe was eleven years old when he climbed the pylon. There was thick snow in the back field that day, and he wanted to see if there was ice on the wires. He'd been going on about dancing conductors ever since the cold weather set in, saying that if the wires got too heavy with ice they could whip together, and then there'd be a huge flashover of electricity.

'They have to melt the ice,' he said. 'They send a phantom load down the wires all the way from Sizewell to overload the circuit. It's like a million kettles being switched on all at once.'

Mum and Dad had only gone up the road to pick up a new washbasin for the bathroom, saying they wouldn't be long.

I was with Ed in the front garden, making a load of snowballs to fire at Pipe when we heard him.

'I can see the water tower . . . Saxtead Mill . . .' We ran round the back but he was already up the pylon by then, well above the danger sign and the barbed wire. 'And so many spires . . . Tannington, Dennington, Worlingworth church over there. Brundish maybe? Fred Bugg has just let Vegas out in the back garden.'

The higher he climbed, the bigger he seemed to get, till he looked like King Kong in that field, standing high on the struts. 'Mendlesham mast . . . some cranes the other way.' His voice was beginning to sound faint. 'I can see everything from up here. A lighthouse . . . Sizewell power station, I can see that all right.' He was more than halfway up when we heard a car skid on the road, and one long blast of a Morris Marina's horn. Mum and Dad were running across the field, the car left skewed across the road with its doors open. It looked like a swan that had crash landed on to the tarmac with its wings spread wide as a brake.

There was only the noise of Dad's rough breathing as Pipe picked his way back down.

In the end, he stepped off that pylon as if he'd just been up a pair of stepladders. Dad didn't tell him off. He didn't say a word. Instead he pushed Pipe with both hands, hard in the chest, and sent him sprawling backwards into the snow. And as he lay there in his black anorak, spread-eagled beneath the 'Danger of Death' sign, there was no telling him or the stickman apart. Dad started crying hard into his hands, and it was only then that Mum started screaming, 'I thought you were dead, I thought you were dead,' over and over, till I had to put my hands over my ears.

GUPPY'S FARM

Mum didn't come downstairs until late the next morning. The first thing she did when she came into the kitchen was peek through a crack in the curtains.

'There's nobody out there,' I said.

'Well, I'm telling you, there was last night,' she said. 'I'm not making it up, I swear. He was so thin, he could have just walked off one of those pylons,' she said, pointing at one of the stickmen signs.

It was the weekend, a good time to catch Guppy at the farm. He'd probably be out in the yard checking over one of his machines and, with any luck, I could talk to him first. Then maybe he could help me with Shirley, have a word with her if that would help. Because I didn't know what I was going to say. It had been so long.

The farm hadn't changed. It was as neat and tidy as ever. The front lawn was a huge square of grass, trimmed so flat and even it could easily have passed for a bowling green. It had been like that for years, waiting for the day it would get covered in swings and climbing frames. Guppy's tractor was in the yard but I couldn't see him anywhere. He was probably in the field nearby, checking his crops for pests.

I was about to knock on the front door when I looked in through the sitting-room window. It was exactly as I remembered it. Everything neat and tidy, Shirley still keeping an orderly house to match the farm outside. The furniture was in the same place, the chairs standing at right angles to tables. Everything was the same except Shirley was about to have a baby. She was on the sofa, lying along the length of it, her feet raised up on a pile of cushions at one end. She had one hand on her belly, and was fast asleep.

It was hard to imagine her with a baby in her arms. They'd tried for so long, nobody believed it would ever happen. And now Shirley was forty-two, old enough to be a grandma, and about to have her first child.

Everyone kept on saying how tiring she was going to find it. '*They take it out of you, babies and small children . . . It's hard enough for a woman half her age . . . She'll feel it in her knees and her back first, all that fetching and carrying . . . Then she'll wake up one morning and feel like she's been hit by a bus.*'

But after all those years of trying, all those miscarriages, there was Aunty Shirley lying on that sofa as big as a sow. She'd want to share her happiness with her own sister, surely. Mum was the only family she had left.

Guppy came into the room, still in his work clothes. He'd come in through the back, straight from the tractor yard. He rubbed his face, looking tired. I was about to tap on the window, not wanting to wake Shirley up but hoping he'd come to the door and we could talk. But he didn't see me and climbed on to the sofa to lie down next to Shirley, moving carefully so as not to squash her. She stirred and woke up, stroked his forehead in a half-sleep. Then she got hold of his cap and took it off, dropped it on the carpet.

He had no hair. Guppy was bald. He'd lost every single hair he ever had. Shirley was stroking the back of his neck, the folds of fat no longer covered by a thick golden fantail. And I wondered if he'd lost the hair off his back as well, the same hair that made us scream as children, the same hairy back I saw at the pig pits that day. I turned away, unable to watch as Shirley cradled his head like a large boiled egg.

'That hair fell out a while back,' Zelma said, when I asked her the next day if she knew what had happened to Guppy. 'Alopecia, that's what he's got. Shirley said it happened a few months back. He woke up one morning to find all his hair on the pillow, laid out like a wig that had slipped off in the night.'

The doctor had put it down to the stress of Shirley's pregnancy. The bigger she got, Zelma said, the more agitated Guppy became. He told

Shirley he couldn't bear to lose another one, not when it had got this far.

'I never realised,' I said.

'Well, people don't talk about these things, do they? He's lucky though. He's a man. He can be bald if he wants. Or he can wear a hat and get away with it. Typical,' she said. 'They get all the luck.' Not seeming to remember that we were talking about a man who'd worried so much about losing a baby, he'd just gone and lost all his hair.

THE SEE-THROUGH HOUSE

The see-through house didn't go away after Sizewell. If anything it got bigger and brighter so that I could see into every room, see every single detail down to the Welcome mat by the door and the pattern on Stan's duvet cover: red and black triangles, shot through with white lines. I liked to think of the house being parked up nearby in the field when I went to bed at night, all the lights left on so that it shone bright as a ferry out at sea in the dark. It was a whole other life ready to move into.

Those nights I could almost feel the weight of him, pressing down on me. Not standing up against a coal shed in the dark but lying down on a bed this time, soft with just the right bit of give in it, and proper bedding.

I was glad Stan had nothing to do with Peewit, though I was no nearer to finding out who did. I didn't like the feeling that she was out on the loose since leaving the church. It looked like she'd already found her way over to our house. The thought of her being outside the back door at night was starting to make my scalp prickle. I wanted to ask her outright. 'So go on then. What are you going to do next and how much damage will there be?'

Instead of wasting time trying to work out who the mother was, maybe I should just gather up all the women in a five-mile radius who were of child-bearing age back then, no matter how young or old they were. Just round them all up in a minibus like the one that went round Worlingworth, picking up women to go apple-picking at Laxfield. They could be bouncing up and down in that bus, chattering away to one another at the tops of their voices, thinking they were off to the orchard, when the bus would divert and take them to Tannington church where they'd be tipped out at the gate. We would see then who Peewit picked out of the line-up as she flew at her long-lost mother, at the woman who till that very moment thought she'd got away with it and left it all behind her in the ditch that day.

On the Saturday I couldn't listen to a word Zelma was saying in the shop. I was going out with Stan for a drink that evening. Couples went out on Saturday nights, married couples, courting couples.

'How about Saturday?' he'd said, as if he'd decided to shift us into a higher gear after Sizewell.

In my head I had started to get a bit carried away. It began with a few small things at first, like Stan offering to help me with the windows one day so I wouldn't have to ring the farm and risk the rent being put up. Then he was doing a bit of work on the Marina so I wouldn't have to take it into the garage. Before long I'd built up Stan so much in my head, he might as well have been in the SAS. I had him turning up straight from work one day, still in his forklift, and using it to bash his way in through the side of our house, cornering my mother in the kitchen with his prongs, then scooping her up like a sack of flour. He knew how to raise her as high as his lift could manage before wheeling her off up the road to get her mended, Mum's arms and legs flailing high in the air like windmills. He'd know to deliver her to Shirley and Guppy's front door, where her sister would take charge and bustle her indoors, chiding her the whole time.

'Fancy getting yourself in this state, Pearl. This has gone on long enough. I'm going to sort you out for once and for all,' she'd say, before wrapping a blanket round Mum and leading her up to the spare room where the bed had already been made up. 'Thank you, Stanley,' Shirley would say. 'Leave everything with me. I'll take care of Pearl from now on.'

I only started to listen to Zelma when I overheard her reading aloud from the paper, a short news piece about a prisoner who'd escaped from Norwich prison and was on the run, last spotted somewhere near

Harleston. I checked the paper I'd put aside to take home to Mum. It said he was serving twenty years for battering his wife to death. Without a second thought, I stuck it back on the shelf. She didn't need to read that so soon after the other night.

Stan pulled up outside the house just as I'd finished getting ready upstairs, and pressed the horn. For a moment he looked as if he was going to stay in the car and wait for Cheryl to come to the window, Cheryl Capon, his first love, with her hair all frizzed up and an empty can of hairspray on her dressing table. But he didn't look up at my window. Instead he checked his hair in the mirror and got out of the car, looking all serious as if he was going for a job interview. He ran a hand around the waistband of his trousers, making sure his shirt was tucked in all the way round. Halfway up the path he must have realised that his trousers were still too loose, because he undid his belt, gave it a quick jerk from side to side, and buckled himself up again.

I was glad Mum was in the back bedroom then; that she couldn't have seen Stan do that. She might have thought for a split second it was the Peaman come back, and looked on with horror as he walked into the back porch, to pick up her daughter this time.

It didn't make for a good start to the evening, having the pair of them crash in on me in all their bright colours. Mum and the Peaman were never going to go away. I slammed the car door too hard as I sat in the passenger seat. Stan looked over at me but didn't say anything.

'I thought we'd try my local, the Plough,' he said. 'It's always lively on a Saturday.'

It was noisy in the pub with a band playing in the back room, but it was too cold to sit outside. Stan sat with his arm round the back of my chair while the band belted out songs by Rainbow and Black Sabbath. His shirt had sharp ironed edges that stood up in ridges, and he smelled of soap and Old Spice, but with the music so loud and us having to shout, talk between us dried up a little till soon we gave up altogether.

'You must be good with an iron,' I said, when the band stopped for a break.

'Why do you say that?' I pointed to the crease on his sleeve. 'Oh, that's Mum,' he said. 'She does all my washing and ironing. I don't even know where the machine is.' And he laughed. 'I know it's in the house somewhere.'

He was too busy with work, he said, too tired when he got home to do much more than eat his tea and sit in front of the television. After he'd been up to his ears all week in kibbled maize and done his overtime, the last thing he wanted to do was housework and cooking.

'Mum says I can't do a job without proper food inside me. She brought over a big casserole yesterday,' he said. 'Should last me a few days at least.'

'So does she come round and help you out a lot?'

'Well, put it this way, she's got a key, and when I get back, there's usually some dinner on the go, or food in the cupboards, washing and ironing done. I tell her not to, but I'm the youngest and she's got time on her hands, doesn't know what to do with herself since I moved out. It gives her something to do. And she's only at the other end of the village. It's a nice walk for her every day.'

The more he drank, the more he talked. It flowed out of him. How he was going to do this and that, the plans he had. I could feel the heat coming off his bare arms like a three-bar fire, and see how his jaw shone filmy with sweat.

Stan knew lots of people up at the bar and stayed there a while, shouting over the music. It was a comfort to look out of the window where I could see the house on the other side of the pub car park. I thought of being in the bed upstairs, crawling under Stan's red and black duvet and looking forward to a Sunday morning lie-in. Then I saw his mother downstairs, tapping her foot. She'd let herself in with her key. She had a hand on his kitchen counter and was staring at the drying wind outside. Her fingers were drumming away. She wanted to get a load on. Tap tap, tap, till she couldn't wait any longer and marched into the bedroom.

'Time you were getting up, Stanley Larter, I need to wash that bedding.' And she throws back the covers to be knocked back by a beery blast of body heat from the pair of us who've been fermenting away under the covers since Friday night.

'Those are some of the blokes I play football with on a Sunday,' Stan said, sitting back down next to me. He was on his third pint, and seemed to have forgotten that he was driving me home. 'Most of them are married now, two with wives in the family way. I thought me and Cheryl were all set to do that. A few more years . . . get married, have children. Then she had to go all arty on me. Good job I cut loose in the end,' he said, 'before it was too late.' And then his leg started up. I could hear it banging under the table.

This story was sounding different from the one I'd heard the week before. But I hadn't forgotten his long face at the party. Donny telling him not to go ruining Cheryl's special night. The break in Stan's voice, 'Please don't go, not like this,' when Cheryl said she was getting her dad to drive her home. I also remembered seeing his black Escort later; how every Friday and Saturday night he'd park up in a field gateway nearby, watching and waiting, thinking he was invisible.

The band had finally packed up for the night and it was quiet enough to talk.

'What are you thinking now?' Stan tapped my forehead, a little too hard this time.

'Nothing much,' I said, remembering him with his head down on the steering wheel crying so hard I could hear it through the rear windscreen, shoulders heaving with every sob coming out of him as he waited to be replaced by another man.

'You know, I've been thinking. Ed really should help you out more. It's not right it falls on your shoulders, all of this. Two women living in the middle of nowhere.'

'What's wrong with that?'

'It's not safe, is it? Do I have to spell it out? All it takes is for some bloke to drive past, see women's washing on the line. It's obvious there's no man about the place. Anyone can see right into your back porch.'

'You'd get on like a house on fire with my mum,' I said, thinking of him coming over and stoking up her fears with a big poker. If they ever seemed in danger of dying down, he'd soon get them roaring away. 'Strange men are the least of my worries right now. I need to find a job.'

'So what have you looked at?' he said.

'Nothing so far. I'm looking in the paper every day though.'

'Well, at least it won't be art college this time,' he said. His juddery leg was making my drink ripple, except now that his legs were stronger it was more like he was hammering at the table from underneath and I feared my drink was about to slop over the side of the glass.

'And whatever it is, it'll have to be round here, won't it?' he said. 'Maybe a bit of factory work? They're always looking for people up at the chicken factory.'

I turned to look at him properly this time, at his face all red with beer. 'What?' he said, in a voice that sounded as if we'd been married for twenty-five years. 'What have I done now?'

His peacock feathers had vanished. Stan had gone back to the way I remembered him underneath all his new fat and muscle. Thin whippy Stanley Larter with the lost-boy look at Cheryl's party, trying to hold on to her as Guppy was about to whisk her off home in the car; going round to have his tea with Donny and Dawn even after she'd moved away, just to get the smell of her.

The house was still standing, parked at the front of the pub, but it looked less solid now. It was more like a see-through egg box, the thin brittle plastic crackling with every gust of wind. Stan's car was sitting on the drive. The freshly washed covers were turned down on the bed. I could still walk out of the pub straight into that house, if I wanted to. Not that there was much room for me. One of Ivy Ling's giant red hens was at the kitchen stove, stirring a casserole while sitting on a clutch of chicks. Stan's big beaky nose was peeking out through the soft feathers, taking one look at the world outside before ducking back inside to the warmth of his mother's chest.

He drained his pint, and stood up to go to the bar.

'You're not going anywhere, are you?' he said. 'Same again?'

I walked back home over the fields in a straight line. I didn't think for one minute he'd miss me. He probably came over to the empty table, wondered briefly why he was carrying two drinks, and went back to his friends at the bar.

SHIRLEY'S KITCHEN

I could hardly get out of bed on Monday morning. I felt like I'd been traipsing over a muddy field all night long, and I'd picked up so much of it, the clay had closed over the top of my feet and was sticking me down to the floor. Mum had started early. She was already talking to herself through the walls.

Elmy didn't look much better when I found him in the shed with the males. He was staring at the kids that were earmarked for slaughter in the next few weeks.

'It keeps going round and round in my head, what I said all those years ago,' he said. 'I can't seem to stop it. I keep going back and changing it, thinking what would have happened if I hadn't said what I did.' He ran a hand down his face as if trying to wipe the memory away.

Elmy was going to turn eighty next year and yet here he was, still fretting over something he'd said as a boy. 'It can't have been that bad,' I said. 'You were only young. You probably didn't know any better.'

He got jealous, Elmy said. He got very jealous because Rosa and Hubert had started to spend more time together after Walter had gone off to war.

'They started talking about things I didn't understand half the time. Rosa didn't want to do the same things as me any more. "Go away, Elmy," she'd say, "stop following me about all the time." She wanted to be reading books with Hubert, helping him look after the peacocks, Percy the First and his new wife Susan, as they were back then, with a clutch of peachicks. I was too young, she said, and I should go off and play with some children my own age.

'I found them together in the straw stack. Rosa was reading to Hubert from a book while he lay next to her, fanning her with peacock feathers. They never saw me.'

Elmy said that Walter Ling came back on leave from the Great War in 1916. He'd marched up the lane to World's End in his army boots, no doubt looking forward to seeing Rosa, expecting to meet her at the gate with a posy of flowers in her hand. She'd have been counting the days and hours to his homecoming the same as him, or so he thought.

Instead the farm was quiet except for Ivy, clattering dishes to cover the noise of old man Ling dying upstairs.

'Walter did find Rosa in the end,' Elmy said, 'because I told him where to look. That he'd find her in the barn over there. The pair of them were curled up together in the hay, wrapped round each other as snug and tight as a nest of dormice.

'As soon as I said it, I knew what I'd done, but I couldn't take it back.'

They were so fast asleep, they didn't hear the scuffles and squawks as Walter wrung the necks of the nearest living things he could find. 'I watched him do it. How he got hold of Hubert's family of peacocks. I saw a look on his face that scared me half to death. He started with Percy, Hubert's favourite. He wrung that bird's neck so hard in front of me, its head came off in his hands.'

'This place will be shut by the end of the summer,' Zelma said. 'You do know that, don't you, Desiree?' I looked around the shop. It had grown an echo in the last week, and the plastic at the window, which had been put up years ago to stop the stock being faded by the sun, had turned everything yellow. Zelma looked liverish, like everyone else who came into the shop.

'Something will turn up,' I said. Shirley's timing couldn't have been better when she appeared at the door just as Zelma was about to launch into her weekly speech about my future. She had to lean against the doorframe for a second to catch her breath.

'I didn't think I was going to make it before you shut for lunch,' she said. 'I had a terrible craving for dark chocolate and had to get a neighbour to give me a lift as Guppy wasn't around.' It was the first time she'd been in the shop for ages, and although she was always friendly to me when she came in and said hello, we never talked properly.

'I'm glad I caught you, Desiree,' she said, walking over to me at the counter. I stood there thinking perhaps she had seen me at the farm after all, and the sight of me walking off that day made her realise we needed to talk.

'You know this baby's due in a couple of weeks,' she said, rubbing her belly. 'Guppy's ready to down tools as soon as it's on the way. We're both so excited. And nervous, of course.' She paused a moment as if uncertain about what she was going to say next. 'You will come and see the baby, won't you?' she said. 'I know it's been a while, with everything, but it would mean a lot to me . . . to both of us.'

'Of course I will,' I said. This pregnancy seemed to have softened her. Even her face looked different, rounder than usual and glowing with colour. I stood there, willing her to extend the invitation to Mum as well.

'And Pipe and Ed, of course, though it's different for men. They don't get quite as caught up in babies, do they?' Shirley opened her purse to pay for the chocolate. 'And how's Pearl?' she said as she passed me the money. 'Is she OK? It's just that I've heard she's not getting out much.'

It was the first time she'd ever asked after Mum. It took me aback just to hear Shirley say her name. She saw the look on my face. 'Pearl's still my sister, Desiree, despite everything.' There was an edge to her voice.

'Would you go and see her?' I said. 'She'd really like to talk, I'm sure.' I spoke in a hurry, wanting Shirley to come home with me right now so things could go back to how they used to be.

She must have seen I was thinking, remembering. She hesitated, and for a moment her whole face slackened and I thought she was going to say, 'Yes, all right then. Let's go, shall we?' But just then the Land Rover pulled up outside the shop.

'That's one worried husband,' Zelma said, looking out of the window. Shirley waved at Guppy then turned to me, the softness all gone.

'No, I don't think so,' she said. 'It wouldn't be a good idea.'

'Oh,' I said, and turned my head away.

'Why don't you ask your mum why?' Shirley sounded tired all of a sudden. 'Ask her what happened.'

It was cool in the church. Quiet. Peewit was skiddering about by the font. It was so easy to imagine that life was completely different outside, beyond the graves and the yew trees. That I'd get home and Guppy's Land Rover would be parked there. Shirley and Mum are round the table, Shirley saying how she and Mum could go to Fram tomorrow, do the jumble sale together and have something to eat. They might even bump into Winona who's now a good friend of Mum's. She's been round to their house, seen all their photos of America, heard all about Melissa who's at college in the States and even met friends of theirs who grew up in Ipswich, New England. Ed's happily married to someone who never went off with Bernie Capon on bingo nights. He sleeps like a baby as soon as his head hits the pillow, while Jason Feathers is in the middle of Dunwich Heath in the back of a camper van, with a girl in a baby-doll nightie. He swapped his motorbike for the van when she said she was worried about him getting killed. They're listening out for nightingales as it begins to get dark, before romping around till the early hours. Dad comes in from the goat shed, the engine of the Morris Marina still warm after his drive back from the farm, the smell of cows mixing in with the goats. 'What's for tea, Pearl?' he says.

Peewit was up to something at the pulpit, the stairs creaking as she rattled up and down, and flicked at the pages of the Bible. She'd be six years old now, creating mischief and getting away with murder, because she's got a way with words and can make people laugh. At the local village school, she'd be getting some special help. 'Strong-willed and high-spirited' the teacher calls her. 'Cheeky and feisty,' the family agree with a smile, always telling anyone and everyone how much of a wanted baby she was, that there was never a shred of doubt, and how they always know where to find her because she sings away at the top of her voice wherever she is, indoors or outside. 'She loves singing,' they say. But her favourite thing would be running full tilt at her mother, who opens her coat so wide that Peewit can hurl herself deep inside as the warm tweed is wrapped tight around her.

There were other women, other suspects, Tina Creasey for one, though I didn't have a chance of talking to her right now, even if I did feel brave enough, since Bella had her sent away a couple of years ago and she was only allowed home for Christmas. But there was someone else, someone closer to home. There was Pam, my sister-in-law. She'd been going with Bernie on the quiet back then, forcing him to hide those tassels in cigarette packets and throw them on to the compost heap. Pam, whose dad kept a twelve-bore under his bed. I wasn't sure how I could get it out of her without causing a family rift, though. I'd just have to march into her house one day when Ed wasn't there and catch her off guard, perhaps when she was in the middle of one of her Tupperware parties and distracted with taking orders. 'Yes, please, Pam. I'll take ten of those plastic tubs, four of the bowls . . . and by the way, did you get pregnant off Bernie and sling the baby in a ditch?'

I shut the church door, left Peewit to roll back into her bed behind the curtain: the nativity crib where she sleeps, surrounded by the sheep and the shepherds, Mary and Joseph looking down at her all night long while she flattens baby Jesus like a cuckoo in the nest.

'You're late back tonight,' Mum said. 'I was starting to worry. I thought you might be out with Stan again.'

'Not Stan, no. I did a few errands, that's all. The same as usual.'

'So who was in the shop today?' she asked. Everything was exactly as I had left it this morning. There was no Shirley at the kitchen table, no Dad in the goat shed. Jason Feathers was still six foot under an empty jam jar, and there never was a girl in a baby-doll nightie or a camper van on Dunwich Heath. Just me and Mum and the shut-up feeling in the house.

'I'll tell you who came into the shop today. Your sister Shirley,' I said. 'That's who.' I wanted to say her name out loud, see what it did to Mum. She flinched, so slightly I could have missed it if I hadn't been watching out for it.

'Anyone else?'

'She's about to have the baby. Two weeks to go,' I said.

Mum turned away towards the window.

'This rape is getting on my nerves,' she said. 'Why couldn't they have grown something different round us this year? The smell of it, I can't breathe.'

'You could always open the windows, let some air in.'

'I don't want to let any more of it in. I can hardly breathe as it is. The stink of it. If only they could have planted something different to break up the yellow. Winter barley, maybe, or peas.'

Peas? After everything we've been through, she could talk about peas as easily as if none of it had ever happened? I'd already had a gutful of Bella Creasey this week, giving me the weekly countdown at the shop. 'Not long to go now,' she says, rubbing her hands. Fresh peas soon, and wouldn't my mother be pleased?

Something started to roar inside my head.

'You know what I reckon, Mum? That if there was a field full of sugar beet, you'd say it was too green. If it was beans, you'd say the smell was too sweet. If it was barley, you'd want wheat, and wheat, you'd want barley. And as for the peas . . .' The roaring got louder till I was having to shout to hear my own voice.

'Desiree, what has got into you?'

'Why did you and Shirley stop speaking? Because she said I should ask you. "Ask your mother what happened," she said. So now I'm asking you. What happened?'

'It's none of your business, Desiree.'

'But it *is* my business, that's the problem. Us here, living together like this. Everything's been made my business, when it's the last thing I want, believe you me.'

'Guppy made a pass at me.'

A tremor started up in my right hand. Mum said it again, thinking I hadn't heard her. 'Your Uncle Guppy, my sister's husband, made a pass at me. In his own house. In Shirley's kitchen. Happy now?'

'He made a pass at you? Like the Peaman made a pass at you?'

She was angry now.

'No, not like him. That was different.'

'Too right it was different. That ruined everything.' She had no right to be angry, not over this.

'If you must know, Guppy made a pass at me when Dad and Shirley were just in the next room. He made damn' sure my sister knew about it. He wanted her to see it. And Tony. He wanted to ruin things between all of us. Though it's still none of your ruddy business.'

I didn't wait around for her to tell me what I'd done, how I'd made things a whole lot worse by telling Dad in the first place. She didn't need to. I knew what I'd done to him. I left Mum crying downstairs.

THE MORGUE

We weren't talking, hadn't spoken a word to each other in days. Mum spent more time rustling up in the bedroom and talking to herself, while I sat in the goat shed in the evenings, watching the sun go down. I could feel us turning into the Ling brothers. We even had our own territories all sorted out.

Rosa went into service not long after Walter found her and Hubert together. She got married, settled down and had a family.

'My sister never talked about those days at World's End,' Elmy said. 'She got on with her life. But the Ling boys, they never got over it.'

And I thought of young Hubert Ling, hiding away in his barn, too terrified to go near another woman after what happened that day. And of Walter Ling out on his tractor on bitter January mornings when by rights he should have been blue with cold, except he sat wrapped up in his flying jacket and churning himself into a hot fury with thoughts of Rosa and Hubert – how they got to lie in Lovelands and Featherbeds together, how Hubert got to fan Rosa with peacock feathers, the pair of them warm and dreamy, while he, Walter Ling, was traipsing through thick trench mud in France.

They were well into their eighties now, those two brothers, carrying on their silent feud over a sixteen-year-old girl, as fresh and raw as if it had happened only yesterday.

'Yes, the job's still open,' Beatrice said over the phone that evening. 'Why not go over in the week and take a look?'

After Dad died, Pipe left home as soon as he could. He got a job at the Marconi factory in Chelmsford, and we hardly ever saw him after that. He'd pop back for the odd weekend but he found it hard to get used to the quiet after living in a town, and always looked forward to getting away. Ed had moved in with Pam and Chubby. The three of them got along just fine in the bungalow, with Ed doing some work on Chubby's car at the weekend. And no doubt he felt better for being in Worlingworth, surrounded by houses and people instead of empty fields. He felt better for holding on to Pam in bed every night, drifting off to the sound of her breathing instead of dreaming about Jason Feathers, night after night, of catching him in his arms like a bride.

That left just me and Mum. Our thin old roof and walls couldn't keep it out then, couldn't keep the sky from reaching down to swallow us whole as the two of us lay tiny in our beds at night, the Milky Way plastered all over my walls and ceiling. My head would get in a tangle under that night sky, thinking of Dad being out there now along with the ditch baby and the boy off the bike, imagining what for ever must feel like.

It was a massive heart attack, the doctors said later. That's what killed him. He didn't stand a chance, even if we had lived just ten minutes away from a hospital.

Dad had only done a half shift that day, and was home by early-afternoon. He'd eaten a sandwich, Mum said, then pushed his chair back from the kitchen table as if he was about to stand up. He had both hands flat on the table top and took a breath as if he was about to make a speech, but then he'd changed his mind and was about to sit back down again except he crashed to the floor, scrabbling at his chest. Dad lay on the kitchen tiles with his legs splayed out.

'There were feathers everywhere,' she said. The white chicken down that flew up in the air came from inside his shirt and overalls, as one of the ambulance men ripped his clothes open to his chest. 'I thought maybe they were thinking I'd done him in, suffocated him with a pillow, because of the feathers stuck to his face and the down which had settled in his hair. He hadn't got changed after work. For the first time ever, he came home straight from the factory in his overalls.' The worst thing, Mum said, was seeing them lift Dad into the back of the ambulance as if he weighed no more than a sack of those wretched chicken feathers.

The doctors had to split him open and have a good look around before they could tell us he had a faulty heart, and that there was probably something in his family history for it to happen when he was still so young. Smoking and stress wouldn't have helped any, they said.

Mum wasn't convinced. She thought there was something going on they weren't telling us about, something to do with us living so close to the pylons, the electromagnetic force fields. That maybe they found something else in the post-mortem but covered it up. In the end, I think she would only have been happy if a lump of cancer had come out of him, with 'Eastern Electricity Board' stamped on it in green ink. It wasn't long after Dad died that she started buying in the kitchen foil.

But it was the feathers that kept bothering at me. Dad never came home with any blood or bits of chicken carcass on him. But in the last couple of months before he died, there'd been the odd feather stuck to him – on the back of his boots one time, like he'd sprouted a pair of spurs – and then there was Mum's talk of the feather down billowing out at the end, as if he'd had a whole chicken down there, stuffed inside his shirt. Till some nights, all I could think was that maybe he really did have a chicken inside him; that one of them got in there somehow from the factory, slid down his gullet on the back of a sandwich, and took root deep down in his stomach.

'I don't know what's got into your father, why he's so irritable these days,' she'd say, when all the time it was growing inside him, a battery broiler with its feathers brushing against his lungs, making him cough and retch till it got too big for him and was scratching at his insides, trying to kick its way out. He'd scrabbled at his chest as he lay on the kitchen floor. And when they opened Dad up in the morgue, they couldn't tell anyone what they saw because they hardly believed it themselves as a ball of black tar covered in white feathers shot out from inside and took off across the cutting table, trying to flap its stubby wings and make a run for it. One of the assistants caught it and, as the others nodded, sawed through its neck with a scalpel because they didn't know how to wring it properly like Dad would have done, with a click and a snap, so it carried on rolling around some more till it ran out of steam and finally they stuffed it into a pickling jar, screwing the lid down tight while its feet still twitched in vinegar.

I was no different from Mum in the end. I didn't want to believe it either: that he'd collapsed on the kitchen floor like an old man, with the insides of him all worn out like someone twice his age.

WELLS-NEXT-THE-SEA

The farm was set back from the road, down a long drive with trees on both sides. Beatrice had never said her brother's house would be this grand. It was like driving up to a manor house, with the gravel turning circle at the front and a sundial above the front door. The panels of plaited brick reminded me a little of the house that Guppy blew up and ploughed under all those years ago.

There was nobody around. It was so quiet, I could hear the birdsong from the woodland which sat on a rise at the back of the farm. I was sure I had the right day. Hilary had barked it down the phone.

'Saturday. Splendid. Yes, do come.' He'd sounded just like his sister.

I went up to the house and rang the bell. A woman answered the door, a cloth in her hand.

'Mr Hilary? You'll find him round the back,' she said. I walked past the end of the house through a rose garden where low box hedges had been laid out in a circular pattern around flowerbeds. Beyond it was a view to the woods over grassland, with sheep and cows grazing right up to the trees. Hilary wasn't there though and I turned to go, thinking perhaps the cleaner meant he was somewhere round the back of the barns.

'Can I help you?' I looked round. It was as if he'd risen out of the ground itself. 'Of course, you must be Desiree,' he said, striding towards me with his hand outstretched. 'Hilary de Fontenay. So glad you could make it.' I shook his hand. He was wearing thick green corduroy trousers and a waxed jacket, but he was still all bone and right angles underneath like Beatrice.

'It's a ha-ha,' he said, noticing I was trying to look past him.

It turned out to be a long smooth grassy ditch that ran all the way along the back of the house. 'Keeps the animals out in the pasture, hides any rubbish, and no unsightly fences to interrupt that glorious view.' He was restoring it, he said, putting the brickwork back in the retaining wall against the near edge. 'Pet project of mine,' he said. 'Like it?' I'd not seen one before, I said. I never knew such fancy ditches existed.

Hilary had to make a telephone call at the house but said that he'd get Keith to show me around the farm. He shouted over to a man who'd come round the corner with a sack barrow.

'Here he is. My right-hand man. I'll show you the accommodation after Keith's walked you round the farm, OK?'

Keith took me to the goat shed first, saying that I'd be helping with the smaller livestock to start off with. There were six Golden Guernseys in one pen, some small pygmy goats in another, though Hilary had plans to expand the herd.

'He'll only ever take on rare breeds,' Keith said. 'He wants to open this place to the public as a working farm, with things all done the old-fashioned way,' he said. 'Ploughing, haymaking, using the horses to do the work. That's my job, the horses.'

I followed Keith around the farm, taking in the barns with cobwebs so big they could have been catching all that dust and chaff for hundreds of years, the worn leather straps and harnesses hanging off rusty nails on the walls. The yard outside was filled with odd bits of machinery, a couple of broken-down old tractors. There was even a fish and chip van parked against the far wall. It wasn't Guppy's idea of how a farm should be, looking more like a junk yard. He'd have got rid of the animals for a start. Then he'd have scrapped the tractors, taken a hose to the place, and given the yard a good scrape with the digger before setting down some proper concrete. Then he'd have gone away and bought in a whole load of new machinery for delivery the next day.

We could both hear Hilary shouting down the phone from where we were standing. 'He's all right,' Keith said. 'He means well with this place, and he'll always step in and help if you need it. Otherwise he'll let you get on with your work. Mind you, he disappears sharpish when his wife has a lunch and the house is full of women.'

Hilary finished his phone call just as we were about to look in the stables. He didn't have long, he said, he needed to go into Holt, but he wanted to show me where I would be staying, should I take the job.

'I can show you the horses later,' Keith said.

The woodland was about a quarter-of-a-mile's walk from the farm.

'It's an old keeper's van,' Hilary said, 'not much to look at, but it's a stopgap for now.' There was a path through oaks and silver birch to where a small caravan stood in a clearing. It had mould running down from the roof, a green stain and leaf drop from the branches overhead. He stood there looking at it with his hands on his hips. 'Oh, dear, this probably isn't going to be suitable, is it? So sorry. I haven't been up here for a while. We could sort out a room in the house, if need be.'

'I'd like a look inside,' I said. It was small, but the van had a bed, a washbasin, and a view from the door straight through the trees to the farm beyond. Hilary looked at his watch. I spoke before I'd thought it through.

'Could I stay a night here? In the van?' Hilary looked relieved.

'Of course,' he said. 'Good idea. Try it out. I'll get my wife Judy to find some bedding and drop it by later.'

I sat down on the bed after he'd gone. It was dark inside the van. The undergrowth outside was growing up against the windows at the back, leaves squashed so tight against the glass, I could see the pattern of their veins. There was an earthy smell of damp coming in through the door, and birdsong echoed deep inside the woods as if in a church. It was my first night spent away from home.

Mum hadn't said a word that morning when I told her where I was going.

'I'm off to see about a job,' I said when she came down into the kitchen. She wrapped her dressing gown around herself, held it closed at the neck in one tight fist.

'It's in Norfolk,' I said. 'I don't know when I'll be back,' and I walked out of the door without saying goodbye.

She didn't watch me from the window as she normally did, giving a small wave round the edge of the curtain.

There was a fine layer of dust on the car, not just on the windscreen but all over the roof and bonnet, and as I looked around, I saw it was on the windowsills, even the rape petals on the other side of the fence. It looked like plaster dust, as if a factory had gone up in smoke some-where miles away. That would be another thing for Mum to worry about once she knew it was there, about breathing it in and clogging her lungs.

If only I'd never mentioned Shirley or the Peaman. Just by saying their names out loud, it felt as though I'd brought them into the house and their presence filled every room. But it was too late now, like it was for Elmy. I couldn't take it back.

I sat in the caravan for half an hour and soon had it all planned out. How I was going to have a walk round the woods first to get my bear-ings, then I was going to find a fish and chip shop at Wells-next-the-Sea, marked on the map. When the pubs were open, I'd buy a couple of bottles of beer to drink back at the caravan where I was going to sit down and make a list of all the things I'd need if I was going to live up here.

There was a well-beaten path to the side of the van which led off into the trees. I'd only walked down it for a few hundred yards when I came to a concrete road. It was overgrown with brambles, and there were weeds and elder saplings growing up through the joints, but it seemed to carry on straight through the woods. The further I walked, the more the wood seemed to be full of them, broken roads, built long and straight like runways.

Hilary had said they were something to do with the war.

'You'll find the woods riddled with them. There used to be ammunition stores up here to serve the base nearby. This whole area was full of bases then. Not much of them left now except for these roads and some of the buildings, which are mainly used as mushroom sheds nowadays, or chicken farms.'

There was a wall at the far end of the wood, a crinkle-crankle wall that curved its way around the trees, with a lane on the other side. I was about to head back to the caravan when I heard what sounded like a truck braking hard in the road just round the corner. There were several thumps, the slam of a door and a whole string of swear words.

I climbed on to the wall. There was a man standing in the lane, surrounded by potatoes which had spilled out all over the road. Several sacks had toppled off his truck and split open, so now he was going to have to scoop them up by hand to load them back on.

'Do you need some help?' I said.

He jumped when he saw me standing on the wall. He was wearing a rainbow-coloured tee-shirt and had a gold stud in his left ear.

'I wouldn't say no,' he said, 'if you've got time?' He pointed at the truck. 'Tailboard's broken. Thought I could get away with it, but the whole lot just slid off coming round that bend.'

We soon had the first sackload back on the truck. He wanted to know how I came to spring out of nowhere like that, so I told him I'd come to look at a job on the farm.

'You'll probably have met my dad, then,' he said. 'He does various jobs there but looks after the horses mainly.'

I told him I'd met Keith, though I hadn't seen the horses yet.

'Dad's training me up to work with them at the moment,' he said, straightening up for a minute and rubbing the small of his back. 'But I'm also setting up my own business, something I can do in the evenings and fit around the farm work. It's a fish and chip van.' And he spread his hands wide at the potatoes in the road. 'That's what these are all about.'

'I think I've seen your van, parked in the yard.'

He'd been doing it up for the last few months, he said, and now it was all ready to go once he'd had a try out with the new fryers. He pointed to a sack of Maris Pipers.

'I'm going to give those a try tonight. But these are my favourites,' he said, looking down at the potatoes by his feet. He picked one up and rolled the pink-skinned potato between his palms as if warming his hands on it. 'So you could be living up here?'

'Maybe,' I said. He was still holding on to that potato, rubbing it like a cricket ball one minute as if he was about to lob it over the wall, running it down his cheek the next. I couldn't take my eyes off it. I was following that potato round and round, and hardly listening to a word he was saying.

'It's a bit out of the way for you up here in the woods,' he said. 'I could easily swing by with the van, deliver fish and chips to your door, if you like?' He held out one hand.

'I'm Aaron by the way,' he said. 'Aaron Bloomfield.' I was still staring at his other hand, at that potato all hot and pink in his palm. 'So what's your name then?'

Judy had left bedding and a gas lamp in the van by the time I got back from the coast that night. I'd had fish and chips on the quayside at Wells, eaten them sitting at the end of a long row of children who were lying on their fronts and dangling crabbing lines into the water below. I watched the wader birds on the mudbanks and the holiday makers who were strolling up and down the path on a high bank that led to the sea. I had only one thought in my head then. I didn't want to go home. I didn't ever want to be stuck in that house with my mother again.

There were teabags for the morning, and a loaf of bread and jam. I sat on the bottom step a while, drinking the last of the beer, listening to the way the wind shook the trees at the very top when it didn't even lift my hair down below. I lost all sense of time as I watched the farm below, and saw a chimney moving along above the top of the hedgerows as the chip van came back to the yard for the night.

Nearly twenty-one years old and here I was in an old keeper's van, about to spend my first night away from home; older than Mum and Lady Diana, who'd both got married, left home, and just had their first baby boys at this age. Diana might have moved into Kensington Palace and Mum into a house in the middle of fields, but was this what it felt like for them? I wondered. Like the feeling you get when you stick your head out of the back window of a car, and you open your mouth wide, feel the full force of the wind snatch your breath away. Was this what Mum felt like when she left Sizewell and her own silent mother?

'I was so happy when I left home,' Mum used to say. 'I had everything to look forward to. The start of married life in my own home . . . having a young family. Then, to top it all, Shirley met Guppy and moved in over the fields. I could hardly believe my luck.'

And now look at her. A widow in her forties, trapped inside her own home. Surely she must wonder how her life turned out this way.

She took a wrong turn with Uncle Guppy in Shirley's kitchen, that was for sure. I couldn't bear to think of how they must have been that evening. Everyone a little bit tipsy after the meal, swapping stories, finding every tiny detail funny. How Dad and Shirley were probably still laughing about something as they stumbled into the kitchen to find out what was taking Mum and Guppy so long with the washing up, seeing them together at the sink. Dad and Shirley still laughing but sounding more uncertain now, before their laughter died away altogether.

No wonder Dad didn't seem that surprised when I told him about the Peaman. He'd probably been waiting for it to happen ever since he saw his wife with his brother-in-law, a thin damp tea towel pressed flat between them. For three long years he'd been marking off the days to D-day. At least there was one surprise held back for him. As he sat in the goat shed with all those chicken feathers frothing up inside him and his heart groaning under the strain, I bet he was thinking, Well, I wasn't expecting that, as it turned out to be his own daughter who broke the news of his wife's betrayal and sliced the pair of them cleanly down the middle.

I lay in bed, wide awake. Mum might just have got away with it, if it hadn't been for me.

The dogs woke me at dawn. I'd only been asleep for a couple of hours when something set them off and they started howling for miles around. They'd heard something. I listened a while, holding my breath, and then I heard it too: a low rumble that seemed to come from deep underground, like a train passing underneath the caravan. The teacups started to chink against one another as they swung on the hooks underneath the cupboard. The noise grew louder and plates rattled on the shelves. An empty beer bottle fell off the sideboard and rolled on to the floor. The whole caravan was being shaken like a money box.

It probably lasted less than a minute, but by the time it finished, my hands were slippery with sweat. There was a stillness afterwards, a brief silence before the birds started up. I sat on the step in the cool dawn. The dogs were quiet. The cockerels were crowing in the yard. It took me a minute or two to work out what had happened: that for all of Mum's talk of tectonic plates thousands of miles away, a couple of them had just knocked into each other right underneath where I was sleeping.

I left a note for Hilary on the table in the van, folded the blankets at the end of the bed, and headed out of the woods just as the sun was beginning to come up.

It was a long drive home. I shouldn't have left Mum on her own like that. I hadn't even bothered to ring her to let her know I wouldn't be back home that night. She probably thought I'd gone for good by now.

I'd treated her worse than an animal. She had food and water, but I didn't arrange for anyone to drop by, check she was all right, that she hadn't kicked over the feed bucket, gone down with swine fever. And it didn't help matters that Stanley Larter was chipping in all the way home as if he was sitting right next to me in the passenger seat.

'*You really should get that door fixed. Two women like that, in the middle of nowhere. It's not safe, is it?*'

As soon as I got home, I knew something was wrong. The back door to the porch was swinging wide open. The house was empty. Mum had disappeared.

THE RAPE FIELD

The dust still lay everywhere from yesterday, gritty underfoot. There were marks on the windowsills where she'd run a finger through it, no doubt cursing the cracks which were big enough to let it in, and trying the window catches to make sure they were locked shut. Except now every window downstairs was wide open

I ran through the house, shouting for her. What if Stan had been right? What if Mum was telling the truth after all, and she really had seen somebody prowling out there in the back field, trying to peer into the house? That man on the run could have been hiding out there the whole time, waiting till I'd gone before he tried the back door.

I checked the door. It was on the latch. Whoever had opened it had simply turned the handle.

I left the upstairs rooms until last, afraid of what I might find there.

'Mum, are you in there?' I opened the door to her room just a crack but the shock of the light blazing inside made me step back, eyes watering. It was as if the entire field of rape had got into the house, blown in through the windows and taken root all over the bedroom.

I opened the door a little wider. It was the tin foil. Mum had pasted it over all four walls. She'd even managed to get it up on to the ceiling, and the back of the door.

I stood there with one hand shading my eyes from the sunlight bouncing off the rape outside. And then through the glare I saw them. They were standing there, faces turned towards me. It was as if they'd suddenly stopped in the middle of what they were doing, to stare at me in the doorway.

It was Mum's mannequins. They'd all been dressed as real people.

I recognised a few of them straightaway from their clothes, and the way she'd arranged them next to others.

'Are you in here, Mum?' I was whispering, not wanting to walk inside. It was as if she had the dead and the living all bundled up in that bedroom together. I kneeled down on the floor to look through the jumble of plastic legs and makeshift stands, feeling like a child lost in a department store, hiding in the clothing rails and trying to spot my mother's feet.

She wasn't there. I'd just stood up when a breeze caught the tops of the flowers outside. The walls started to ripple and I hung on to the door, fearing the house was about to tip sideways.

The tremors must have woken her up. Fearing the house was about to split open, she'd made a run for it. And if she was running out of the door in blind panic, she would have bolted for cover into the rape field where at least the flowers would have closed over her head.

I ran downstairs to the back porch and soon found her size-four footprints in the dust. They led straight to the back fence where they disappeared into hundreds of acres of rape.

'Can you hear me, Mum? Are you in there?' My voice sounded small and flat as I shouted into the field. She was out there somewhere, cowering in terror from the sky overhead and the ground shifting beneath her feet. She must have been desperate to leave the house like that, realising there was nowhere else for her to go.

Ed arrived ten minutes after I'd called. He had Pipe in the car, who'd happened to drop by the night before.

The three of us stood by the back fence for a moment.

'She'll have dived into the field and gone up one of the tractor tracks,' Ed said. 'Let's spread out and take one each.' We climbed over the fence and plunged into rape which came up to our waists in an instant.

'We'll never see her over this,' I said. 'She's too short.' The rape was choppy in places, one minute barely up to our knees, the next rising fast up to our chests. Ed was by far the tallest, but some of the flower-heads were up to his shoulders.

'If she was frightened, she could have fallen,' I said. 'She could be lying anywhere in this field right now with a broken ankle.'

'She'll be somewhere up one of these tracks,' Pipe said. 'We just need to keep going.'

We shouted for Mum as we chested through the flowers with our arms held over our heads.

This was the worst sort of sky for her. High, blue and clear, nothing between her and heaven, the sort of sky that made her crawl around the house, find dark corners, burrow away in the bedroom upstairs. I should have done more to help her. Instead I threw the windows wide open to let the air in, and frightened her half to death. I hardly dared look up when we came to the power lines overhead, for fear of seeing her up there, blown into the air like a sheet of newspaper and caught on the underside of the wires.

After a while I noticed we weren't alone in the field. There were other people out there with us. Donny had appeared over in the distance, Fred Bugg not far behind.

'I rang Donny before I left,' Ed said, 'just in case he'd seen her.' There was Elmy and Zelma's husband Michael out there as well, till I must have counted at least ten people in that field, a ragged row of heads and arms gliding above the flower line.

There wasn't much talk in between the bouts of shouting. Ed cursed every time a pheasant flew up and set our hearts racing, and there was a distant sound of engines that seemed to stop and start as if there were cars going slowly along the road, following the hunt. But the further we got out into the field, the quieter it became, as if even the hares didn't make it this far in.

Pearl . . . Mum . . . where are you? Our thin voices rose high above the rape, sounding like the rise and fall of skylarks in the silence of that endless field.

'I'm just taking a look over there,' I said, and cut over to the farthest pylon where I knew there'd be a box of bare land underneath, in case she'd washed up there. I didn't like the look of the cracks in this part of the field. The soil was dry as old bones, split open in places where any rainwater must have run straight down, missing the roots altogether. I remembered the food that had vanished without a trace and felt cold sweat running down my back. Maybe the tremors had loosened the whole field, and Mum was out here as the earth opened up beneath her, and she fell in feet first, just as the ground closed over. And none of us would spot her brush of hair, left sticking up out of the soil like a few stalks of old stubble.

We needed a way of looking at the field from overhead, a bird's-eye view, so that we could spot any tracks if she'd veered off the tractor ruts and cut through the rape. I looked up. I'd only have to get a little way above the barbed wire and the 'Danger of Death' sign. Any broken rape from that height would be as clear as a moorhen's path through pondweed. It would lead us straight to her.

The pylon was buzzing overhead. I felt dizzy just looking up through the struts and wondering where to start. Then there was the sound of a horn, someone pressing on it long and hard.

'Desiree . . . this way!' Ed and Pipe were waving at me through the fog of flowers. 'We've found her.'

And there was Pam in the far distance, except she looked so tall she seemed to be standing on top of the rape itself, the flowers holding firm beneath her feet.

'She's fine,' Pam was shouting. She wobbled a moment on the roof of their car. 'She's at Shirley's house.'

EL ALAMEIN

Mum was standing in the front garden as we came out of the field, a small figure like a doll set down in the middle of Guppy's vast lawn.

'You had us all worried back there, you know,' Ed said.

'We thought you'd been kidnapped,' Pipe said, 'that you were halfway up the A12 by now.'

'I'm sorry,' Mum said. 'I didn't mean to cause such a fuss.' Her face fell as more people waded out of the field behind us. Every one of us was covered in yellow pollen, rape petals stuck fast with sweat to our faces and arms. 'I certainly didn't mean for other people to get involved,' she said.

I put a hand on her arm.

'I'm glad you're safe, Mum. I'm glad you're out.' She smiled.

'So am I, Desiree,' she said. 'So am I.'

Ed said he'd give people a lift back to where they'd left their cars, but first everyone must stay and have some tea. Mum wouldn't let any of us go inside the house though. 'Shirley's just had her baby up at the hospital,' she said, 'so they're not here right now. I'll bring tea out for everyone, shall I?'

But there was something else going on, the way she stood there as if barring the door. 'It's just a bit of a mess in there at the moment,' Mum said to me. 'Shirley would be mortified if anyone saw the place. Let's talk later, shall we, once everyone's gone home? I'll explain everything then.'

People hung around the edge of the garden, not wanting to walk on Guppy's lawn in their heavy boots. Instead they stayed by the ditch, the men with their hands in their pockets, scuffing at the grassy bank with their boots.

Elmy and Fred Bugg were already in the middle of some argument about field names.

'And I'm telling you, we were walking through Spion Kop back there. That's where the plane came down,' Fred was saying. 'In Spion Kop. Not South Sea. I can remember it as clear as anything.'

'Spion Kop wasn't round here. You've got it all wrong,' Elmy said. 'It was South Sea back there.'

'What plane?' I said, passing them tea.

They were talking about a bomber, Elmy said, the one that came down during the war in the fields behind our house.

'It happened in 1942,' Fred said. 'The crew survived, everyone except for the pilot. They found him miles away, near World's End. I'd forgotten how our kids were up here all the time, rooting about for bits of plane. A great big four-engined Liberator, it was, belly-flopped right into the mud. Took them ages to dig it out of that field. It got known as El Alamein after that, as I remember.'

Mum was heading over the garden with a second tray of teas, Pam following behind with a spoon and a bag of sugar.

'It's wonderful news about Shirley, isn't it?' Pam came to a stop next to me. 'How lovely to have a little girl. I always thought me and Ed should carry on trying for a girl, but after the twins . . .' She looked past me at their four-year-old boys, Carl and Paul, who were fighting with sticks out on the lawn. 'But, God, all this talk of babies, it's making me feel broody. I thought I was done with that side of things by now.' She looked behind us into the ditch. 'I sometimes forget you found that baby that time,' she said. 'I didn't realise until I had my own children how it must have been for you. Did it bother you, finding her like that?'

'She's never gone away,' I said.

Pam glanced down at her chest. It was the first time she seemed to notice that her bra was showing and she pulled at the neckline of her tee-shirt.

'You know, I've done some things in my time I'm not proud of.' She didn't look at me when she spoke. She was staring at the bag of Silverspoon in her hands, staring right into it as if seeing a whole pile of filthy sugar beet inside it. 'But I was young then,' she said. 'I'd never do something like that though, would you? Abandon a baby. What woman would?'

'I don't know,' I said, watching Mum as she threw the last of the tea dregs into the ditch.

Fred and Elmy were the last ones to leave. They were still going on at each other as they got into the car with Donny.

'And I'm telling you it was South Sea, you daft bugger,' Elmy was saying. 'You're way off the mark.'

It was only when I followed the boys indoors that I could see why Mum hadn't wanted anyone to come into the house.

'Bloody hell. What's been going on here?' Pipe was staring through to the lounge where the sofa and chairs had been tipped over. The curtain pole was hanging down to the floor and there was a strong smell of whisky from a bottle which had been knocked over on the carpet. It was just as bad in the kitchen. There were broken plates on the floor and food up the walls as if there'd been a fight over dinner the night before.

We stood there, looking all about us, hardly recognising the place.

'I think Guppy did this,' Mum said.

Pam made a start on clearing up the kitchen while Mum explained that she'd first tried to ring Shirley yesterday morning after I went off to Norfolk.

'I felt it was time me and Shirley sorted things out, with you gone,' she said. 'But the phone was engaged all evening, so in the end I went to bed. I got woken up by the earth tremors and then I was really frightened. I thought the house wasn't going to make it. I actually heard it crack.'

After the tremors had stopped, Mum tried Shirley's number again but it was still engaged.

'It was easy in the end,' she said. 'I opened the back door and set off through the field by myself.'

When Mum got to the farm and saw the state of the house, she thought they'd been burgled or squatted. And the phone was hanging off the hook.

'I thought something terrible had happened,' she said. 'I was about to ring the police. But the phone rang as soon as I put it back on the hook. It was Shirley at the hospital. She was looking for Guppy. She said he'd disappeared.'

The boys had a good look round the farm but said there was nothing out of the ordinary. Guppy had been busy burning stuff in his incinerator, but there was nothing unusual about that. He liked to keep on top of things that way.

'You think Guppy did this?' I said. Ed shrugged his shoulders.

'He could have done if he was really drunk, I suppose.' But it looked like more than drunkenness. It looked like panic, as if he'd gone and lost something valuable and turned the house upside down looking for it, and when he couldn't find it, he flew into a rage.

'It's only been a few hours,' Pipe said. 'He's probably gone off on a bender and passed out somewhere. He'll drag himself home later on.'

'Oh, he'll be back all right,' Mum said. 'Guppy will never cope on his own, not without Shirley.'

Mum said she was going to clean the house from top to bottom before Shirley got back. She was due home with the baby tomorrow. Mum was also going to stay the night so she could ring Shirley when Guppy turned up with his tail between his legs.

'I'll keep you company then,' Pipe said. 'We don't know what state he'll be in, do we?'

'The strange thing is,' Mum said, 'I had a feeling Shirley wasn't telling me everything. She said something odd on the phone. She said Guppy looked really frightened when he walked out of the delivery room. Undone, was how she put it. He looked undone. How could he be frightened when they've just had a baby, and one that he's wanted for so long?'

It was quiet back home. Ed offered to stay with me a while after we left Mum and Pipe at the farm, but I told him I'd be fine. I wanted to know what it felt like to be alone in the house, to sit there with the windows and doors open wide, and let the evening air run through every room.

I didn't go upstairs though. I felt uncomfortable at the thought of them all up there, waiting for me, staring at me. Of walking straight into Mum's loneliness. I could feel it starting to seep through the ceiling, heavy and suffocating. In the end I put the radio on for company as I lay down on the sofa. The pylons were quiet that night. There was no interference, no foreign voices breaking through the music. Even Peewit had decided to keep away that night.

THE SAHARA DESERT

The chicken boys were not in their usual place the next morning. I went to feed them on my way over to the farm to help Mum with the tidy-up before Shirley and the baby got home, but they'd shifted over the road and gone a little way up towards the old straw clamp. After all these years of living in the same hedge, they seemed to have wandered a few extra hundred yards and found a whole new territory to scratch about in.

They didn't come to me this time. I'd left it too long. So I sat against the clamp to wait a while. There was something worrying at me. I could feel it squirming away at the back of my head. Walker was in the distance. I recognised his springing walk as he headed off some place, probably Kettleburgh or Easton, though he could reach Woodbridge by lunchtime if he kept up that pace.

And then I remembered. It was Dad's feet. I'd fallen asleep on the sofa, wondering what he'd been up to on the night of the stubble fires that his feet had got so filthy with soot? The same night that Melissa Makepeace had smouldered away in Drunken Mary. What had happened to Dad's socks?

The confident bird finally came a bit closer and I threw him some corn. But he wasn't hungry. It looked as if someone else had taken to feeding them, making sure they were all right. I was surprised at how put out I felt that they didn't come running like they used to. They'd managed to cope just fine all these months without me. World's End was only just up the road. Perhaps it wouldn't be too long before they found their way to the farm, and maybe one day soon I'd find two white leggy capons in amongst Ivy's fat hens.

I watched Walker disappear into the distance. He must have seen it all on those walks of his. All those years tramping round and round, knowing every square inch of verge, every culvert, every pothole in the road as surely as if he had a map on the inside of his skull. He'd have cocked his head at flattened nettles, a smell of perfume, the red Vauxhall Viva well off its usual beaten track. Snatches of private conversations carried to him out of doors and windows as he sped past, as see-through as a ghost. He'd soon piece it all together. Walker probably knew more about most people's lives than they did.

He might have been waiting for years for me to ask. It wasn't as if I'd have to say much. Just one simple question. 'Did you see anyone that day on the Straight?' All I had to do was slow him down for one fraction of a second. 'Just tell me it wasn't my mother.'

I took the long way round to the farm, going down Watery Lane, still flooded as always, to the flower meadow which I knew would be in full bloom. At least I could pick a handful of wild flowers to brighten up the place for Shirley. Every year there was the same clump of ox-eye daisies, the same grasses I'd wanted to lie in with Bernie all those summers ago, where Walker liked to take a rest and blow smoke rings as big as circus tops.

I saw the Sold sign first and then the board which someone had hammered into the long grass by the gate. It was a picture of what the development was going to look like. They were going to dig up that meadow, sling all the wild flowers, the root balls and the worms into a builder's skip, and bury it under tarmac to build four identical houses, each with a square of front garden. There was a family of four in the picture who looked so happy standing in front of their double garage, they could have just won the Pools.

There were tracks through the grass where people had been coming and going, people with clipboards and measuring tapes. It took a few minutes and some hunting around but I found Walker's den in the end, over by the oak tree in the far hedge. The grass was flattened around the base of the tree, and in odd gaps in the bark and between the tree roots there was a collection of things: a pile of cigarette ends in a neat pyramid, birds' eggs, and flints shaped like arrowheads. There was a tobacco tin, and some rolled-up paper pushed tight into an old tree hollow. I didn't want to get too close or touch anything. I was worried he'd pick up my scent and never come back. He had this place for the summer at least, then he'd have to find somewhere else to go.

I'd been wrong about his route though. Instead of being ten miles away the other side of Framlingham, he came through Watery Lane just as I was sitting on the bank above it. He was never usually so close to home at this time of day, but perhaps he'd changed his routes and was doing more fat laps on the roads close to the village rather than his long oval walks to places fifteen miles away. Maybe he was getting old, slowing down. He couldn't walk those long distances for ever, and what would happen to him then?

I never called out to him in the end. Instead I sat still and quiet up there on the bank, watching him as he passed through Watery Lane, leaving a V-shaped wake like a mallard.

'So Guppy's not back then?' Mum shook her head. She'd tidied up all his mess though. She'd scrubbed the floor and the carpets but there was still a smell of whisky on the living-room carpet, and two of the kitchen chairs were broken. 'You could give me a hand cleaning the windows, if you like. Your father helped Shirley do all this for me when I was in hospital.' She'd just finished drying up and shook the tea towel to straighten it. 'It's what new fathers do for the homecoming of their wife and baby.' And she snapped that cloth so hard it sounded like a smack round the face.

'Shouldn't we phone the police?' He'd been gone for two days. I thought someone should be out having a proper look for him.

'Shirley can decide what to do when she gets back,' Mum said. 'He's still her husband, if a cowardy one.'

Clean, upright, solid Guppy, all starched and white in his spray gear and riding about on his huge tractor, turned to jelly by a baby? I couldn't help thinking we'd all missed something.

There was nothing unusual on the farm that morning. There was no sign that Guppy had gone off in a hurry or that he wasn't coming back. Everything seemed to be in its place, as tidy as ever. He had only recently cleared the weeds by the drinking pond as there were browned patches of scorched grass all the way around the edge.

Mum had brought the Moses basket from downstairs and put it in a corner of the kitchen. She'd made soup, and there were fresh flowers on the table.

'Pam gave me a lift to the shops this morning,' Mum said. 'I didn't want to bother you.' She stopped folding clothes and looked at me. 'Pam told me the shop's closing. You never said.'

'I didn't want to worry you.'

'But you'll have to get another job. What about the place you went to look at?'

'It's a long way away,' I said. 'North Norfolk. I'd have to move.'

'Well, is it a good job? Would you like it up there?'

For a moment I thought of the woods, the goats and the chip van in the yard. But Mum wasn't thinking things through properly. Shirley and the baby would be home any minute now, and when Guppy turned up, she'd have to leave. Shirley might have forgiven her, but she wouldn't want Mum staying in the house around Guppy, not after last time.

'I'll find something else,' I said. 'Something round here.' I still had the house to sort out. I was none too sure it was even safe to live in any more.

'I won't be going back there, Desiree,' Mum said. 'I know it's been difficult since Dad went, but we'll sort something out. Don't worry.' But I couldn't stop worrying, that was the problem. Now that she'd stopped, she'd passed it on to me like a baton, till it seemed all I could do at the moment was fuss and worry. Somewhere along the way, we seemed to have swapped places.

We cleaned Shirley's windows, front and back, then sat in the garden, breathing in the scent of washing.

'How come you always end up covered in seeds and bits of blossom?'

Mum was brushing my shoulders down. 'Look, you've still got rape petals in your hair from yesterday.'

I sat at her feet on the grass. It was like the old days, sitting with my back leaning against her knees. I couldn't see her face but I could feel her through the tips of her fingers, slow and thoughtful. She was somewhere else as she untangled the burrs from my visit to the chicken boys earlier.

A breeze blew across the field.

'Why was Dad so late getting home on the night of Cheryl's party? And what happened to his socks?' I took a deep breath. 'Was it something to do with the American girl?'

Mum was quiet for a moment. 'Yes, I suppose it was,' she said.

Dad had stopped that night to help the American man. He was on his way home from work, Mum said, when he found Lance Makepeace out on the road near Stradbroke. Dad had nearly run him over because Lance was wandering across the road, jabbing at the air as if he was in the middle of some almighty argument. Except he had tears streaming down his face. And he wasn't wearing any shoes, just a pair of socks which were half flopping off his feet.

'When your dad got out of the car and asked Lance if he could give him a lift home, Lance just took off over the fields. Dad was worried he was heading straight for the stubble fires. So he went off after him, managed to steer him back to the road, but he couldn't get Lance into the car. In the end, it was easier to walk him home, Dad said. Lance was calmer then. He'd stopped crying, though he'd lost both his socks. Dad couldn't bear to see the man walking home barefoot so he gave Lance his socks. "He stood there like a toddler," Dad told me later. "He had a hand on my back while I kneeled in the middle of the road and helped him get dressed."'

Mum's hands were resting on my shoulders as she spoke. There was a neat pile of burrs and leaves on the grass next to her.

'So Dad was late home because of Lance?' I said. 'Because he stopped to help him?' I couldn't see anything wrong with that, certainly nothing that was worth fighting about.

'Your dad didn't say a word about it at the time. He wouldn't say where he'd been, what he'd been up to. I thought he'd stopped off at the pub, forgotten all about the party. Forgotten about me.'

'But why didn't Dad say anything?'

'Because Lance got him to promise. He pleaded with him not to say anything. It was about his daughter.'

I turned round to face Mum. She was shredding the rape petals in her lap, tearing them into tiny pieces.

'What about her?'

'Lance had just found out from his wife that evening. She'd been keeping it from him for months. They both had. Her and Melissa.' Mum looked at me then, and tucked a strand of hair behind my ear. 'You know the baby you found that day? In the ditch? That was Melissa's baby.'

In the end, it was as simple as that. My mother had known all along. She'd known that Peewit's mother was a fourteen-year-old American girl from San Diego.

Looking back, I should have realised something had happened to Melissa to make her look like a winded horse. She'd been so full of herself in the beginning, so pumped up with air. But then there was the time I saw her in Tannington church with her thumb in her mouth. I remember thinking their move to Suffolk was turning her simple, that it didn't look as if she was coping too well away from her skyscrapers and her burger bars as she lay there unblinking, legs curled underneath her, that suck-sucking of her thumb. But she could have found some other place of her own to go to. It wasn't as if we were stuck for quiet out-of-the-way churches. There was Bedfield church just up the road, or Brundish. They weren't used much any more. They were lovely and quiet. Why couldn't she just mess off somewhere else? I was thinking. When all the time she must have been emptied out by what had happened, remembering what it felt like to let slip a baby long before she was ready. Melissa was lying on that pew and wanting to disappear into the poppy field, just the same as me. I walked out of the church in a huff and less than four weeks later she was dead.

There was a crunch of gravel as Ed and Shirley turned into the drive. Mum gave me a final pat as she ran her fingers through my hair.

'There, you're done. You'll do.' But I didn't move. Peewit's mother had been dead for the last six years. So why was Peewit still hanging around? I knew she had something in mind. She'd been far too quiet lately, as if she was carefully planning out her next move. And at that moment I could almost feel the shudder of that crazy runaway train as it changed direction out there in the fields somewhere, the shower of sparks and black smoke as it hurtled straight towards me, full steam ahead.

Shirley looked stiff as she got out of the car, slightly bow-legged as if she'd just climbed off a horse. She was pale with tiredness.

'I haven't slept for two days,' she said, holding Mum first and then me. She looked past us towards the house as if hoping to see Guppy standing there. Sheepish, apologetic, his big meaty hands held out to her in a 'sorry for everything'.

Mum shook her head.

The baby was fast asleep in Shirley's arms, wrapped up tight in a blanket.

'Could you hold her for a moment, Pearl?' The baby was tiny with just her face showing beneath a white cotton hat, blanket tight under her chin, a few strands of dark hair.

'What's her name?' I said.

'Jennifer Rose,' Shirley said. 'I think that will suit her.' She gently touched her daughter's nose. 'She's like a little Jenny Wren, don't you think?'

I didn't stay long. Mum and Shirley were already closed in tight over the baby's head, taking in every part of her face.

'I'll come back tomorrow,' I said. They tried to get me to stay.

'We've got plenty of room,' Shirley said, but I needed time on my own to think about Dad and the Americans. About Peewit. I needed to start over again from the beginning.

Mum came to the door as I got ready to leave. She stood on the step and cupped the top of my head with both hands.

'Dad knew about me and that man,' she said, quietly. She kissed the top of my head, very gently. 'I told him the night of Cheryl's party. I was so furious, it just came out. How lonely I'd been, how desperate. How it was just the once. You didn't tell him anything he didn't know already.'

I sat on the couch where Dad had spent that night, drunk, worn out, crushed like a beetle, the soot on his bare feet rubbing off on Mum's best cushions.

He must have come through the door, carrying Lance and the ditch baby heavy in his gut, but thinking they could still make it to the party. They still had time. That is, until he walked head first into Mum's fury.

Why did he have to be so loyal to that American when he barely knew him? When Lance and Winona had never even stopped to give him the time of day? If only he'd told Mum what had happened, told it quickly enough, then he could have stopped her before she coughed it up in front of him, that terrible gobbet that was working its way up her gullet like a fur ball, speeding towards daylight. How he didn't think of her, ever, or care about her. How she should have known better than to expect any different. As if it wasn't enough to be stranded in this place, relying on him for a lift everywhere, now she'd missed a party because he couldn't be bothered to come home on time. He knew she'd been looking forward to it for ages. All he had to do was let her know he was going to be late, one simple phone call, and she could have got a lift with Ed. But then he never thought of her, did he? He didn't know she was there, half the time. She was just part of the furniture to him. Well, another man had noticed her. He'd taken an interest in her. So what did he think of that? Your wife turning to another man? A big strapping peaman. Right here in your back porch.

Dad sat in the Crown that night, tipping beer down his throat, pint after pint, so he could fill himself up to the brim and drown the pair of them. He drank till he no longer cared about them, the Americans or anything else.

Chubby Hawes had been in the pub as well that night. He told Ed afterwards that he'd seen Dad in the corner by himself.

'He didn't want to talk to anyone,' Chubby said. 'He was shut away with some trouble or other, so we left him alone. He couldn't have had more than three pints of Broadside, but he looked like he'd drunk ten times that amount, the way he was staggering when he got up.'

Chubby reckoned he hadn't seen anything like it, the way Dad fell into the car and set off at three miles an hour. He was clipping all the bends, then zig-zagged his way up Tannington Straight, bumping from one bank over to the other. It was a miracle he didn't end up in the ditch, Chubby said, but then he wasn't going fast enough. Chubby was right behind him on his pushbike, shouting at him to pull over. 'We all knew there was a copper about,' he said. 'Everyone did except for Tony.'

The policeman had been watching all this from the top of the Straight, with plenty of time to put his car across the top of the road. When Dad was twenty yards away, he gave him a squirt of his siren.

'That stopped Tony dead in his tracks all right. He must have known he was for it then,' Chubby said. 'And I got a bollocking for riding without lights. What a night that was! Thing is, I swear I didn't see him drink more than a few pints down the pub. Guess he just couldn't hold it that night.'

But then Dad never could hold his beer, like Mum said. And he wouldn't have wanted to hold it either, not with those two laughing at him in his head. So when the beer didn't work, he had to get away somewhere else, a place where they couldn't reach him.

I knew how Dad would have been in the car as he left the pub, head bent low over the wheel, gripping on to it tight with both hands as he saw double and rounded the bend on to Tannington Straight. Black banks rising up in front of him whichever way he turned the wheel, the blackness of the dead fields all around him. Till suddenly, from out of nowhere, this blue light on his face. In that moment knowing it was all over for him then.

And as everyone rolled home from the party, the rum and black now sponged off Cheryl's white dress and all but forgotten, as Winona tucked Lance up in bed still wearing Dad's socks and Mum bubbled away with bitterness at the kitchen table while my father lay unconscious on the sofa, Melissa had jumped the ditch straight into the flames of Drunken Mary.

I wondered if Peewit had caught up with her then, as Billy the Kid reared up in the air and Melissa slid off Billy's back, all buttery with sweat. If Peewit had managed to fly back into Melissa's arms and the two of them had floated to the ground and landed as gently as if on a bed of feathers, everything feeling right between them for the first time.

It was two in the morning by the time I went upstairs. I took a deep breath outside the bedroom, and opened the door slowly. The room was lit by the moon outside, a pale blue light falling on all the people Mum had made, the dressmakers' dummies and old shop mannequins; the homemade ones she'd knocked together herself with coat hangers and broom poles, spare parts, anything she could find. Some people were just pieces of cardboard, their bodies flat against the wall, more like shadows, but she'd had someone in mind by the way she'd cut out the shape of their head. Some people she'd only known by sight but she still caught their likeness. There were others in the room, people I recognised from the way she'd laid out the clothes or hung them on the wall.

The Capons were there, Donny and Dawn, standing close together, Donny's leather tool belt brushing against Dawn's bare thighs as she leaned into him in a low-cut top and a yellow mini-skirt. Fred Bugg was in his grey trousers and cardigan, a bundle of fur at his feet that was Vegas. The Rumseys were there, the Bullocks, even Fidelis Fairweather in a long red linen dress. It was like looking at the inside of my head made real, seeing some people in clothes whose description I'd come up with on the spot just to try and make Mum happy.

Bernie hadn't grown up much beyond seventeen. He was still in his flame shirt and oily jeans. Cheryl stood next to him with her big candy-floss hair. Stan Larter was on the other side of the room, sitting down, resting his juddery leg up on a stool. Mum must only have dressed him recently as he was wearing black jeans and a woman's blouse in royal blue.

There were so many people in the room, I didn't spot them at first. They were in the far corner of the room by the bed. I caught sight of them through a gap between the Americans. I pushed past Lance, Winona and Melissa, to where Mum and Dad stood by the bed with us three children.

Dad was in his stockman's clothes, his brown overalls. She'd kept them all this time. They still had the smell of him, of cows and beet nuts, fresh hay. Mum was in her sunflower dress, the same one she was wearing on Sizewell beach that cold autumn morning, the day they first met. We were still children, not more than eight or nine, in a tumble of arms and legs and duffel coats. The globe was next to us. She'd never got rid of it after all, or the atlas which was on the bedside cabinet, lying open at North Africa.

I lay down on the bed, sank deep into layers of our clothes: Mum's old-fashioned dresses and mini-skirts, Dad's shirts and trousers lying on top. Mum must have done the same thing, burrowing her face into the clothes at night, taking one last breath of him before bed.

'It was the dust,' Mum said. 'That's what got me out of the house in the end.' It had been on the local news, how strong southerly winds had picked up red sand from the Sahara Desert, carried it for nearly two thousand miles and scattered it over parts of Suffolk and Norfolk.

'There it was. Right here in our back porch,' she said. 'I could hardly believe it. I was able to stand in the Sahara Desert in my bare feet. And after the earthquake, the fear just lifted. I didn't even think about it. I just opened the door and walked out of the house.'

How many thousands of times must she have spun the globe over the years, willing the Atlantic to shrink away and dry up, the English Channel to become a muddy ditch between us and France? And then one day it happened. Because as those tectonic plates had shifted and ground against one another deep underneath the house, and sand from the Sahara blew into the back porch to settle in drifts over the concrete floor, she knew she'd been right all along. The world had just got smaller and landed at her feet.

THE RAILWAY

The tremors only lasted a minute and were never big enough to cause any real damage. They didn't snap the Orwell bridge in half or move London that bit nearer. They did topple a few roof tiles though, and brought down a shelf of bottles in the Railway pub in Fram, the expensive ones with optics.

'It could have been a lot worse,' people said. 'At least nobody got hurt.'

But they put a crack in our house that tipped Mum out like a raw egg straight into the rape field, and they were strong enough in Tannington to set the church bells ringing – only faint and muffled as if ringing out from under the sea, but loud enough to bring the local farmer to his window. That was when he saw the straw rolls.

He told Zelma the day after how he watched it happen from his bedroom window, saw the whole stack in his yard come tumbling down, and how those rolls, which must have weighed half a ton each, bounced on to the ground like a dozen soft toilet rolls, and then kept on rolling straight out of the yard and into his field. There was only a slight slope in that field, he said, but it was enough to give them some momentum, one roll pushing behind another, going faster and faster till they were thundering over the sugar beet like a steam train, straw and dust flying behind. He'd never seen anything like it in his life.

'I had to rub my eyes,' he said. 'I thought I was dreaming.'

The straw rolls got up such a speed that by the time they reached the bottom, they sped off that field and crashed into the back gardens of two cottages like an engine come off its tracks. The plastic netting split as the bales ploughed on over flowerbeds and runner beans, and into the churchyard till there was nothing left of them but a barley-straw carpet that reached all the way up to the door of the church.

'It was like seeing one of those old railways come back to life,' he said.

Mum rang early the next morning, saying that Shirley wanted me to come over.

'She feels it's about time you and Jenny met properly. And we can wet the baby's head while we're about it,' Mum said. She reckoned that, knowing Guppy, he'd probably turn up the moment they'd got the baby off to sleep and were about to open a bottle.

'I'd love to come,' I said. I was still half asleep but something was different: the way I imagined her looking at the other end of the phone, a comforting ordinariness to her voice. Something had happened in the night as I lay asleep on the bed with Mum and Dad standing over me, my brothers and younger self watching from its foot. The colours from that afternoon in the porch had slowly drained out of me. They'd stayed so bright and so real for all these years, I thought they were going to stain the inside of my head for ever. But Mum and the Peaman seeped out in the night as if a bucket of soapy water had been swilled over the porch floor, and with a final sweep of the broom, they were gone.

THE SLURRY POND

Mum and Shirley were upstairs in the baby's room. I could hear their voices, low around Jenny. The table had been set in the kitchen as if for a party. There were candles, a bottle of sparkling wine, the smell of roast chicken filling the house. They came down the stairs, giggling.

'She's asleep,' Mum said. 'Now we can relax.' She opened the bottle and poured the wine. 'Here's to baby Jenny,' she said.

Shirley was looking better. She'd lost that look of shell shock she came home with, and she no longer winced every time she sat down.

'You seem more your old self,' I said.

'Do you think so?' She smoothed the hair back from her face, and pinched the flesh on her cheeks. 'I feel like I've aged a hundred years, and I was no spring chicken to start with.' Shirley put one hand on Mum's arm. 'I'm just so happy that Pearl's here. I haven't had to think about a thing except looking after Jenny.' It didn't look as if she was thinking too much about Guppy. 'Here's to some good luck at long last,' she said.

The wine went to our cheeks till we were sitting at the table as red as hips and haws.

'Jenny's the spit of your mother when she was a baby, you know,' Shirley said. 'We found these photos earlier.' She showed me a black-and-white picture of a baby being held up to the camera by a man in shirt sleeves on a beach. 'That man is your Granddad Clifford,' Shirley said. 'Your mum could only have been a few weeks old when that picture was taken. She's got the same dark hair as Jenny – look.' And she pointed to the spikes of hair sprouting out from beneath the baby bonnet.

'Do you remember Mother telling us that story of how you came about, Pearl? She'd been losing her marbles for a while then, hadn't she? Started coming out with all sorts. She told us about the night of the ribbons, remember? How Father came back from fishing at sea with his arms full of silver ribbons, saying they'd fallen out of the back of a plane. He'd watched these strips of foil come twisting down out of the sky, catching the sun as they corkscrewed through the air in slow motion. So silvery bright, he told her, he could hardly look at them. The boat was festooned with them, and the water glittering all about.'

Mum was tilting the photograph at the light to get a closer look at her father's face.

'It was something they used in the war,' she said. 'The Yanks called it chaff . . . long strips of foil wound into coils. They threw them out of the backs of planes and, when they unfurled, the foil messed up enemy radar. They gave off a signal that looked like there were hundreds of planes in the sky, and made the real planes disappear.'

'Father hung the foil everywhere apparently,' Shirley said, 'strips of it from the kitchen door like a silver fly curtain. Lengths of it trailing from his trouser pockets.

'And the whole time Mother was telling us that story, she was laughing away. "It was like Christmas come early that day," she said. "That was when we made Pearl, somewhere amongst all those silver ribbons. They got everywhere, they did. We were in a right tangle." She was remembering it right in front of us, reliving every moment of them making a baby. I didn't know where to look.'

There was no talk of Guppy all evening. I was starting to wonder if there'd be room for him whenever he did crawl back. If Shirley would even take him in. There was a calmness about her, a steady quiet, as if she were already making plans for life without him.

I helped Mum clear away in the kitchen while Shirley went upstairs. She came down with the baby while I was washing up, and was fussing over her, wondering whether she was too hot or too cold. She decided to strip off the blanket and shawl and lay Jenny down in the Moses basket in just a long-sleeved vest, under a sheet, but thought maybe she was too cold then and added two blankets, just to be on the safe side. Or maybe she needed changing after all, and then she'd go back to sleep.

'Would you like a hold, Desiree?'

She was in a soft pink suit, warm against my chest as I held her close. She smelled of milk and washing powder. And then I noticed the sleeves. They were empty. Little Jenny Wren had no arms.

The pylons were spitting and hissing by the time I got home. The smell of wet weather was blowing in over the back field, and I had a headache coming on that felt about ready to split my head in two.

It could only be him. Two babies and not a single arm between them? My uncle had been with a girl, had sex with a girl the same age as his own niece, and then gone and had a baby with her.

It must have been so easy for him. A fourteen-year-old girl who didn't know anyone in her new home, and had nothing to do except ride around on her horse all day long. He probably made her laugh in the beginning, told her a few jokes and some funny stories, the same ones he used on us that made us laugh so much we wanted to follow him everywhere. Then he checked that she was good at keeping secrets, said some nice things to her about the way she looked, and that was it. All he had to do after that was couple her on to the back of his tractor like a big old empty trailer, glancing over his shoulder now and again to check she was still bouncing along behind him wherever he went.

It was raining hard by the time I went upstairs to the bedroom. Sheet lightning flashed in the distance and the walls had turned silvery-green. Guppy stood there by the window, firm and steady on his wooden feet next to Shirley. His face was hidden by a spray mask, but it was like he was watching me in the doorway, watching me work it all out.

I wondered how many times he went with Melissa, how many secret out-of-the way places they managed to find, all the pillboxes and rundown cartsheds, the sugar-beet mountains. Or was it always at the pig pits, hidden away amongst piles of farm rubbish and rusting machinery? Billy the Kid's hoof prints were everywhere by that wall.

Shirley was never there that day when I stumbled across Guppy with his trousers round his ankles. She wouldn't have gone and lain flat on her back in a freezing cold field of sugar beet when they had a warm comfortable bed back home. Nobody in their right mind would want to do that . . . nobody except breezy, confident American Melissa.

Billy the Kid would have been nicely hidden from view behind the wall as Guppy held on to Melissa and turned her head till a college education back home was the last thing on her mind, and all she could long for was Uncle Guppy and a promise of their next date by the slurry pond. Maybe I was even there that day, just a few hundreds away in the bottom of a ditch, at the very moment Peewit sparked into life amongst the stench of dead pigs.

It was like connecting up a string of fairy lights, tightening the bulbs and replacing the dud ones. Everything fell into place. It was so clear, I could have drawn a line of arrows between all the bad things that had happened and seen how they all pointed back to Guppy. And here he was in the room with me, looking stiff and awkward in his whites, watching me work it all out as the first crack of thunder broke.

I pushed through the mannequins to get to him. If he'd left Melissa alone, I'd never have found their baby in the ditch; Dad wouldn't have come across Lance strewn over the road in pieces at the news of what his daughter had done. Dad would have got home in time and made it to Cheryl's party. Mum and he wouldn't have rowed. They'd have gone to the party and had a good time, and she wouldn't have told him about the Peaman. He might even have disappeared altogether. Dad wouldn't have got drunk and lost his licence. Ed wouldn't have had to pick up the goat feed that night. Jason Feathers would have made it home to Stowmarket on his new Yamaha.

Melissa may have told her mother about the baby when Winona got suspicious about the bleeding and the crying, but she hung on to Guppy right to the end. It wouldn't ever be over with him, not while he was still a secret. Until the night of the party when she saw him in the car park, offering Cheryl a lift home.

Was that how it started for Guppy and Melissa? The offer of a lift? *'Come on, jump in. You're miles from anywhere. I'll have you home in minutes.'* And there he was, spinning the same line to some other girl when Melissa's body was only just starting to knit back together after the baby. She knew it was over then, as the drink sank into Cheryl's dress and Melissa raced off over the fields on Billy the Kid, heading straight towards Drunken Mary who was waiting for her with open arms.

If it hadn't been for Guppy, they'd probably all be alive right now. Melissa Makepeace, Jason Feathers, Dad. It was Guppy who lay at the root of everything that had gone wrong, not Peewit. She'd just been caught up in it along with the rest of us

And the worst of it was, he kept Shirley hanging on for all those years, losing baby after baby while he pawed at other women and went off to douse himself in pesticides every day.

I opened the window. He was out there somewhere, hiding away from what he'd done, shaking like a coward. I shouted into the wind and the rain.

'We've lost everything because of you! Every single thing . . . our whole family . . . ruined because of you.' I picked the mannequin up and threw it out of the window, watched it break as it hit the ground. The arms flew off and landed in mud a few yards away from the rest of him.

At least Shirley would never find out about Guppy's other baby. I closed the window. Nobody else would work it out either. I'd never told anybody about the missing arms. I looked down at the crooked whites on the concrete below, at the mannequin arms sticking up in the mud as if held out in surrender. But Guppy knew all right. I sank down on to the carpet. He knew everything about her. That was why he ran away from the hospital. He'd seen a baby like Jennifer Rose before.

I woke at dawn under Mum and Dad's bed. The storm was long gone, the sky fresh and clear after the rain which had fallen steadily through the night.

That was when I spotted her. She was just inches away from me, on the floor by the bed. It was just a bundle of newspaper, but I knew it was also Peewit, from the way Mum had wrapped the paper around her like a cot blanket. I picked her up and put her deep inside her American family, between her mother and her grandparents, and shifted them all a little closer to us.

Guppy was a man of fixed routine, Shirley always said so. He had the same routine every morning. He picked up his lunch and flask that Shirley made up for him the night before. He picked up the paper from the mat. He liked to read it in his cab over a sandwich with the heater turned up, that, and the Sunday papers. He always made them last all week. Then he left quietly so as not to wake Shirley who still had another hour in bed. Except there's something different on this particular morning in March. He finds Melissa curled up in his tractor cab, fast asleep. She's been there all night, bunked off from school. She's still got her leather satchel slung over one shoulder.

'This can't go on,' he says. They'll both get into serious trouble. He can give her a lift near to home if she keeps her head down.

He says they need to let things cool for a while, just for a few weeks, so nobody gets suspicious. She doesn't want him to get into trouble, does she? He says just enough, uses the right words so she won't get all upset and blurt out his name to anyone, and drops her off before heading back to his fields the long way round. It's a beautiful calm day, and for the first time that year the sun feels strong enough to take the chill out of the ground. He can get some serious spraying done today if he's lucky.

Halfway down Tannington Straight he notices her school bag lying on the floor. She's left it there for him to find, for him to poke through like a parent and come across a bad school report she didn't dare show him to his face. He reaches down and opens it, and finds her lunchbox, full and heavy. He opens the lid. There's a baby inside, swimming in blood. Guppy slows right down, steers with his knees for a moment while he takes his paper and sets it on his knees. He tips the box upside down, taps it like a pie dish, and she lands face down on the *News of the World*, on Prince Charles and Lady Diana in her blue engagement suit.

He can see for miles sitting high up on his John Deere, can see that there's nobody around. He wraps her up like a bag of cold chips, opens the window and tosses his baby into the ditch.

Guppy drove off that day, no doubt wiping the sweat off his forehead and cursing away to himself in the cab, but he never stopped for one instant to look back. He didn't even check his mirrors to see where she landed, how her body splashed into the filthy water and sent a small surge up the ditch which carried on and on like a tidal wave.

Guppy had been missing for three days before I realised that none of us had thought to check the pits. Nobody did. Local people didn't go up that way. They'd forgotten it was even there. And they wouldn't have known that the brick wall was high enough and at just the right angle to make most things invisible from the road.

The Land Rover was there, behind the wall. I parked a little way away and walked over to the pit, past a large hole which had been freshly dug at the edge of the field. The air felt so clean after the storm. The rain even seemed to have dampened down the stink of slurry. It was very still, very quiet.

There were canisters everywhere. Guppy's neat stack of oil drums had given way at one end. A few of them had rolled off the top and made it all the way across the concrete to the pig pit, bobbing in the slurry like bottles at sea.

It looked like a dead pig at first, lying on the surface, blown with gas. Guppy looked as if he were in a swimming pool, floating on his back with his arms outstretched.

I sat a little way away from him for a while, and watched a lapwing take off in the distance.

MILLY DOY'S BATHROOM FLOOR

'That poor girl,' they were saying. 'Desiree White. She found him, didn't she? Her own uncle over by the pits. How awful to stumble across a dead body like that. Like last time, remember?' The reek of death had come back, just enough of it clinging to my clothes that, if people got too close, it made them take a step back. After years of silence, they could suddenly remember the ditch baby. 'But they never did find the mother, did they? Or the father? Or why they chose to dump the body there in the first place?'

'I'm sorry to hear about Guppy.' Elmy was in the allotment watering his beans when I went round to tell him that I was taking the job in Norfolk. 'Terrible way to go,' he said, 'and leaving a wife and child behind.'

'I think Shirley will be all right,' I said. She wasn't short of money, and she did have Mum and the baby.

Elmy filled up two buckets from the water trough and started on the second row of broad beans. He looked different somehow, younger, as if twenty-odd years had slid off his face.

'You've got rid of the chickens,' I said.

'It was too much work,' he said, 'having to come up to the allotments to feed them every day, check the runs and make sure the foxes couldn't get at them.' It had been getting too much for him for a while, he said. 'Dolly prefers those big brown eggs from Ivy Ling anyway. We go and get them up there now,' he said.

I couldn't help thinking how pleased Miles Fairweather would have been to see those chickens go. No doubt he'd have punched the air at the sight of the empty run and poured himself a large glass of wine back home to celebrate. It was too late for him now though.

'You know, Walter would probably have found out about Hubert and your sister in the end,' I said. 'He might even have guessed there was something going on by the time you told him.'

'You could be right,' Elmy said. 'But you don't think like that when you're a child, do you? And before you know it, you're an old man and all those years have gone by with you feeling responsible for the way other people's lives have turned out. It's what I'd like to believe though.'

It was Ivy he felt sorry for, caught up in the middle of two brothers not speaking, another one deaf as a post, and no other women to talk to, not even a sister-in-law, and the whole time having orders hollered at her by Old Man Ling. 'He'd have sent Ivy the same way as his wife if he hadn't gone and died first. Do you know what he did when he lost his gammy old leg to the poison? He had it buried in the church-yard, right on top of his wife, before he joined it less than a year later.'

'It sounds like your sister had a lucky escape,' I said.

I filled the last few buckets to finish watering, and Elmy said to help myself to a few new potatoes while I was about it, and pick a bunch of sweet peas for back home.

'You heard about Milly Doy, I suppose,' he said. 'That was a rum do. They reckon she had that stroke on the morning of the earthquake. Strong old bird to have survived so long on the bathroom floor like that.'

Nobody had missed her for over two days – nobody except Walker, and he'd gone and disappeared. The neighbours were feeling bad about it but said, there again, she did keep herself to herself, and they never saw much of her boy. He flitted in and out. They tried to make light of it in the end, they were feeling so bad.

'Gone on his holidays. Probably in Yarmouth on the waltzers by now, having the time of his life,' they said.

'Poor old bugger,' Elmy said. 'Wherever he is, he won't have gone far.'

I should have realised something was wrong, that I'd been seeing

Walker too many times in one day as he stuck close to home. Even Zelma had mentioned that Milly had been getting vague for a while, leaving things behind in the shop, wandering around as if in a daze. It turned out she'd been forgetting to unlock the door as well to let Walker back in for his tea some nights.

Guppy and Milly Doy were both lying there on the ground as the tremors died away, no doubt wishing they'd done things differently. I hope Milly Doy was lying on those cold tiles wishing with all her might that she hadn't just booted her son out of the door minutes before, and locked it behind him as she'd done every day for the last fifty years. I hope she was flooded with regret as her head filled with blood and the ground beneath shook her so hard it made her teeth rattle. She'd never recover, people said. She'd lost her speech, her movement, everything. But I hoped her brain was still ticking over, that she was locked away deep inside herself where her memories were as clear as day, and she could go over every single thing she'd said and done until the day she died.

'There's one good thing though,' Elmy said as I was leaving. 'My worm's buggered off. I sleep through the night now. Dolly's relieved, I can tell you.'

The newcomers to the village, they didn't like all this talk of death flying about the place, of farmers drowning in their own pig muck, of elderly women on bathroom floors, not being missed by their neighbours for days. They didn't much like hearing the stories from before their time either, of a dead baby being found in some ditch hereabouts, or of an American girl thrown by her horse in a stubble fire and burned to a cinder. Village life wasn't meant to be like this. Where were the fêtes and the babies in bonnets, the village shops and the pubs buzzing with life? Where were all the animals that were meant to be out in the fields? The flower meadows and the kindly old women who snapped open the clasp on their purses to give children a ten pence piece to buy penny chews at the shop? And, good question, where was the shop?

Instead they found Milly Doy who kicked her son out of the house every day and Sadie Borrett who didn't have a kind word to say about anybody, especially them.

All this death and unpleasantness, it just didn't sound very nice, especially as they'd moved to villages like Worlingworth to get away from all of that. But at least they kept a decent distance, a respectful silence, unlike Sadie Borrett who couldn't help herself as usual. She was in the shop every spare moment, telling Zelma the latest, trying to work it all out.

'Just imagine it. To be lying out there in the open, concussed and breathing in all sorts, trying to crawl for help and landing up in a slurry pond.' She sucked in her breath through pursed lips, sucked it so hard the end of a stray till roll flapped towards her. She didn't know I was only round the corner, cleaning out the stockroom.

'And it happened so close to where that baby was found. Less than a quarter of a mile away. I wonder if there's any relation. Hmmm.'

She was getting far too close for comfort. I came out from round the corner and stood by the counter so that she'd see me. So that she might stop.

'They never did find the mother, did they?' Sadie wasn't looking at me directly. 'Or the father.'

Sadie and Zelma were looking at a stag beetle in the window. It was upside down in the dust, pedalling on its back. 'Somebody round here must know something, don't you think?' I might not have been a fourteen-year-old girl like last time, trapped in a cage to be poked and prodded, but Sadie wasn't going to give up that easily.

'Oh, I should think so,' Zelma said, nodding in the direction of the beetle. 'Bound to in a place like this.'

'It must be such a strain, having to keep other people's secrets for years on end.' Sadie threw it to me side on, like a chunk of raw meat that slid across the floor and landed at my feet. 'It would be a real weight off their shoulders after all this time if they could say what happened . . . who it was. Give them real peace of mind.' She cleared her throat. 'There was talk about that American girl a while back, wasn't there? The one who died. Her family rented Guppy's old farmhouse, didn't they?'

Sadie was so close, all she needed was a detail like the missing arms, and she and Zelma could slot it together in minutes. Then for the next forty years Shirley could remember her dead husband as a dirty old man who preyed on an underage girl and dumped their baby in a ditch like she was just another pest to be got rid of. And one day Jennifer Rose would be in the school playground, wishing she had fingers like everyone else so she could stick them in her ears, because she didn't like hearing what those girls over there were saying about her father.

'You knew her, didn't you, Desiree?' Zelma had stopped staring at the beetle and was looking straight at me. 'That American girl could have got herself in a spot of trouble, don't you think?'

I shrugged my shoulders.

'Never heard that one,' I said, and reached past the pair of them and righted the beetle.

SUCKLESOME

The Fairweathers were packing up and leaving. Seven years on and the same removals lorry from Basingstoke had come back for them.

'I will miss some things about living here,' Fidelis said. She was going to miss the village school and the walks she went on with her children down Watery Lane where they liked to sail their wooden boats on the water. 'And I'll miss living in this brand-new house.'

In all the time they'd lived there, Fidelis never knew about the pull their house had on Charlie Breeze. She'd never once seen him climbing over the fence or marching straight through the children's sandpit. She had no idea that Eunice always managed to yank him away by the collar just as he was about to go through the verandah doors and walk over their cream carpets in his muddy boots.

'No, you don't, Charlie Breeze,' his wife would say, and he'd follow after her as soft and dewy-eyed as a lovestruck calf.

In that shrunken brain of his, Charlie must have thought he still owned the place. He didn't see a brand-new house with plate-glass windows, a whirligig washing line and a three-piece suite. He saw a cow shed in a field called Sucklesome, and a herd of red cows that needed to be fed and watered, mucked out. There was a pile of wet straw to be pitchforked on to the heap by the back door, a water trough to be filled, fresh bedding to be laid down, and a swinging slap to be given to the rump of the animal next up for milking.

Fidelis Fairweather never had any idea how close she came to having her house turned inside out, her soft furnishings forked into a heap by the back door, a pitchfork left standing upright in her tapestry cushions, and Charlie Breeze crooning at her, 'Come on, girl, in you come,' his hand swinging back just high enough into the air for a good ringing slap. 'Let's give that big old udder of yours a wipe, shall we?'

'We'll be closer to family with the move,' Fidelis said. There was no mention of the real reason though, that Miles Fairweather had gone off like a bomb after all. It was in the paper the day after, a few lines reporting how a man had gone beserk at Ipswich station, and that it took four police officers to restrain him after he'd caused over a thousand pounds' worth of damage.

Miles had come back on an earlier train out of London that day. It was a Wednesday at the end of June, and he was looking forward to a large gin and tonic at home in the garden, a whole two extra glorious hours of a summer's evening to enjoy, the smell of mown lawns and roses in the air as the children played nicely because they'd been promised they could stay up later to be with Daddy. He'd been looking forward to it for a week, Fidelis said, had it worked out to the minute how he was going to make the most of all that free time before the sun went down and he found himself back in the car the next morning driving to the station.

Miles got off the train at Ipswich, headed straight to the station car park almost at a run so he wouldn't lose any of those precious minutes, only to find his car wouldn't start. Those watches up his arm wouldn't have helped any as they ticked away not just London but New York and Tokyo time, minute by minute, making it three times as bad as he tried to start the engine until the starter motor packed up altogether. He ended up kicking that Volvo, bashing in its headlights, swearing at it the whole time like some old workhorse that wouldn't get up. Then he started on the cars next to his. If he couldn't get home, so his reasoning went, then neither could anyone else.

'He never got over those chickens, did he?' people said, as the removals lorry drove out of the village.

THE DELIVERY ROOM

Shirley was quiet after the news about Guppy. She'd worked it out that he'd probably been poisoning them both for years; that every time she took a dip in the old drinking pond, soaking in the dirty run-off from the yard, she'd been frying her eggs to a crisp. She believed that was the real reason for him running off from the hospital in such a hurry.

'I think Guppy knew what he'd done,' she said. 'He hung on to all those pesticides after they'd been banned, when he shouldn't have. He reckoned they were the only ones strong enough to do the job properly. It must have been why he started burning up all his chemicals when he got home from the hospital that day.'

All those babies she could have had. I didn't know how she could bear it.

But there was still one thing Shirley couldn't understand, she said. 'I know it was a shock to him, to see our daughter born the way she was.' She looked down at baby Jenny in her arms. 'But what I don't understand is why he looked the way he did when he left the ward. It was more than just shock or guilt. It was terror. He looked frightened near to death.'

But I knew all right. I had a very good idea of what was going through Guppy's head at the hospital that day, as Shirley laboured away by his side. He was thinking this was a chance to put things right at last, that this new baby would help put the past behind him. *'Come on now, Mrs Savage, one last big push. We can see the baby's head.'*

No wonder he was terrified, because suddenly there she was. The baby he thought he'd got rid of, once and for all, was being born all over again right before his very eyes. Except this time she was coming out of his wife.

It was a very bad dream, a nasty joke surely as he waited for the arms to appear. Maybe they were following behind. Doctors could do all sorts these days. But the arms never came, and after the midwife had cleaned her up and wiped her head with a towel, Guppy was handed a baby bundled up in a blanket. She had the same black hair as before, sticking up in feathery tufts.

He must have careered down the hospital corridors thinking he could still get away from her. He just needed time to work things out. But by the time he speeded down Tannington Straight, he could only have been certain of one thing. This child of his was never going to let go. She was going to haunt him to the end.

Guppy opened a bottle of whisky when he got back from the hospital, and started burning his chemicals in the farm incinerator. And when the incinerator was full, he took a load more up to the pig pits. He had stacked the drums by the wall, then started to dig a great big hole so that he could pour them straight into the field. He wasn't wearing his whites or his mask that night, but then he wouldn't have been thinking straight with that amount of whisky sloshing around inside him, so the police said.

Guppy was covered in mud from digging the hole. He could even have been in the bottom of it when the earth tremors started up, terrified he was about to end up buried alive. He ran for cover by the wall, something safe and solid, and crouched down by the far end. He was probably bracing himself against the bricks when the first pesticide drum got rocked off the top of the stack and hit him on the side of his skull, followed by another, then another, some splitting open as they hit the concrete.

He had crawled around for a while, breathing in fumes. He probably had no idea where he was by the time he slid into the slurry pit like it was a warm bath.

The spilled chemicals had seeped over to the edge of the field where they left long trails of scorch marks in the grass, some in neat parallel lines like train tracks.

GRANDDAD CLIFFORD'S TUBES

It didn't take long to clear our house. Donny Capon offered his van for the move, and came over with Bernie to help load it up.

They took the furniture over to Shirley's place, where it was being stored in one of Guppy's tractor sheds. 'Just till we sort out what's going on,' Mum said.

She couldn't bear to come back. 'I don't want to see the house being cleared out,' she said. 'I'd like to remember it how it was when me and your dad first moved in, and brought you three babies home from the hospital . . . seeing you grow up there.'

By the time we'd finished, half of Worlingworth was standing in the back garden. It was unsettling to see them like that, out of the bedroom. They looked so much smaller outside, lost and ragged as they stood in a huddle under a big open sky. One or two people looked like nothing more than clothes hangers, just something to hang a jacket on, or a linen frock. No longer solid.

Our family was in a group set apart from the rest. Although they were the sturdiest ones, made from the proper wooden dressmakers' dummies with three feet apiece, they looked wobbly standing alone with nothing to lean against except each other, as if the next breath of wind would knock them flying like a bunch of skittles. They stood there staring in different directions. It made them look uneasy, like there was something bothering at them, something just outside the group. It must have got to Donny as well because when he thought me and Bernie weren't looking, he started to rearrange everyone. He pulled us closer together in a circle, the smaller ones on the outside, and made us all face outwards. Mum and Dad looked so slight, he stuck half a sack of King Edwards on their wooden feet to anchor them down. When a breeze did get up and sent the Fairweathers crashing to the ground, Fidelis's linen frock blown up round her ears, my family stood firm and rocked into the wind.

The last few were stretchered to the van on an old shed door. To anyone else they would have looked like the broken ones, body parts which had dropped off and couldn't be fixed. A hand with no fingers, a damaged head, a pair of leather boots laced with baler twine. But I recognised Marcus Chapman from the chicken factory, Jason Feathers, and the small bundle which Donny carried in his arms like a baby.

'So you're going then?' Bernie said. 'Dad says you'll be living in the woods. Won't you be scared out there on your own?'

'After growing up here?' I said. 'I don't think so.'

I saved the goat shed till last, waiting till after Bernie and Donny had gone. Everything was rotting in there. The weather had been getting through a gap in the roof at the back. The straw walls had stood up all this time but were riddled with rat holes. Underneath a pile of old feed sacks, there was a neat bunch of lengths of baler twine, the one thing not to have rotted.

I threw everything out of the door, kicking up dust and chaff as I reached the bottom. Pallets covered over with potato bags. A paper matting of Saxons, Maris Pipers and Desirees with King Edwards making up the last layers. The shed was completely empty. Four walls of grey bales, a hollow straw stack with a corrugated roof laid over the top.

The house didn't look much better. It felt like it was on its last legs without any furniture left indoors to hold the walls up. The crack in the outside reached from the downstairs window up to the eaves, so wide I could almost fit my hand into it. Even the seagull had finally flown off, the big brute of a bird who'd been at the window every day, eyeing up food on the kitchen table.

The sun was going down. This was the best time of day to sit in the bedroom, when the sun could set the walls on fire, make them flare red and orange until they turned back into gold leaf, then silver.

I left the foil on the walls. People could think what they liked when they found the room that way. I didn't care. All I knew was that Mum had felt safe in there, wrapped in foil, as if she'd gone back in time and was still swimming around in Granddad Clifford's tubes, like it was Christmas come early.

There was nothing left indoors apart from an old packet of chicken Paxo which had been at the back of a cupboard for years, and a box of firelighters under the sink. I took them with me as I locked up the house.

It was almost dark when I set fire to the goat shed. It was better this way than have someone else kick the walls in, bash the roof to bits. It went up in a blaze with the potato sacks forked on at the end.

THE NORTH SEA

It took a while, but I worked him out in the end, the man who Mum saw in the back field that night. There was never a stalker or a prisoner on the run, but there was Walker. It was him who'd been wandering up and down those fields in the dark, passing the time as best he knew how and hoping his mother would remember to open the door as she did so on her way up to bed, his tea sitting stone-cold on the counter.

But that same night after the earth tremors, he must have thought he'd been kicked out for good while she lay unmoving inside the house, hearing him scratch at the door. The neighbours felt bad. 'But what can you do?' they said. He was in and out of that door so quick, first thing in the morning, last thing at night, they never saw him half the time. They only knew something was up when they saw the milk was being drunk off the doorstep. It was nothing to do with blue tits this time as the foil tops were left neatly on the path.

I couldn't bear to think of him going round and round in circles in those days after the earthquake, slowly wrapping himself round Worlingworth. How he'd have been on that final night of the storm, circling the house, closer and closer, till he was rounding on the spot by the back door, legs splayed out in fright as the storm roared around him. Then something snaps and suddenly he breaks away, strides straight over the field opposite, walks in a plumbline over fields and ditches. Over Shoulder of Mutton, Sucklesome and Neathouse Pightle. He walks as the crow flies, ignores the boundaries, the bends in the road.

His feet never touched Drunken Mary, didn't pick up one speck of her as she tried to clutch at him passing overhead. Even the demented Creasey dog was silenced as Walker sped past, going over fields and farmyards, ignoring the *Do Not Trespass* signs, *Keep Out* and *Beware of the Dog.* On this one night he walked for all the world as if he owned the land, over Roman roads and railways still laid out beneath him.

A couple of young boys found Walker in the end. They were headed for a pond in a small field just outside Bruisyard, clutching their fishing rods, talking non-stop about the carp and the rudd they were going to catch that day. They found him tucked tight under the hedge which ran between two fields, Montserrat and Seldom Seen.

He'd have had a soft bed there on old leaves, staring up at the night sky after the storm passed, at stars that were so close at night you could feel you were in heaven. He'd have heard the wires singing from way across the fields. He had a last smoke, blew that smoke ring as big as a tractor wheel that had circle upon circle set flush inside, a flat spiral that opened out as the breeze caught a hold of it. He'd have turned round and round on the spot, making a bed of dry oak leaves where he curled up underneath dog roses and speedwell, his feet twitching in his sleep, as he flywalked over fields far beyond World's End, heading for Dunwich and the North Sea.

TANNINGTON CHURCH

It's early-July and the fields are full of poppies as I drive up to the farm that morning. Somebody has cleaned the caravan and put fresh flowers on the table inside. A new gas cylinder has been hooked up, so I can cook on the stove and have the fire on when the evenings turn cool.

The two horse chestnuts at the edge of the wood have grown so thick, they touch at the top and make an arch like a window. Sitting on the steps to the van, I can see through it to the farm and the fields below. It's mid-afternoon but there's still not much sign of life down there, apart from chickens scratching about in the yard, pigs out in the field.

The farm was deserted when I turned up earlier. Hilary and Judy weren't at the house. There was no one around in the yard. The place didn't feel quite the same now things were different back home. I didn't have the same sense of excitement or the feeling that anything could happen as I got out of the car this time. It just felt a long way away from everyone I knew, everything familiar.

'You could always stay here, you know,' Shirley had said. She stood in the front garden that morning to wave me off. 'If it doesn't work out, you know where we are. There'll always be a bed for you here.'

I still had the car keys in my hand. Nobody need ever know I'd turned up. The driver's door was wide open, all ready for me to climb back in. I was just thinking I could easily be back in Suffolk by dinner-time when a noise started up in one of the barns at the far end of the yard. Someone was banging at the wall. It was so loud there could have been someone in there, trapped under machinery, trying to get help.

Thump thump thump. The ground was shaking as I drew close to the door. I could feel the vibration coming up through my feet. I was half expecting to see Keith stuck under the prongs of a hay turner as I opened the barn door. But instead there was a row of horses' backsides pointing straight at me. Ten Suffolk Punches were kicking away at the stalls around them. They had their tails braided up with all colour ribbons, and bells in their manes which rang out so clearly with every toss of their heads they made the dark barn and the cobwebs fall clean away. And suddenly I was sitting in Worlingworth church behind Elmy's mother and sisters. There was Flora at the top end, the eldest, head-strong and bossy, then May next to her who broke her arm falling off a hay rick. After Ivy, Iris, Daisy and Rosemary, there was Violet who wanted to see the world and ran away from home till they found her up the road in a ditch near Rishangles, sobbing for her mother, and Dottie, who looked after their parents to the end. And then there was Rosa, the one who got away. She was at the end with green ribbons in her hair, kicking at the pew in front of her, not wanting to be there in her Sunday best but at World's End, riding the hogs with the Ling brothers.

Those horses dragged me over like a one-sided tug-of-war, drew me in with their big old elephant feet kicking away, making that concrete yard shake beneath my feet.

'We're in here. Don't you forget about us.' I could still hear them halfway up the track to the woods.

If it hadn't been for the horses, I wouldn't have gone past the goat shed and seen inside. I spotted her straightaway amongst all the other Golds. I recognised her by the lumpy beer-pull teats. Nancy came to the bars and I gave her a good rub on her withers, just the way Dad used to do it, before she wandered off and went to stand with her feet in the food bowl as if nothing had changed.

The sun has come out on the fields below, the wheat about ready to be cut. It's going to take a while to get used to this, living in a caravan by myself. There's a chiff-chaff somewhere overhead and a steady drone of insects in the branches between me and the sky.

Judy must be back and having one of her lunch parties, because Hilary has taken to his ha-ha, thinking he's invisible down there as I watch him go backwards and forwards, the hump of his back just breaking the surface as he ploughs along like a human mole.

I don't have to worry about the stack of secrets in my head any more, about keeping them safe and herding them back in, the minute it looks as if one of them is about to escape from the bottom and bring the whole lot crashing down. Nobody round here is going to be interested in dead babies, or who takes the *News of the World*, or who did what with the Peaman. It wouldn't interest them in the slightest to know that he left an inch of rubber on the road in his desperation to get away from the stink of loneliness that clung to his hair, his clothes, or how that fresh lorryload of peas made it to the Birds Eye factory in record time that night. How he told her she'd never see him again because he was off to Iceland. There'd be less of the peas and more of the frozen TV dinners from now on, he said. Out here, the straw bales will turn grey and after a few years they'll sink into the ground and get ploughed under.

And one evening, when the nights are drawing in, perhaps Aaron Bloomfield will clamber over the crinkle-crankle wall and drop by with some food for a meal, and I'll tell him a story – not the usual sort that people tell each other, about a trip round the world or an affair gone wrong, but one about a baby in a ditch.

'It's a ghost story,' I'll say. And I'll tell him it when he's sat there peeling potatoes. But I'll know he's listening all right. I'll know he can hear every word as the branches knock and scrape at the roof of the caravan, and the gas jet in the fire sputters like an engine flying low overhead with a bellyful of bombs. And along the way I'll tell him tales of men ploughing fields in flying jackets, of rotten legs getting buried on top of wives, and a worm that can burrow into your skull and grow up to ten foot long. I'll tell him about fields that can turn bad and take a grown man down feet first, and when I feel ready, 'There's a story about a baby,' I'll say, 'a baby that bathed every night in a font, and slept in a manger.'

I went to see her after I found Guppy. At least I could tell Peewit where she came from now. I could tell her that her father was so good at jokes, children thought he was the funniest man in the world, and that her mother came from a faraway place where the skyscrapers were so high, they reached all the way up to heaven. But as soon as I opened the church door, I knew she'd gone. She didn't roll out of her crib to see me this time. She wasn't lying in the colours on the floor, moving this way and that, gurgling with delight at the way the stained-glass colours rippled over her body. The smell of ditchwater had disappeared. There was just the scent of wild flowers which someone had placed in a jam jar by the font.

A chill from the graveyard had crept into the porch. There was straw still lying around from the runaway rolls, caught against the porch door and the headstones. I knew then that Peewit had been astride the train as it did its last damage across the neighbouring fields and gardens. But there was no more careering about in all directions for her. She was headed in a straight line. She was leaving Guppy far behind, up to his neck in slurry at the pig pits, until finally she ran out of steam as she drove that train to its resting place at the church.

Mum was walking Jenny Wren over the front lawn when I went to say goodbye this morning, the baby fast asleep in her pram. Mum picked her up to pass her over to Shirley. There was just a single tuft of dark hair sticking up out of the blanket. I stood and watched as Shirley opened her coat wide to fold it around her baby, wedged there safe and warm at last.

I'm about to go and unpack my bag in the caravan when there's some movement out in the top field next to the farm. A team of horses is starting to make its way across the stubble in the practice area. I can see the horseman following behind the Suffolk Punches as they plough against the horizon, a flash of light every time they turn at the end of a furrow as the sun catches their harnesses.

I set off towards the opening in the trees, arched high above me like a church window, about to walk through it into the bright sunshine. I head for the horses on the horizon, along a path through a wheat field full of poppies. There are butterflies everywhere, a cloud of Peacocks criss-crossing the track just ahead of me. The ploughman waves. Aaron Bloomfield has spotted me as he turns the horses at the end of a furrow. The flower heads waver in the breeze, so close to me now, I can see their black seeds as I make my way towards him.

ACKNOWLEDGEMENTS

The following books made essential and enjoyable reading throughout work on this book: *Akenfield* by Ronald Blythe; the works of George Ewart Evans, including *Ask the Fellows Who Cut the Hay; All About Goats* by Lois Hetherington; and *English Field Names: A Dictionary* by John Field.

I am indebted to Arts Council England for its financial assistance and the support provided by staff at the Writers' Centre Norwich through the Escalator Literature scheme, and by my fellow participants (2009/10). Special thanks are due to my mentor, Michelle Spring.

Thank you to friends and family for all their advice, expertise and encouragement along the way: Reg and family, Nicky, Ellie and Will; Chris Ridgard, John and Joan Ridgard, Margaret Farrell, Sandra Deeble, Kathryn Simmonds, Jill Valentine, Frankie Duggan, Mark McPhail, Catherine Butcher, Vicki Dunleavy, Sara Eltringham and Esther Spence; my editors, Jocasta Hamilton, Stephanie Sweeney and the team at Hutchinson; and my agent Veronique Baxter.

And finally, with much love and gratitude, to John, Eva and Laura for all their support, understanding and such good humour. Thank you.